CW00864662

The characters and events portrayed in this book are fictitious. Any similarity to
real persons, living or dead, is coincidental and not intended by the author. Any
reference to real locations is only for atmospheric effect, and in no way truly
represents those locations.

Copyright © 2021 by R.A. Casey

Cover design by Damonza.

WHEN I FIND YOU

R.A. CASEY

RyanCaseyBooks.com

PART ONE

CHAPTER ONE

I think about my life in two distinct segments.

The days before Charlie went missing, and the days after he went missing.

I remember it well. Too well. Freddie tells me it's not good for me to keep on revisiting it all in the detail I do. Even my therapist used to say to me I'm somewhat obsessive about the details.

But how *can't* I be obsessive about the details?

My six-year-old son went missing in the middle of the day. In my care.

Nobody saw him disappear.

Nobody saw a thing.

How could I *not* be obsessive?

I remember how warm it was, for a start. The middle of summer. July 17th, in fact. There was an event on at Charlie's school, Ashworth's in Broughton. The summer fete. Always happened every year. Barbecues, bouncy castles, organised water fights, and a big local band on in the afternoon to round off the day, a moment the kids always went wild for. It had everything. The whole lot.

I used to walk past there on those warm summer days before Charlie was even born. I'd stand at the gates of the school, and I'd smile. Smile as I listened to the children's laughter. Smile as I felt the warm sun beating down against my skin. Smile as I pictured myself pushing a pram with Charlie inside it, or walking through the fete with him, his hand in mine, the stickiness of melted ice cream between his fingers against my palm.

Or watching him play football from the side of the field. Dribbling like Messi. Charging forward, scoring a goal. All his friends lifting him up and cheering, a smile on his face. And pride inside me.

The thought of a life I hadn't even lived yet. And yet it felt true to me, even then. The anticipation of having a child alone was like living it and experiencing it for real.

I'd always wanted a child. A son in particular. Not sure why. I'd always got on better with boys, and obviously, you hear all the rumours about girls being more difficult. And I suppose from my parents' perspective, I wasn't exactly the easiest of kids either. Not exactly the most... well. Cooperative, let's say.

So something always drew me to have a little boy. A feeling that it was just the way it was meant to be. A feeling that it was just... right.

I think about the first time I ever saw Charlie, and I feel a lump swelling in my throat.

His little crying eyes staring up at me in that summer warmth.

But back to the day now. July 17th. The day he went missing. The day my life changed, forever.

Walking through the school fete with him.

Hearing the laughter of the children all around us.

The sound of joyous music from the carnival games.

The smiles on everybody's faces.

The smell of meat cooking somewhere behind the school. The meat from a barbecue.

But the thing I remember more than anything as I walked through that playground was how hot it was.

And how *off* Charlie seemed.

"You okay, young man?"

He had his head down, but his beauty always filled me with warmth. His short dark hair. His tanned, olive skin. His yellow Brazil football T-shirt and his white shorts, which were still mucky from football with Gregg, his dad.

And I'll never forget the way he didn't look up at me this time, with those brown eyes. With his usual smile. He was going to be a heartthrob when he was older, that was for sure. Destined to break a few hearts along the way.

"Hey," I said. "Speaking to you, buddy. You okay?"

He glanced up at me then. Looked at me, just for a second. And then he nodded. But it was pretty much the least convincing nod I'd ever seen.

"You sure? You don't look like you're so happy. Something bothering you?"

He rubbed the back of his head. Moved his fingers through that short dark hair. "It's just..."

"Just what?"

He sighed. Shook his head. "It's nothing."

"You can talk to me, you know? If something's bothering you. Is there something wrong with your friends? Alan being mean to you again?"

"It's not Alan. Alan's fine."

"Then what's—"

"It's nothing, okay?"

I never saw Charlie angry. Never saw him mad.

So seeing him staring up at me like that... that's the first sign I had that something wasn't right.

Something wasn't right at all.

I stood there. Looked at him, the warmth of the sun covering us. The sound of laughing children all around us. A tombola raffle machine rattling just up ahead. A kid holding on to a set of kitchen scales she'd won, clearly just some a teacher found surplus to requirements.

And yet still, the kid looked happy. Bemused but happy.

Such a beautiful day.

A beautiful happy day.

I often think back to that moment. The moment where Charlie told me he was okay. Told me it was nothing. Snapped at me.

I often wonder if I'd asked him, pushed him a little more, if maybe something would've worked out differently.

If it had anything to do with *anything* at all.

Freddie says it didn't. Gregg, my now ex-husband, said it didn't. Everyone says it didn't.

But in my mind, there was something in Charlie's voice that day.

There was something in his eyes.

There was a question he wanted me to ask him. Like a missing piece of a puzzle, he wanted me to find.

And I didn't even bother to look.

I remember it so well.

The way I looked into his beautiful brown eyes. Smiled. "Come on, little man. Fancy a burger?"

He opened his mouth. Looked like he was going to say something.

And then he closed it, and my little smiley prince was back.

"Sure," he said.

We walked together, hand in hand, towards the burger stand.

The maize fields in the background standing tall.

And a feeling inside me that it was going to be a good day.

I remember walking to get the burger right before we headed over to the stage to watch the band.

The worst part of the whole memory.

The part of the memory that fills me with fear. With dread.

Because the memory of the stage, the memory of the band, is the memory of the last time I ever held my little prince's hand.

The memory of letting go.

The memory of losing Charlie.

CHAPTER TWO

PRESENT DAY: THREE YEARS LATER

Moving home is supposed to be a happy day, but I can't help feeling a little bit sad seeing the moving van unloading everything in front of me and Freddie's new home.

"Well?" Freddie says. "What d'you think, Sarah? Looks even nicer in the sun, huh?"

I look out of Freddie's Ford Transit van window, and I want to feel excited. It's such a beautiful neighbourhood, after all. And Freddie's right. It looks even more beautiful in the sun. A semi-detached house on the outskirts of a new development in a place called Cottam, just outside Preston. 19 Fairworth Avenue. Not one of the shitty new builds—a robust old house, and one of the few remaining around here in this jungle of new houses. Needs a bit of work doing, some of it structural, but Freddie is handy like that, so it's right up his street.

It used to be a pretty rural area back in the day. All fields. All clicky residents. But naturally, the need for new homes took over the needs of the clicky residents for their "green spaces."

And nowadays, it is something of a suburban metropolis.

But mine and Freddie's place is in a really nice spot, the last semi on a row of five. There are no houses across the road, just a quiet street and then some rare green space. Directly in front of the houses, there's a little pond area where ducks float. And while it's all admittedly a little artificial, it looks nice. Especially, yes, on a day like today.

"Sarah?"

I look around. See Freddie sitting there beside me. He never fails to make my heart skip a beat, my dear boyfriend. God, "boyfriend." What a word. I sound like a bloody teenager. But what better word is there for it, really? Partner? Too sappy. Significant Other? Wow. Sexy.

No. Unfortunately, we have to submit to the teenage classic that is "girlfriend and boyfriend."

He has dark brown eyes. Short, jet black hair. That stubble, which makes him look so attractive, and that little neck scar, which I find weirdly endearing. And he always has this smile to his face. A smile that warms me inside. That calms and soothes me in my darkest moments.

I am so grateful for Freddie. My marriage to Gregg was collapsing before Charlie went missing, but Charlie's disappearance was the icing on the cake. Gregg couldn't handle it. The shock and grief of losing his son. But something else, too.

The resentment.

The resentment directed at me because *I* was supposed to be the one looking after Charlie that summer's day, July 17th, just over three years ago.

Charlie was in my company when he went missing. I'd let him out of my sight, let his fingers slip from mine, and he was gone because of me.

The sex with Gregg, already limited, dried up to nothing. That was an immediately foreboding sign. I'm not going to lie; I've always had a high sex drive. Caused a few problems with Gregg and me in the first place. He was way more laid back about the whole endeavour while I needed it, craved it.

But we loved each other. For over ten years, anyway. We worked through it.

Until we couldn't work through any of it anymore. And in our moment of grief, we went our separate ways.

It was difficult; I'm not going to lie. Mostly because I still, to this day, find it hard to accept Charlie is gone. Even though the police told me he's most likely dead. Even though everyone around tells me in various, gentle ways that he's gone. Even though deep down myself I know it's the case, I still have this feeling that he's going to walk through the door and slot right back into my life again as if no time has passed at all.

And just when I thought I couldn't be more alone, I met Freddie.

Freddie is the opposite of Gregg, and I say that in the sweetest way possible. Gregg, nice as he was, wasn't a *conventionally* attractive guy. He was a bit nerdy. Traditional family man. A very safe pair of hands. Sweet, cute, all those nice things. Freddie, on the other hand, is a bit of a rough diamond. His family history is somewhat complex and unclear. Estranged from his mum, and his dad died when he was young. He's someone who had a bit of a wild youth and early twenties but is finally putting all that aside to settle down properly now.

Yet, he still has that spark about him. A spark that reminds me of being twenty again.

The sex is great, too.

I think back to when I met him in a bar eighteen months ago. I was drinking alone as a quest to get myself out of the house and build some confidence. I remember how he just wandered into my life out of nowhere and seemed so perfect. So confident. So self-assured. Just what I needed. I'd only been out of my marriage to Gregg for six months, so it seemed a little early and fresh. I'd sworn I wouldn't get involved with another man. That I'd spend some time to just focus on myself for a while.

But there was just something about Freddie, right from the off. Something that drew me to him. That *allured* me.

Like he knew me so, so well, even though we'd only just met.

And yet, despite all that... despite how great Freddie is, how understanding he is of me and my needs... there is still an itch unscratched.

"You're not feeling it. Are you?"

I look around at Freddie again as he sits there in the driver's seat. I realise I zoned out. I take a deep breath. "It's—it's not that I don't like it. I love it. Obviously."

"But it's not Broughton," Freddie says, his face turning a little. A look that could be interpreted as annoyance, but I've known Freddie long enough to know he's just unhappy because he wants me to be as excited about this as he is.

I think about shaking my head. Leaning over and kissing him and telling him I love him and that it's perfect, the perfect little semi-detached house in a nice little suburban neighbourhood I've always wanted, with perfect white-tooth-smiling neighbours and perfectly cut lawns and perfect little children running around like Charlie and—

"It's not Broughton," I say, lowering my head a little. "I'm sorry. I'll... I know it sounds crazy."

"You don't have to explain yourself," Freddie says, putting his big hand on top of mine. "Really, Sarah. I get it."

I look up at him, right into those chocolate brown eyes. And I see love. I see someone who cares about me dearly. I see my protector.

"You had a lot of links to Broughton. Especially with that being where... Yeah. I get it. Well. I don't *understand* because I haven't been through it. I can't pretend to get it like you do. But it must be hell. And I'm sorry it's something you've had to go through. Like I say, it must be hell. And I get that it won't be easy moving someplace new at first. I get that it won't be easy settling in. But I'm here for you. Talk to me, okay? Talk to me. Because that's what I'm here for."

I look into Freddie's eyes, and I want to tell him he is right. That this is all about Broughton. It is all about Charlie's disappearance. I want to tell him this isn't going to be easy for me, but in time, with his support, I'll make it through.

I want to tell him everything.

Every.

Single.

Thing.

But I can't.

I can't even begin to scratch the surface.

So instead, I just close my eyes.

Instead, I just make myself smile, even though I am aching inside.

Instead, I nod, then lean over and kiss him, right on his salty lips.

"I love you," I say.

And I mean that. I really do.

He looks me in the eyes. Then he kisses me on my forehead in that way that feels so warm, so caring, so *paternal,* almost.

"I love you too, Sarah. Now come on. We'd better get inside. Can't keep the moving guys waiting all day."

I look outside at the gorgeous, sunny day.

At this perfect street.

Birds singing.

The sound of sprinklers firing water everywhere.

Of kids laughing and playing.

I look out, take a deep breath of the warm summer air that seeps in through the open van door.

I look at my red Mini Cooper, sitting there on the pavement.

I look at the little old woman peeking through the curtains of the semi-detached house attached to us, cigarette dangling from her lips, and I know she'll be quiet. She'll be no trouble.

I look at it all, and I smile.

"It's perfect," I say.

And I mean it.

CHAPTER THREE

I'm there again.

The sun is hot. So, so hot. I can feel a bead of sweat rolling down my forehead, over my eyebrow, touching my lips, so salty.

I can feel his hand in mine. And it's so sweaty.

So sweaty that I want to let go and wipe my hand and...

No.

I don't want to let go.

I can't let go.

Because if I let go, I know what'll happen.

I know it'll be the last time.

We've eaten our burger, and we've moved on. I can feel the crowd of people all around me. The rush to see the band—The Bandits, they are called. So many kids around us. All screaming and sweaty and shouty.

And me there, Charlie's sweaty hand in mine.

I remember looking down at him. Remember seeing him looking ahead and seeing that smile on his face. The concern of earlier, gone now. Before we went to the burger stand. That weirdness. The way he'd looked at me with concern like he wanted to say something. Like he wanted to tell me something.

He was happy again. My happy little boy again.

So that's why I didn't ask.

I know I should've asked, but I didn't.

I see him holding my hand and know how sweet it is. He's only six, but I know soon he'll see it as uncool to be holding my hand around other schoolkids. I need to be grateful for moments like this. Savour them while I still can. Because there will be a last time. And I won't know when that last time is. Nobody ever knows when it's the last time they'll do anything at all in life. All the more reason to be grateful and kind to those around you.

People pushing behind. A teacher speaking over a loudspeaker. "Can everyone stay in an orderly line, please? The band will only start when everyone is in attendance."

But it doesn't even cut through. The excitement. The rush. All for this band—this imitation of BTS, or whatever they are called.

I see Charlie look up at me. Excitement in his little brown eyes.

"Can I go, Mum? Can I go to the front?"

And as I'm here, as I'm witnessing this now, with what I know and how I know it all plays out, I want to tell him: no. I want to tell him I'm not letting go of his hand. I'm not letting him go anywhere.

I want to tell him I'm holding his hand forever, and I'm not losing him.

I'm not letting go.

But I know how this goes.

The same way, every single time, I know how it goes.

I try to tell him no. I try to tell him I'm not letting go. I try to stand my ground.

But then I nod.

And I smile.

Because I'm powerless.

And then the next thing I know, Charlie's hand slips out of mine, and he's gone.

My hand immediately cools, like he was never even holding it at all. The only trace of him is the sweat on my palm.

He's running.

Running through the crowd.

And then suddenly, in the rush, he's out of my sight.

But what harm can it do?

He's in this crowd.

He's down by the stage.

The maize fields surrounding the stage, making me feel strange, uneasy...

We're all gathered around in the heat and the excitement and the buzz, all watching this band, all happy and laughing and loving life.

What can possibly go wrong?

What can possibly fall apart on a day like this?

You should know, Sarah. You know better than anyone what can fall apart on a day like this.

I hear that thought now. Not then, but now.

And it haunts me.

Makes the hair on my arms stand on end.

No. You're wrong. I couldn't have known. I couldn't have—

You should know better, and you know it.

I shake my head. And I look around for him. I fight the bind my body finds itself in. I fight the rails this dream always seems to progress along. All so hazy. Almost... artificial.

I fight it, and I push against it, and I tell myself I can change things.

I can change history.

I can—

You're never going to change anything.

I shake my head and suppress that thought when finally, I see the crowd has reduced.

I'm back again.

Back to that day.

July 17th.

Only it's later now.

The band has stopped playing.

The kids are all wandering back to their parents, the crowd much thinner now.

Burst red balloons on the grass.

Sweet wrappers everywhere.

I look around for him. For my Charlie. And at first, I feel just a mild panic. At first, a sense of slight unease, but nothing major. 'Cause he'll come back. Of course, he will.

He's in the crowd. He knows where I am.

And besides, there are loads of people around. People who would've seen him. Who'd know where he was.

But as I stand there and wait for longer and longer, I realise I don't see him. I realise he's nowhere.

And I start to entertain the fact he isn't here at all.

I scratch my itchy elbows and see grass stains on my knees and see people looking at me strangely.

I feel a little sore. I feel a twinge of embarrassment.

I feel in a haze.

In a cloud.

And then I see him.

Alan. His friend. His best friend. Bit of a shit with him sometimes, but they get on in that love-hate way kids always do.

I run up to Alan. See him with some other kids. Fully expect Charlie to be with these kids.

And then I stop.

Because I realise Charlie isn't there.

Alan looks up at me. His eyes widen. And for a moment, just for a moment, it looks like he's hiding something.

It looks like he's been whispering something.

Something about Charlie.

"Alan?" I say. "Have—have you seen Charlie anywhere?"

Alan looks at me like he wants to say "yes."

Like he knows something.

And that's a moment I revisit a lot.

That's a moment I return to, again and again.

But it's somewhat unclear.

It feels somewhat grainy.

Somewhat... out of reach.

Because every time I think back to it, it always returns to what Alan said next.

He looks me right in the eyes and shakes his head.

"Sorry. I... I've got to go."

I want to reach out and shake the little shit and tell him he's lying because I know he's lying he has to be lying he must be lying he knows where my boy is my Charlie my—

I gasp.

Launch forward.

I'm covered in sweat.

Someone is touching my back. Stroking me.

"It's okay, Sarah," Freddie says. "I've got you. It's okay."

I lower my head. Realise I've had a nightmare. A dream. Nothing more.

I sit there in the darkness. All these shapes surround me, unfamiliar shapes of the new bedroom.

I clutch my legs.

Wrap my arms around them, tightly, and hug them, hug them like they're Charlie, like he's here.

Freddie keeps on moving his hand up and down my back. Saying things to me. Reassuring things.

"It's okay, Sarah. It's just a nightmare. You're right here. I've got you. You're right here."

I want to tell him that's exactly the problem.

I'm right here.

I'm right here, and Charlie isn't.

And it's all my fault.

But instead, I just clench my eyes shut, and listen to the attic creaking in the wind.

Instead, I just think of nice things, like the sun and laughter and beaches and holidays and ice creams.

Instead, I just take deep breaths in through my nose and out through my mouth.

Instead, I cry.

CHAPTER FOUR

I bury my face in icy water and try to wash away the grime of three hours of sleep.

When I look back up at the mirror, I'm still pale. My dark hair is greasy. I can see the bags under my eyes, bags that never used to be there, and I know I'll never hide them again. My skin, which used to have such a glow to it—something everyone always commented on—has faded. In all truth, it's hard to believe standing here and staring at myself that I am only thirty years old. I used to look young for my age. Girlish. Now, I look weathered and old.

I see the grey hairs dangling down my fringe. They are multiplying by the day. Stress, Freddie says. Manage my stress, and I'll manage my grey problem better than any hair dye.

Problem is, I am beyond hair dye at this stage. I'm beyond covering up my true self. No matter how much I try to hide behind makeup or hair dye, the truth always comes out in the end.

And I can see it staring back at me right now, threatening to burst from my skin.

"Sarah? Can you give me a hand with this?"

I hear Freddie's voice, and I sigh. Last night, the first in our new home, was rough. I'm not going to lie about it. Not going to pretend it was all rosy. It wasn't. I barely slept a wink. The sleep I *did* get was tortured by the same dream I'd had for the last three years.

The dream of holding Charlie's hand.

The dream of letting him go. Letting him run off into the crowd.

The dream of him disappearing into that crowd of people.

The dream of him never coming back.

I stand by the mirror in a daze. Because I'm thinking of another part of that dream now. Or the memory, anyway. It's right around the part where Alan walks over to me. Where he looks up at me. Where I ask him about Charlie, if he's seen him today, if the pair of them chatted, whatever.

The moment I feel that rage towards Alan, 'cause I feel like he's lying. He *has* to be lying.

It's a memory of someone standing by the side of the stage.

Someone looking right over at me.

A figure.

I see the memory in total clarity now. Feel the warmth of the sun. Taste the remnants of vanilla Mr Whippy ice cream on my tongue. Smell the sunscreen in the air.

And that figure.

By the stage.

Why haven't I thought of them before?

Why haven't I—

"Sarah?"

I jump. Spin around.

Freddie is at the bathroom door. He's leaning on it.

"Yes?"

He narrows his eyes. "I shouted you. Need you to give me a hand with the ladders. That okay?"

I nod. "Sorry. I... I was washing my face. Didn't hear."

"You sure you're okay?"

"Why wouldn't I be?"

He opens his mouth. As if he wants to push for more information. Then he closes it. Half-smiles. "It's okay. Come on. Give me a hand with the ladder. The sooner I get this doorway glossed, the better."

I finish washing my face and hear creaking above. I look up there. See the slight darkened hole in the ceiling towards the attic. My stomach sinks. Freddie told me about that. The loft's in a state, apparently. Real structural issues up there. Told me not to go up there because it's really rickety. Fortunately, as well as decorating, he's a dab hand at pretty much anything manual, so he'll get it sorted. Said it might take a while, though.

I look up there and see a speck of dust fall towards me, and I take a deep breath.

Then I step away. I smile as I follow Freddie out of the bathroom. We've only been in the house a day, and already he's putting his painting and decorating skills to the test. It is his trade, after all. Runs his own business, hires two people. And he's got two weeks off work to really put our own stamp on this place. Enough money in the bank and a couple of reliable people working for him to afford the time.

Before we moved in together, he'd tell me about his plans for this place. All the work he was going to do, all the decorating. And it made me feel happy, hearing about all these future plans. Hearing all these visions of our shared future. It made me happy how into me he was. How much he clearly cared about me. He was so proud of this home. So proud finally to be settling down after years of apparently failed relationships followed by a sole focus on the business. Proud to be putting his bachelor ways behind him.

But I also feel guilty, too.

Because as much as I love him—and I do love him, dearly—there's a lot about me he doesn't know.

There are things about me he *cannot* know.

Things I can barely acknowledge about myself.

I hold the ladder in the lounge for him as he climbs it. I feel a bit irritated that he's given me such a menial task, but he is a pretty traditional guy. Not in a knowing sense. Mostly out of naivety. I decided not to point it out to him today though, because I'm really knackered and not feeling up to helping too much.

He dips his brush into the can and starts glossing the top of the doorframe. The smell of paint fumes is strong, makes me smile. Reminds me of moving into our little Broughton cottage, Gregg and I, and planning on starting our own little family.

I remember standing in that cottage, those low ceilings, that dark interior, that dust hanging in the air and catching on my chest, and despite all its flaws, despite all the work that needed doing, I felt so happy about the future. So happy about what lay ahead.

"So what's the plan, Batman?" I say. Showing an interest. I fully realise I've been a bit insane since we moved in here. I don't want to scare Freddie away. We've been together eighteen months now, and yet at times, I feel like we barely know each other.

And in a weird kind of way that suits us both.

Freddie smiles, clearly in his element. "Gloss the doorframes. Then give this wallpaper a good old covering. I've heard a lot about those painting skills of yours, so I'm expecting a real schooling there."

I raise an eyebrow. "Oh, you have, have you?"

"I mean, if you can drag yourself away from your tutoring plans long enough to pay me some attention?"

I smile. I haven't even started up the online French tutoring again yet. Both teaching English kids French and French kids English. It's in the planning stages. It's been a handy little business for me over the years. Made a bit of cash, plenty in savings to get me by. Back in the day, I got my teaching qualifications and taught at a few schools. But teaching online definitely suits me more these days.

"Pay *you* some attention?" I say. "I thought we were talking about giving the wall attention here."

"We can get to the wall," Freddie says, looking at me in that adoring, desirous way he always does.

The way that touches me right where it feels best.

I look down. Smile on my face. "I'm sure the French students can wait a little while for their tutor ..."

I stop.

Because on the newspaper beneath my feet, I see him staring up at me.

Charlie.

His brown eyes.

His cheeky little smile.

A headline.

A headline from when he went missing.

"Sarah?" Freddie says.

I look down, and I am trapped.

I am trapped in that fete.

I am staring into the distance, beyond Alan, towards that figure by the stage.

Towards that man.

Clearer than I've ever seen him.

I am there again.

"Sarah? What's..."

I reach down without thinking, and I tear the paper.

"Sarah!"

I tear it up. Tear it to pieces. Dig my nails into it and rip it apart, like a feral dog tearing into a rabbit.

Tear and tear and tear and keep tearing until it's all gone until it's nowhere until it's gone gone gone—

And before I know it, there is no trace of Charlie there.

Before I know it, I've shredded it all to pieces.

But I am on my knees.

I am gasping.

I am deep underneath the ocean without oxygen.

Freddie is beside me. Big hands on my back. The smell of paint not pleasant anymore. Strong. Too strong.

He holds me with those hands, and he whispers words of reassurance into my ear.

"It's okay, Sarah."

"He—he was there."

"It's okay. It's over now. It can't hurt you anymore. None of it can hurt you anymore."

I crouch on my knees, struggling to get my breath back, heart racing in my skull, and I want this nightmare to end.

But all I see now is the figure by the stage.

The new detail in the memory.

And as much as I want to settle and ease into our new lives, I know what my latest obsession is.

I know I am not going to be able to let this go.

CHAPTER FIVE

I sit at the dinner table and want to be present with Freddie.

But I can't stop my thoughts wandering to what happened earlier.

I know it was an innocent mistake. The newspapers Freddie used to line the carpet, to stop the paint splashing onto the floor.

And yet... what are the chances, really?

A three-year-old story. Where did he get the papers from? Surely he saw the papers when he laid them down?

And there's the confusion. The way it's unsettled me. Deeply. In ways I can't even begin to explain.

And yet every time I look up from my dinner of lentil bolognese—one of the nicest vegan dishes I've ever tasted, courtesy of Freddie himself, who's all for a few meat-free days a week—I can see the guilt in his eyes, and it breaks me a little.

"Sarah, I'm sorry," he says.

"It's okay." What else can I say, really? What else is there to say? Obviously, it's not okay. It was careless; that's what it was.

But as upset as I am, I can't torture him for it. Not when he so clearly regrets it.

He puts his fork down. A little of the tomato sauce splashes onto the brand-new IKEA table we're sitting at. "I can tell you're upset."

"What do you want me to say?"

"I want you to tell me you know it was a mistake. And that—and that you're okay."

"I've told you I'm okay a thousand times."

"Well, say it like you mean it, won't you?"

I can tell from the tone in his voice that he's in one of his self-pitying moods. It's a shame. One of his flaws. He has a way of turning somebody else's upset into his own. Making you feel guilty for making *him* feel bad about something *he* has done wrong.

It isn't with ill intent; I'm sure of that. He's a good guy.

But it's something that always irritates me.

"Look," I say, deciding honesty is probably the best policy at this point. "I'll be honest with you. I'm finding it hard to believe you didn't notice the article when you laid the papers down."

"I didn't notice *anything*. Like, it's just old paper."

"Where did you get it?"

"What?"

"The paper? Where did you get it?"

Freddie scratches the back of his head. "Gary, I think." Gary is his friend from work. "Or maybe it was Russ. One of the boys I work with had a load in the back of the van. Might've even been a customer who gave it us. I don't know. Anyway, what does it matter? You think somebody gave me it to get at you or something?"

"I didn't say that. You said that."

"Oh, Sarah, don't start this again."

"Don't start what?"

He lifts his red wine and sips back a little too much. "This is our second night in here. And already you're..."

He stops. I can tell he's regretting the path he's walking down right away.

"Go on," I say.

"Look, do we have to do this?"

"It's our second night, and I'm ruining it. That's what you want to say, isn't it?"

"I don't want to say it," he says. "But... But yeah. Yeah. You're putting a real fucking dampener on things if I have to be completely honest. There you go. All cards on the table, like you usually say."

I'm hurt. And yet, I understand it. When I look at the facts, I really have put a dampener on our move so far.

This is supposed to be our big step. Our new life.

And here I am, acting like a bitch, having night terrors, and kicking off at Freddie all for an innocent mistake.

I open my mouth to bite back at him when I think better of it and close it.

"I'm sorry," I say.

It takes Freddie by surprise, I can see. He's bracing himself for an argument. Readying himself for conflict. My apology startles him.

"It's... Look, it doesn't matter, Sarah. I'm sorry too."

"You don't have anything to be sorry about."

"No. I was careless. I was an idiot. But I just... Well. I didn't see the paper. I didn't look. There wasn't anything in it. That's all I can say. I'm sorry."

He reaches over the table. Takes my hand in his. And when I look up into his eyes, I see that diamond in the rough. I see that caring gaze. I see the man I love. And I am so, so grateful for him.

"It's okay," I say.

And this time, he doesn't question it.

This time, he knows I mean it.

"The pasta's lovely," I say, returning to my food.

He smiles. Rolls a big spiral of it around his fork. "Chef's special. Know it's your favourite."

I smile at that. He's not exactly the best cook in the world. But what he cooks, he cooks well. The first thing he ever cooked for me was this curry he hyped up for weeks on end. Turned out being nothing more than a jar sauce, a few vegetables, and some Quorn chicken. Taken the piss out of him for it ever since.

But he tries, and he cares. And that care is worth more than anything.

I tuck further into my pasta as he talks to me about his plans for the house. But I drift in thought. Lose myself in that flash-back, that dream.

The figure.

The figure by the stage where the band was playing.

Has my memory inserted that to taunt me?

Or have I missed a vital clue?

"When're you getting back to work anyway?" he asks.

"What?"

"I asked when you're getting back to tutoring. I know you're doing your plans, but like... Well. It'll be good for you. Sure there's plenty of little Frenchies looking forward to saying bonjour to their favourite Mrs Evatt again."

I smile.

I've always liked working with children. But as much as I hate to admit it, Charlie's disappearance made returning to any kind of school in a professional capacity difficult for me.

But that suits me. I prefer it this way anyway.

"I figure it'll be good for me to take a week or two off and keep working on plans," I say. Hoping he believes me. Because I don't want to have to go into the full truth.

He smiles back at me. "Good for you."

He raises his wine glass, then. And I think of mentioning the figure in my dream. The figure that has inserted itself into the memory.

But in the end, I think better of it.
I raise my wine glass.
"To our new future," Freddie says.
"To our new future," I say.
We chink the glasses against one another.
Red wine spills out over the white tablecloth.
Like blood.

CHAPTER SIX

The last two weeks have been blissful.

I'm happy. I never thought I'd say those words again, but I really am. Ever since we moved to our new home on Fairworth Avenue, things have been a delight.

Of course, we had our hitches at first. The reluctance I had about turning my back on my past, moving away from Broughton. And the squabble we had that second day about the newspaper with Charlie's face staring up at me.

But since then, we've got on like a house on fire.

The sex has been fantastic. I hold on tight to Freddie's big, rounded shoulders as he slides deep inside me. I smell the wine on his breath. Hear his little moans. And I moan with him, too. Not because I'm climaxing. I find it hard to lose myself in the moment enough to climax, especially these days. But because I know it will make him feel better about himself. I know it will reassure him that I am okay.

And I *am* okay. Really, I am. I love our new home, the nights in front of the television, feet up, lying in his arms. I love the newly decorated living room and the grassy garden, such a sun trap. I love every bit of our new lives.

But today is different. Today, Freddie's gone back to work. He has a job decorating over in Fulwood. A big job, apparently. Some idiot kid had a house party, and the place got trashed. Posh Fucker Parents, as Freddie calls them, footing the bill for their spoilt brat of a son's mistakes, as always.

I felt sad when he left. When he stood there at the door in his work gear, smile on that perfect face of his.

"Are you going to be okay?" he asked.

I smiled back at him. Nodded. "Course I will."

He opened his mouth. Like he wanted to ask me something. "Are you sure?"

"Honestly, Freddie. I'll be fine. Don't you worry. I might grab a coffee with Cindy, anyway. And I've got a book to finish. Seriously. Don't worry. I do actually have a life that doesn't include you, you know."

He raised an eyebrow at that. "Oh really? Well, in that case..."

He opened the door, paused, walked over to me. Held me tight and kissed me, right on the lips.

"I'll miss you."

"I'll miss you too."

"Can't wait for later."

"Yeah. Me too."

He looked right at me and smiled. And I felt my body melt. Felt my knees go all weak. And I wanted him, right then and there.

But then, just before I could act on these impulses, these desires, he pecked me on the cheek and walked out the door.

He stepped back in not long after. Fumbled around for his Stanley knife—his favourite one, which I find bizarrely adorable. He seemed really miffed to have lost it. I kept on telling him it would show up in time, but he didn't seem happy. Eventually, he went out the door and left, being sure to give me all the affection before he did.

That was three hours ago. It's midday now. I text Freddie to tell him I met Cindy for a quick coffee in the Costa around the corner. She was going to bob around, but she had a call from a client—she works in social media marketing or something similar. All I know is that it keeps her really busy all the time. Or something like that. The details don't matter, as long as they're close enough. Whatever.

So I'm standing here now in front of my front door. Heart racing. Because I'm bracing myself to step outside. Out into the outside world, all on my own.

Yeah. It might seem like I'm making a bigger deal of this than I should. But the truth is, I'm a nervous wreck. And I know what you're thinking. You went for a coffee with a friend earlier, right?

Yeah. Sure. But you can't account for when anxiety is going to take hold or not. Any anxiety sufferer knows that too well.

I never find leaving the house easy. Especially back in Broughton because everyone knew who I was there. Everyone looked at me in that judgemental way.

And, I know. Best thing I could've done was get out of there a lot faster than I did. But you know what attachment is like. When you've loved and lost someone, your mind plays tricks on you. It convinces you you'd be better off staying put. That you're betraying that someone for turning your back and walking away.

That's what I've always felt with Charlie.

A feeling he might just walk right in through my front door again.

A sense that if I just stay put, at least he'll know exactly where to go, exactly where to find me.

The feeling deep down that he's still out there and that he'll show up again.

One day.

That's one of the many things I was so thankful to Gregg for when we split up. He let me keep the house. I had a lot in savings, and even when my teaching gig ended, I made more from the tutoring than I expected.

So I could get by on my own.

People told me I was insane for staying there. Mum and Dad offered to take me back. Cindy asked me to move in with her. Even my estranged sister, Elana, who lived over in Sweden, offered to fly me over there to spend some time with them.

But that alone time was my healing time. That's what I told them.

Deep down, it was my punishment time.

Exactly what I deserved for losing Charlie.

This is the story I tell myself.

The concerned family.

The worried friends.

Their caring advice.

All of it.

But here I am now, standing at my door. Sweaty hand gripping the cool, golden metal handle. I'm going for a walk. A walk around the neighbourhood. Freddie said it'd be a good idea to meet the neighbours. He'd bumped into a couple of them over the last couple of weeks, said they were nice. But he said I should probably show my face, too. I don't get it, really. Why do neighbourhood friendships have to be a thing? Why can't people just get on with their own lives? Mind their own business?

Because neighbours bring problems.

They only ever bring problems.

I remember what it was like in Broughton after Charlie went missing. The visits from Karen and Andy next door. The constant stream of kids' parents coming around, passing on their sympathies, saying the usual "I'm sure he'll turn up" crap, again and again and again until I couldn't take any more of it, and I just hid away every time the doorbell went.

But it's different here. I have a chance here. A chance for a new start. For a fresh beginning.

I turn the handle, and I'm surprised to see somebody standing there.

It's a man. He's older than me. Probably in his sixties at a glance. He has dark brown eyes, bushy eyebrows, and furry ears. And he's smiling at me with these yellow teeth. I can smell his onion breath from here.

"Oh," I say. A little startled.

"Didn't mean to bother ye, lovey. Name's Calvin. Your fella, Freddie. Met him the other day. Top bloke. Champion."

Calvin. Did Freddie mention meeting a Calvin? I've no idea. But it adds up.

I move my hair out of my eyes, fully aware of how greasy it is. "Calvin. Hi. I think he did mention meeting you."

"I live over the other side of Cottam. Fairhawk Avenue. Number 19, just like you two. Problem is, postie always gets us two mixed up." He holds out a small, rectangular parcel. "Think we might be seein' a lot of each other."

He laughs. And I laugh, too. Or at least I attempt my best impression of a laugh. Truth is, I'm shaken up. I need time to prepare myself for any human interaction these days. Calvin here took me by surprise. And I'm all sweaty, all flushed, all... disgusting.

"How you two findin' it 'ere anyway?"

"Oh," I say, fiddling with my fringe again. "It's nice. Really nice. Thank you."

"Good. Beautiful spot you got 'ere, with the pond in front of you and all that. Cracking on a sunny day like today."

"It is," I say. "It really is." I want him to go away. I want him to leave. I'm not sure how much longer I can pretend I'm a normal functioning person here, that I can pretend I can sustain ordinary small talk for longer than a few seconds.

"Anyway," he says, and a weight lifts off my shoulders. "Like I say. Parcels droppin' at ours all the time. You'll get a few for us, too, if Stacey and Mike's record have owt to say about it. 19

Fairhawk. Other side of Cottam. Right by the fountain. You'll know it."

"What did you say your name was again?"

"Calvin. Calvin Hooper. Only me lives there, so you've only got one set of post to worry about."

He laughs again, and I smell that onion breath. His laugh a little too loud, almost inappropriately so.

But he's leaving. And that makes me feel relieved. So I laugh along with him, humour him.

"Anyway," he says.

"Yeah. Nice—nice meeting you, Calvin."

"See you around, Sarah. Hopefully not too soon, anyway. 'Cause that means the postman's cocked up again."

I nod. Smile, watch him turn his back, and walk away.

I close the door, close my eyes, and I sink to the floor.

I'm dripping sweat. My heart is racing. My throat is tight.

I take deep breaths. Deep, calming breaths.

It's over.

He's gone.

Everything is okay now.

I open my eyes, inhale deeply, and then I look at the parcel.

Two things strike me at that moment.

Two things that seem a little... well, off.

First, the parcel is unaddressed. Completely unaddressed.

Not a name in sight.

I frown. Turn the parcel over in my hands. It's small. About an inch thick, six inches wide.

No name.

So how did he...

And then that second thing hits me like a punch to the gut.

If there's no address on the parcel, how did he know it was for us?

And if there's no name on the parcel...

How did he know I'm called Sarah?

I stand up. Shaking. Look out through the little window at the top of the door.

Calvin is nowhere to be seen.

CHAPTER SEVEN

I stare at the parcel on the kitchen table, and I'm not sure whether I want to see what's inside.

I haven't stopped shaking since Calvin dropped the parcel off. Sweat streams down my face. I can taste its saltiness across my lips, and it reminds me of that day.

The fete.

Holding Charlie's sweaty hand, then letting him free into the crowd.

Watching him disappear.

The crowd dispersing, and no sign of him.

The grass on my knees.

The tenderness between my thighs...

And the weird feeling in my stomach I sometimes get, like Charlie's hand was totally dry, and it was mine that was sweaty.

Or sometimes I wonder if I was even holding his hand at all. Maybe he let go sooner. Maybe he didn't hold my hand that day at all. Maybe he was embarrassed holding my hand in front of his friends.

Memory is a fickle demon.

I stand in the kitchen. It's darker in here. Cooler in here. I know that logically, but it doesn't *feel* it. It feels roasting hot. Like it's getting hotter and hotter like someone's ramping the heating up in here. I keep on staring at that parcel. The little cardboard box, six inches by an inch. And I know I should just open it. I know I should just look inside it.

But something bothers me.

Two things bother me.

Calvin. The man who dropped the parcel off. He said my name; I'm sure of it.

But there's no name on the parcel. And there's no address on the box.

And when I turned around to see if he was still outside, Calvin was already nowhere in sight.

I take long, deep breaths. I need to pull myself together. I'm being irrational, and I know it. Chances are, the parcel came in some kind of external packaging, and Calvin removed it before realising it wasn't for him. And the whole him knowing my name thing. He said he'd met Freddie already, right? So there's every chance he got my name from him.

There're all kinds of reasons. Loads of potential explanations.

And yet I can't help feeling like something is wrong.

I walk over to the table. Lift the parcel, shake it. Something moves around inside. Doesn't feel heavy. Doesn't sound like there's much in there at all.

I'm being ridiculous. I'm shaken up because I wasn't expecting Calvin, that's all. He took me by surprise, and that's why I feel so anxious now. So paranoid. So fucking insane.

I want Freddie here with me. I want to call him and tell him to come home because I need him. I think he's coming home for lunch, but I want him here earlier.

But I know how ridiculous that sounds.

I know, even though he will come home, even though he'll do anything for me, he'll look at me like I'm some special precious flower who needs protecting.

No.

I need to pull myself together.

I need to step the fuck up.

I'm strong. I've always been strong, all my fucking life.

It's just a parcel, a parcel with a totally logical explanation, nothing more.

I open the tab at the side of the box. It's one of those red tabs where you pull it off, and it tears some of the box away. Which reassures me a little because at least it means it's been sent from some online store or something. Certainly looks pretty official, anyway.

I can't think if I've ordered anything. My mind's a bit of a blur lately. I might've ordered something off Amazon. A new book, perhaps?

But no. I haven't ordered any books, I'm sure of it.

And besides, this doesn't feel like a book. It's too light. It's too...

And then it hits me, and I smile.

A bookmark. A bloody bookmark, that's what it'll be.

I went on Etsy and ordered a cute artisanal bookmark a few days ago. I'm a bit of a traditionalist in that way. Never been a fan of Kindle, digital books. And I can't just make do with a piece of old card to keep my page. And God forbid anyone folds over a page in my presence.

It's a bookmark. That's all it is.

It makes total sense now.

And as I turn the box, I notice something else. A little plastic wrapping, where a delivery note looks like it's been stuffed, but fallen away. My smile widens. I'm so relieved. Such a bloody idiot. There must've been a delivery note, and it must've fallen away while Calvin was bringing the parcel round or something. Loads of potential explanations. No need to lose my shit.

I tear the cardboard box open, and I lift the flap.

I feel my stomach sink.

I feel the walls closing in.
I feel my face heating up like it's burning in an oven.
I feel my heart racing at a thousand beats per minute.
I feel all these things, but I see nothing.
Nothing but the contents of the cardboard box.
I drop it to the kitchen floor, and I scream.

CHAPTER EIGHT

I think about my life in two very distinct segments.

The days before Charlie went missing, and the days after he went missing.

* * *

I AM BACK THERE AGAIN. The hot sun beating down. The sound of screaming, laughing children all around me. And the sound of a band playing up ahead. It feels fantastical. It feels... blurry. It feels dreamlike.

But it is real.

So, so real.

I can hear a microphone screeching as one of the band members holds it too close to the speaker. I can smell burgers in the air. Taste ketchup on my lips. I feel full. Not bloated, just nice.

And at this moment, I am happy.

Not a care in the world about my boy.

Because we're at a school fete. He's surrounded by other kids. He's safe. Everyone is safe. That's what I keep telling myself.

Things are safer these days.

Not like when I was younger.

Not like...

No.

Not now.

Not in this happy moment.

I stand there on the grass, and I feel a cool breeze against my face. And that's when I sense someone beside me. I don't usually remember this part. I remember things in fragments, see. I always remember the key parts. Charlie running off to the front of the crowd. The crowd dispersing, and no sign of Charlie. Asking Alan if he's seen him, with no luck.

I remember the panic. I remember searching everywhere for him. Asking parents if they've seen him, if they've seen any sign.

And then I remember ringing the police.

I remember their confidence that he would show up again. That he'd probably just gone home with a friend.

But that wasn't like Charlie.

He didn't do anything without telling me.

He'd never run away. Not without telling me.

But the police reassured me all would be fine. They sent out a search party but were confident he'd show up. That most kids showed up within a few hours. Especially around here, in this perfect little community.

But he didn't show up within a few hours.

And that's when they started to worry.

That's when *everyone* started to worry.

That's when...

"Beautiful day for it, int it?"

I hear that voice and a shiver creeps down my spine.

Because I don't remember this part.

I never remember this part.

I never told anyone about this part because it seemed so irrelevant in the grand scheme of things.

It seemed like it didn't matter.

Or maybe I didn't tell anyone because this is the first time I've remembered it…

But that voice. That northern accent. That jolly manner of speech.

It takes on a new relevance now because I recognise it.

I turn around and see him smiling at me.

Beaming smile.

Yellow teeth.

Onion breath.

And I want to scream at him because I recognise him.

Because this man, it's Calvin.

This is the man who came to my door.

This is the man who delivered the parcel.

Oh God, the parcel, the contents of the parcel.

Oh God oh God oh God don't think about it don't go there don't do it no no no—

But I smile back at him because all I can do in this memory is go along with how it went.

"Beautiful."

And I remember then; he turns around. Looks ahead at the band.

Or is he looking somewhere else?

Is he looking at the children?

The children at the front of the stage?

Or is this just my memory playing tricks on me?

I want to scream at him. I want to ask him who he is. I want to beg him to tell me where my son is. Where my Charlie is.

But I can only turn to the crowd.

Turn to the stage.

And then suddenly the crowd has dispersed again, and I'm back there searching for him.

And I have stains on my knees.

I feel week.

Sore.

I feel...

And now I see the figure.

I can't see him properly. I'd be lying if I pretended I could.

But seeing Calvin here, at the fete.

And then seeing that figure by the stage...

It all comes together.

Crashes together.

Calvin.

Is Calvin the man involved in Charlie's disappearance?

Is he the figure I saw by the stage?

And then I think of the parcel, and I'm right there in the present again, only I can smell smoke and hear ringing and—

"Sarah? Sarah!"

Someone is shaking me. I am on my back, lying on the floor. My head hurts. I feel stiff all over. Nothing quite feels right.

Freddie stands over me. I can hear bleeping and realise it's the smoke alarm. There's a smell of burning in the air, and I realise I must've left the hob on.

But I don't remember cooking anything.

I don't remember turning the hob on at all.

"Sarah," Freddie says. His eyes are wide. He is sweating and covered in paint. He looks worried. "Are you okay? Jesus. You must've... you must've passed out. You left the stove on. You know how iffy it is at the moment. Bloody hell. Good job I came back for lunch, or the place might've... anyway, that doesn't matter. You're okay. I'm here. Come on. Let's get you on a chair."

I let Freddie help me to my wobbly feet when a bolt of fear shoots through me.

The parcel.

What's *inside* the parcel.

"The—the parcel," I say.

Freddie frowns. "What parcel?"

I can barely speak. I can barely bring myself to say what's in it.

"Sarah? What parcel?"

"It—it was here."

"Where?"

"I was... I was holding it. And then I must've..."

I look down at the checkered tiles of the hard kitchen floor. See a speck of blood where I banged my head.

But I see nothing else.

No cardboard box.

No parcel.

No nothing.

"Sarah?" Freddie says.

I look up at him. Frown. "But..."

"Sarah, there's no parcel. There was nothing in your hands when I found you here."

I sit in the kitchen chair, and I shake.

Because as much as I know what I saw, as much as I know it's real... I see no parcel in sight.

CHAPTER NINE

"I know what I saw, Freddie. I know what I saw."

I'm sitting in the living room, on our new two-piece leather sofa. There's a throw over it, but I've pulled that back so I can feel the cool leather against my skin. I need something to cool me down. Anything. I'm hot. So hot.

And I can't stop thinking about the parcel.

Freddie is by my side. He's taken the rest of the day off work. I sense he's probably a bit annoyed about that. At the end of the day, he's self-employed. But he has two other decorators working for him in the firm. He thinks he can get one of his workmates to step in, but it's going to slow the whole job down, and that won't exactly impress his clients. Especially when he's only just gone back.

But he doesn't say anything. Because he is sensitive, and he is attentive, and I love him so much.

He sits with his hand on my back. That big warm hand, stroking my spine. He gives the best back strokes in the world. Even when I'm feeling ill at ease, those back strokes have a way of settling me. Of filling me with confidence again.

But that parcel.

I don't understand what happened. I went to the door. I took the parcel from Calvin. I felt awfully weird about it—how he knew my name, how he knew where we lived when there was nothing addressed to us.

And then what was inside the parcel.

My head spins. I taste vomit collecting in the back of my throat.

And then I remember the memory.

Calvin.

Calvin standing beside me at the school fete.

Or was he?

Was he actually there? Or was that all in my head?

Is this something I remember?

Or am I just confused and sleep-deprived and...

But then there's the other kicker.

Waking up.

Freddie standing over me.

The parcel being gone.

"I think we need to get you down to the doctors," Freddie says. "For a blood test or something."

"I don't need a blood test."

"I found you passed out on the kitchen floor, Sarah. You're bleeding out the back of your head. You'd left the fucking hob on. I already warned you about how iffy it is at the moment. You could've burned the house down. You could've died."

He's pissed. I know he is. But he's concerned more than anything. Concerned about me. He looks at me in that fearful way. Like he worries about me. Like he is afraid of me, somehow.

"And you keep going on about this parcel. A parcel you didn't have. What the hell's this parcel business all about?"

I close my burning eyes and take a deep breath. I haven't told him what was in there yet. I can barely bring myself to acknowledge what was in there myself. How can I? Where do I even begin?

I can barely explain it to myself. So how the hell am I supposed to explain it to Freddie?

Especially when I'm pretty sure, deep down, I didn't leave the hob on.

After all, why would I?

I was leaving the house.

Although... shit. I did scramble a couple of eggs earlier. Maybe it's from then.

I contemplate another option, just for a brief moment.

Maybe someone is trying to hurt me.

I shake my head at that thought. No. That can't be it. It can't be true.

"A man dropped by," I say.

"A man? What man?"

"I... I nipped out. Nipped out to see Cindy for a coffee. Didn't stay long. I came back here. I was going to take a walk. Maybe chat to a few neighbours while it's nice. But before I could get out..."

I remember his dark brown eyes.

His onion breath, so pungent it makes me want to vomit.

That yellow-toothed smile.

"Beautiful day for it, isn't it?"

"Sarah?"

"Huh?"

"You were telling me about this bloke. He's not done something, has he? 'Cause if he has, I'll rip his fucking head off."

I shake my head. "It's... It's not like that."

"Then what the hell is it like?"

"He... he came to drop a parcel off. He said—he said he was from number 19 Fairhawk or something. That he was always getting mail from the old neighbours."

Freddie nods. And I see he is trying to believe me. Trying to get on board with me.

"He... he gave me this parcel. Small parcel. I can see it like it's in my hand right now. An inch thick. Six inches wide. And then... Freddie, the weirdest thing is, he said my name as he left."

"Why's that weird?"

"My name wasn't on the parcel. Neither was the address."

Freddie stares at me with narrowed eyes, waits for me to continue.

"So I... I took it into the kitchen. I opened it. Figured there must've just been a delivery note with it or something. And then..."

It clicks.

Hard.

"Wait," I say. "The man. Calvin. He said—he said he'd run into you. Chatted to you the other day."

Freddie frowns. "What?"

"A man called Calvin. Slicked back hair. Real smelly breath, like—like onions. Broad Lancashire accent. Always smiling with these yellow teeth. Do you remember him?"

Freddie shakes his head. "I... I mean, I've chatted to a few people. But I don't know, Sarah. Maybe?"

It hits me again that maybe that's how he knew my name. Maybe Freddie introduced himself and mentioned I was called Sarah. He's always doing that, Freddie. Introducing himself to people, forgetting he's even met them. Absolute social butterfly, if ever I've met one.

"But what does it matter, anyway?" he asks.

"It matters because of what was in the parcel."

"And what was in the parcel?"

I open my mouth. And the silence hangs there, like a rotten smell.

Freddie stares at me with these big, wide eyes.

"Sarah? What was in the parcel?"

"This... this man," I say. "This Calvin. He... he was at the fete."

"The fete? What're you talking about?"

"He was at the school fete. The day—the day Charlie went missing. He was there, Freddie. I'm sure of it."

His look changes, then. I can see it, even though it's only momentary.

A look of sympathy and fear changing to one of pity.

He lowers his head. Sighs. "Sarah. We've been through this."

"You think I'm making this up? I know what I saw."

"You haven't been right ever since we moved in," he says.

"That's not true. That's not true at all. I've—I've had my issues settling, sure. But I've been okay. Don't you believe me?"

He looks at me with pity, and he half-smiles. "I trust you're telling me the truth, Sarah. But... but the truth is... there is no parcel, Sarah. And it's like I said. I don't remember anyone called Calvin with any onion breath."

"Then go on bloody Google Maps then," I say, dragging my phone out of my pocket. "I barely fucking know the street names around here. Go on Google Maps and tell me how some bloke from 19 Fairhawk just so happens to come round here with a parcel for us. How I'd possibly know the name of that street."

"You're telling me there's absolutely no chance you've come across a street with that name round here in all the time we've been here? Come on, Sarah. Come on."

I open my mouth to argue. But I'm determined. Determined to prove to Freddie that this isn't all in my head. That I am not insane.

"Let's see," I say, typing in Fairhawk Avenue. "Fairhawk Avenue. Right by the bloody fountain, which I've never seen in my bloody life. Then you'll believe me. Then you'll see."

I hit search. Wait. Wait as the WiFi lags, the time stretching on, far longer than it usually does. Fibre broadband, my arse.

I glance up at Freddie. See him looking at me with those same pitiful eyes.

"You can stop looking at me like that, too," I say.

"I'm not looking at you like anything."

"Yes, you are. And I..."

A bleep emits from my phone.

I look down.

And I see the words staring up at me.

Words I don't expect to see.

Did you mean Fairworth Avenue, Cottam, Preston?

I dismiss the suggestion. Search for Fairhawk again.

Wait.

And again, the error message.

Did you mean Fairworth Avenue, Cottam, Preston?

I frown. My heartbeat picking up again.

I cancel the message.

I zoom out from Fairworth Avenue.

I scan the area all around us.

The streets wrapping around us in this suburbia.

I don't know how long I search, but when I finish, I feel cold inside.

I look up at Freddie and tell him what I don't want to admit.

What I don't want to face.

"Sarah?" he says.

I look into his eyes. "Fairhawk Avenue," I say. "It... it doesn't exist. The road Calvin said he lives on. It doesn't exist."

CHAPTER TEN

I feel the needle pierce the vein in my forearm and watch the dark red blood splutter out into the vial.

It's a day after the incident with the parcel, and I'm sitting in the doctor's surgery. It's boiling in here because there's been some problem with the air conditioning. Apparently, this doll of a doctor—Doctor Murray— doesn't want to open the window because she's scared of wasps getting in. Big nest behind the surgery, apparently. I don't want to remind her that just months ago, her lot was advising us to stay as ventilated as possible because of the coronavirus. But of course, a rogue wasp is a much more tangible threat in this instance.

She smiles at me as she holds the needle to my arm. She's a new doctor. She's in her twenties, and she already looks like she's had more work done than I've had in my entire life. Big lips. Hair extensions. Even her eyes look too blue to be legit. Must be contacts. Nobody's eyes are that blue.

"That's it, Mrs Evatt. Shouldn't be too long now."

I nod and smile politely. She looks the sort that likes to small talk, which irritates me. I'm not here because I want to be here.

Fuck, is *anyone* ever at the doctor's surgery because they want to be?

But I especially do not want to be here. I'm here because Freddie made me come. After the fainting incident yesterday, he wanted me to have a blood test to check I'm okay. As well as "ask to see if your head's okay," which I knew didn't have any intentional double-meanings deep down, but I can't help view it that way.

The back of my head is fine, physically. A little scab where I'd banged it on the kitchen floor, but nothing serious. Definitely didn't need any stitches.

But the insides of my head...

I tense up. I know what I saw yesterday. I know a man called Calvin came to our door. I know he handed me a parcel. I know he claimed to be from 19 Fairhawk Avenue, and I know he called me by my name and called Freddie by his name, too.

And I know what was inside that parcel.

A parcel that went missing.

And I know he claimed to live on a road that didn't exist.

But naturally, Freddie had questions. And he had concerns. So he wanted me to head over here, to get my blood taken.

And to have a chat with the doctor about my experience, too.

"Your partner mentioned something about a fall?" Doctor Murray asks.

"Oh," I say, hating Freddie for mentioning it. Bastard. "Yeah. I slipped. Banged my head on the kitchen floor."

"Want me to take a look at it?"

"Really, it's fine."

"I'm the doctor, lovey. You should let me be the judge of that."

I sigh. Shrug. I decide I don't like her. She's too jovial. Unprofessional for a doctor. Yeah, she might be young, and she might be pretty, but that's nothing to do with anything. She's just playing the novelty character role too much, and it pisses me off.

Fuck. I sound like a real grumpy bitch. When did I get so miserable?

She looks at the back of my head. Winces a little. "Ouch. You took quite a tumble, didn't you?"

"It's not so bad. It's my boyfriend. He worries about me."

"I can see why with a little bump like that! Anyway, you should be okay. No need for stitches. Obvs, if you have any worries, you should come back and see me for a chinwag."

Obvs.

Chinwag.

Who the fuck does this moron think she is?

"I'll do that," I say, standing. "Thanks."

Doctor Murray taps away on her keyboard for a few seconds. Stares at the screen. And then I see her turn. See the way she looks at me, eyes slightly widened. The way she does a double-take, back at the screen.

"Okay," I say. "Well, I'll be heading off—"

"Is there... is there anything else you'd like to talk about today? Any... any concerns? About the fall? Or... Or anything?"

I know what she's asking. I know what she's getting at. And the way she can't just be straight and frank about it pisses me off, too.

She's unprofessional. And the sooner I get out of this place, the better.

Because she can't help me.

"I'm fine," I say. "It was just a fall. Hot weather. You know how it is."

She smiles back at me. But I can tell she's not totally convinced. "You would speak to me, Sarah? If you felt like something wasn't quite right. You would speak to me, wouldn't you?"

I look at her, and I want to scream everything at her. I want to tell her about the memory. About Calvin.

I want to tell her about the parcel.

But I know what she will say.

I know how she will look at me.

And besides.

There's somewhere I have to be.

"I know I can trust you," I say.

This seems to appease her. She smiles back at me with those unnaturally white teeth. Walks up to me. Holds out her perfect little hand with all those false nails.

"Well," she says. "Have yourself a smasher of a day! We'll be back to you with your results in no time."

I take her hand.

Squeeze it. Tight.

"Thank you, doctor," I say, smiling back at her.

I snap one of her false nails in my tight grip.

And I can't help feeling somewhat happy about it.

CHAPTER ELEVEN

I stand opposite the school, and I try to convince myself what I'm doing is totally sane, totally okay.

Okay, I know it's probably not cool. I know I probably shouldn't be here. It's not exactly healthy for me. Not exactly a productive use of my time. I know what Freddie would say if he knew I was here. Especially after the fainting incident yesterday and my trip to the doctor's earlier today.

But it was the anniversary of Charlie's disappearance three weeks ago, and I still haven't been back here. That has to count for something, right? I've done so well to stay away. So, so well.

But I felt the call inside me the second I woke up this morning. And I knew there was no way I could resist it.

Because it would make me feel better again.

It's such a beautiful day. So warm. Bright sun beaming down. Perfect blue skies above. Birdsong filling the air. A light breeze, so cool against my skin. It feels so like that day. The day Charlie went missing.

And maybe that's partly why I'm here. Not just to recreate the scene from that day in my mind. But to see if I can piece together some of the missing sections of the puzzle.

I lean against the school's iron gates. It's the summer holidays, so the kids are off. The school grounds are empty, but for a couple of teenagers playing football at the top end of the field.

As I stand there, I can see it again. All of it, in its glory.

I can see the flurry of children racing towards the stage.

I can hear the sound of the band singing. The cheering and laughter.

I can smell the burgers and sausages cooking on the barbecues.

I can feel it all.

But it's that man I see more than anything, now.

Calvin.

I close my eyes, see myself standing there three years ago. And I am certain. Certain I *did* see Calvin. Certain he *did* speak to me.

But it wasn't something I thought anything of at the time. I just let it go. Because why wouldn't I? What relevance did it have, really?

I knew now I was so wrong to dismiss it.

Because I don't give a shit what anyone says or thinks.

Calvin came to my front door yesterday.

That man who was there on the day Charlie disappeared came to my front door and handed me that parcel.

It was him.

It happened.

As batshit crazy as I know deep down, it sounds.

I think back to the days after Charlie's disappearance. It's all quite a blur. A blur of fear. Of sickening nausea. Of crying uncontrollably through the night, not a wink of sleep.

I think of the taste of alcohol to dull the pain.

I think of Gregg sitting there on the sofa beside me. So cold because he can't even bring himself to look me in the eye. He can't even bring himself to comfort me.

Because he blames me.

And God knows I blame myself, too.

I shouldn't have let Charlie go.

I should've kept hold of his hand.

I should've—

"Sarah?"

I jump. Turn around.

There's a man standing there. I don't recognise him. Not at first. Thinning brown hair. Thick moustache. Big blue eyes. Fluffy brown dog by his side. A cockapoo or labradoodle or whatever the hell these weird new bastardised breeds of genetically engineered teddy-bear dogs are called.

I'm about to ask him how he knows me when I realise exactly who it is.

"Glynn?"

Glynn smiles at me, really wide. "Sarah. I thought it was you. How the hell are you doing?"

I nod at Glynn. Smile. Alan, Charlie's old friend's, dad. I've not seen him in years. Truth be told, I don't know why he's here at all. He never used to live around the Broughton area. And I haven't seen him here for a long time.

I tend to avoid the school these days. Tend to avoid anyone once associated with Charlie.

Too many memories.

Too much pain.

Memories I want to push away.

Memories I want to suppress...

"I'm... Yeah. I'm doing good, actually."

He smiles at me. But I can tell he's just humouring me. I see from the way he looks at me that he doesn't believe a word I'm saying. "Wow. Absolute, umm, blast from the past. So what're you... What're you doing round here, anyway?"

I realise then how weird I must look, standing here, eyes closed, leaning against the school gates.

Glynn realises too, so quickly shakes his head. "Sorry. None of my business."

"No. It's okay. New dog?"

Glynn smiles. "Monty."

"Monty," I say, crouching down, patting his fluffy head. "He's a cutie."

"Wouldn't say that if you saw him in his natural habitat. Absolute terror. Chewed up one of Holly's dresses. Crunched on Alan's new Xbox controller. Not exactly the best impression for a pup to make."

I smile. Stand up again. "How are Holly and Alan?"

Glynn glances away. "Oh. They're umm, good, you know? Holly's involved herself with some interesting new friends from her air hostess stuff. They find deals on holidays and share the info with each other for referral money. I don't know how it works really, but she seems happy, and it brings a few extra pennies in, so who am I to complain?"

"Sounds a bit cult-ish."

"Not tempted to join up?"

I smile, a bitter taste in my mouth. "Nah. I'll give that a miss."

He laughs. And an awkward silence hangs in the air, just for a moment. A silence I have to fill.

"Still... still away from home a lot, then?"

Glynn looks me in the eye. I can see he knows what I'm getting at. "Better, now, actually. A lot better. Anyway. Alan. Yeah. He's doing good at school. Top of the class."

"That's good," I say, smiling. Wanting to feel sincere. Wanting to feel happy for Alan.

But a small part inside me knowing Charlie was always brighter than Alan.

That *he* should be top of the class.

"Anyway, how about you?" Glynn asks. "You and Gregg. Sorry to hear what happened there."

I shake my head. "It's fine. The stress. Of what happened—"

"You don't have to talk about it."

"No, it's okay. Everything... everything that happened. It came between us. Never really recovered from it. And things weren't... they weren't great before then, anyway."

Our gaze holds for just a little too long.

"But anyway," I say, looking at the ground. "I've met someone else. Freddie. He's a real sweetheart. Bit of a doofus. But he makes me happy. We're good for each other. Well. He's good for me. I do my best."

"I've no doubt you'll be great for him," Glynn says.

I can see something, then. Sadness in Glynn's eyes, just for a second.

And the memories come piling back in.

Memories I am trying to suffocate.

Memories I am trying to hold back.

Memories I hope will not surface.

"Anyway," Glynn says, clearing his throat, cutting through the awkward silence. "I should probably get walking."

"Sure. I... Same here."

"It's been lovely seeing you, Sarah."

"You too, Glynn. Pass on my best to Holly and Alan, won't you?"

He smiles. Nods at me.

But I know right away he won't say a word about seeing me to his wife and son.

Why the fuck would he, after all?

He walks past me, Monty in hand. And I swear he walks a little closer to me than is appropriate. I swear his arm brushes against mine, just for a moment.

And that's when I turn around and sense an opportunity.

"Glynn, you and Holly were always pretty in with the parents at Broughton. This sounds really weird, but... well, do you know anyone called Calvin? Slicked back dark hair? Big brown eyes? Sort of... yellowish teeth? And I... I know it sounds horrible, but I've got to say it. Breath stinks of onion?"

Glynn stares at me for a few seconds. Longer than feels comfortable.

"Why do you ask?"

"Nothing," I lie. "It's just... Well, I guess I had a memory. Just wondered if anyone comes to mind."

Glynn stares at me again. The seconds roll on. I feel the tension. I feel the discomfort.

And I feel like he has something to tell me.

And then he shakes his head.

"Sorry, Sarah. Nobody like that I can think of."

I want to tell him I think he's lying.

But for the sake of my own dignity, I can only nod.

"I'll see you around then."

"Yeah," he says, smiling at me. "See you around." And then he pauses. Hesitates. Just for a moment. "Stay well, Sarah."

And then he turns around and walks away, Monty in hand.

And as he disappears, as my face flushes, I feel the flurry of memories rushing out.

Glynn holding onto me.

Kissing my neck.

Fucking me. Hard.

And my phone buzzing with sweet messages from Gregg, all while it happened.

CHAPTER TWELVE

Okay, so Glynn Maynard might've fucked me once.

I know, I know. I'm not the innocent person you wanted me to be. But I'm human. And you have to understand that mine and Gregg's marriage wasn't great, even before Charlie went missing.

Gregg worked away a lot. He worked for a microchip company, TruCorps Technology, and often went over to the Netherlands on business matters. Leaving me alone, at home, with little Charlie.

I don't know how Glynn and I got into each other's circles. To be honest, it all happened very naturally. We'd see each other at school when we were picking the kids up. I'd have Alan over at mine to give Glynn a hand while his wife, Holly, was away. She worked away a lot too—she was an air hostess, so it was the nature of her job.

But it was just a friendship between two adults. Nothing else.

I've no idea how things got so illicit so quickly. So sordid so quickly. Everything was always very friendly. Very cordial. There was nothing dodgy about a thing. Even though the grounds were there. After all, Glynn never mentioned me to Holly. And I kept

Glynn a secret from Gregg, too. I should've known things might take something of a turn, right from the start.

One night, Glynn got around to mine to pick Alan up, and there was just this sad aura about him. I could smell booze on his breath. And I swore I saw a bruise around his eye.

And seeing him, standing there, in this daze, I couldn't help asking him in.

We told Charlie and Alan to play upstairs for a while. I'd bought Charlie a new PlayStation game recently anyway, so no doubt they'd snap up the opportunity of a little extra time playing.

I sat Glynn down. Asked him if he wanted a drink. Initially, he resisted. But then the red wine opened up, and we both had a few glasses, and I hadn't eaten much, and before I knew it, my head was spinning and...

Yeah. Well. Glynn told me he'd had a rough time at home lately. That he didn't want to go into it. Holly. And even though he was being so cryptic, I felt sorry for him.

And when he spoke of his loneliness, of missing Holly, I felt it. I understood. I knew what it was like to be without my husband for half the week.

And even though Charlie was a delight, even though he was six, so hardly a baby, and even though I couldn't exactly complain when there were single parents out there doing a damned sight harder a job than I was... still, I felt it.

It began with a kiss. I don't know what possessed him to do it. He leaned over and kissed me on the lips, and before I knew it, as much as I wanted to hold back, as much as I wanted to resist, we were tangled up in one another, and he was kissing my neck and stroking my thighs, and then he was between my legs and inside me and grunting and pulling my hair and coming inside me and—

The door creaked.

I remember looking around.

Remember that fear.

A fear that someone was there.

Charlie. Or Alan. Or both.

We stopped, then. Got dressed immediately. And Glynn left with Alan, barely saying a word.

Alan never came around after that.

Glynn and I did our best to avoid one another.

We tried. We really, really did.

I still feel guilty about it now, right to this day. It was wrong. I know that.

But I'm human. I made a mistake. I'd had too much to drink, and I was lonely. It was one brief encounter, and that was that.

Honestly.

I contemplated telling Gregg about it. I really did. I sat there prepared to tell him when he got back from work, and I braced myself. Really.

But I'll never forget how he walked in. Smile on his face. Flowers and chocolates in hand.

I'll never forget how he leaned over, kissed me on the cheek.

"Happy anniversary, angel."

I'll never forget the guilt I felt right then. The tears I cried in the bathroom. The way I washed, right inside myself, to get rid of any trace of Glynn; to scrub him from myself.

And I'll never forget telling myself that it didn't matter that Glynn had come inside me. I wasn't at my most fertile. Gregg had come inside me so many times without any repercussions. I'd be fine. Besides, he'd pulled out before the bulk of it had gone inside me.

But I'll never forget the increased need to pee that picked up in the weeks after that, too.

And the tiredness.

And the spottiness.

And then the missed period.

I'll never forget taking the pregnancy test on my own in the bathroom. Waiting for that line to show itself. And knowing it couldn't be Gregg because Gregg had had the snip—we'd decided one was enough for us.

I'd never forget sitting there and waiting for that line.

And I'll never forget the positive result.

I stuffed it in a load of tissue. Heart racing. Panic taking over. Feeling sick. So, so sick. Knowing I needed a trip to the doctors. Knowing I needed to get rid of the baby immediately.

And I'll never forget composing myself by the bathroom door before opening it.

And as I opened it, seeing Charlie standing there.

Staring at me.

"Are you okay, love?" I asked.

A little shaken up. Not expecting him to be there. Not at all.

I saw him open his mouth. Saw his wide, brown eyes peering right at me.

Then, I saw him nod, and close his bedroom door, and disappear.

That's the first day Charlie started acting weird with me.

That's the first day I started suspecting he knew something about what happened with Glynn and me, after all.

And that was just a matter of days before he went missing.

Before the stress of his disappearance caused a miscarriage, taking abortion out of my hands.

That was the day everything spiralled apart.

CHAPTER THIRTEEN

I'm standing in the middle of the school field and trying to remember that day in full detail.

It seems like the perfect opportunity. After all, it's so sunny. I can feel the sweat rolling down my face. Feel my hands, slightly damp and greasy, just like they were three years ago, almost to the day. If I really focus, really take deep breaths, I can fully convince myself I can still smell the barbecue. I can hear the children. I can feel the buzz all around me.

But whenever I open my eyes, I see nothing but bright green grass, nothing but birds flying overhead, nothing but a few teenagers kicking a football around.

I see emptiness.

No matter what I do, I cannot rewind to that day.

And I cannot change things.

But maybe I can remember something.

I walk slowly along the grass. I see myself here, just three years ago, with Charlie's hand in mine. I see the way he is distant with me. Detached with me. And I realise that's why I never brought it up. That's why I never attributed any relevance to his behaviour.

Because deep down, I knew.

He must've seen me. He must've seen something going on between Glynn and me. And that's why he was being so weird with me. So distant with me.

At the time, as much as I didn't want to admit it, I told myself it was probably because of the whole Glynn situation. And the whole pregnancy situation, too. Even though I didn't know how he could possibly know about that.

Whatever the case, I didn't think it was particularly off at the time for him to be a little weird with me.

But what if I were wrong?

What if Charlie's behaviour was something to do with his eventual disappearance?

That's something I'm starting to entertain more and more by the day.

But how did Calvin fit into the equation?

Was he even here even though Glynn seemed adamant that he knew nobody by Calvin's name or description?

Still. He didn't seem particularly convincing on that front.

I walk through the grass. Reach a slight slope. I can see the stage up ahead, even though there's nothing there anymore. The fete hasn't taken place in the last three years. They decided not to have it the first year, in honour of Charlie, I like to believe. Nothing to do with not having the funds to cover it, being a small failing school reliant on donations to stay afloat.

And it seemed like that tradition of no summer fete prevailed. It makes me sad, in a way. Because the fete should still go ahead. What happened to Charlie shouldn't stop the rest of the kids having fun, enjoying themselves.

But it stood to reason that naturally, parents were fearful after what happened.

I remember the police. The lead detective, Brian McDone, a thoroughly unpleasant man who smelled of body odour and seemed more interested in internal police corruption than a missing child, according to the notes I saw scattered around his desk. I remember when the detectives finally started to take the case seriously. When their initial blasé, laissez-faire approach turned into one of panic. When they began to search—truly search—for my son.

And when that search stretched on, and eventually, they concluded he was officially missing.

I often wonder how much that initial delay in searching for my son cost things. There could've been evidence pointing towards his disappearance on that first day. Evidence that was cleaned up in the dismantling of the fete. Apparently, it sparked a major inquiry. But naturally, like all inquiries, it came to nothing. A few slaps on the wrist, a few admissions of negligence, but a stance of solidarity that the department "did their best".

But they didn't find my son.

They didn't find a single fucking trace of my son.

How could that be "doing their best"?

But now I'm here again. I'm staring at the area where the stage was placed. Behind it, I can see the tall maize fields shaking in the wind. I remember running through there with Gregg and Charlie once, hand in hand. The maize is so high it towers above your head, no matter how tall you are, at this time of year. We ran so far into it that we lost our bearings, got totally lost. Took us an hour to find our way back.

I reach the edge of it. Stare at it. Sometimes, I wonder if that's what happened. If Charlie went running into there and got lost. Never came back.

But the police searched it. Had the dogs out. Had the helicopters out. And there was no trace of DNA or footprints or clothes or *anything* that pointed towards Charlie.

I stand here opposite the maize, listening to it rustling in the breeze when movement catches my eye over to the left.

I see someone at the edge of the woods.

It isn't a thickly wooded area, so it isn't particularly ominous.

Just a small bunch of trees, not tightly packed together. People often walk their dogs through there. So again, it isn't anything I should be too concerned about.

But for a moment—just for a moment—I swear I see someone there.

Standing there.

Watching.

And I don't know why, but it feels like this figure is looking right at me.

I walk towards them. Faster now. Up the slope in the grass. Past the two teenagers playing football, their Bluetooth speaker blaring out some shitty rap music.

And as I get closer to the trees, I realise I don't see that figure anymore.

I don't see *anyone* anymore.

I step into the woods.

Feel the atmosphere shift straight away.

It is sheltered in here, so it is cooler.

The warmth of the sky is gone.

The light and heat from the sun.

I look around. I saw someone. I'm sure of it. Man? Woman? I don't even know. It was so brief I could barely even take that much in.

But there was someone here.

I'm sure of it.

I start to turn around, to head back towards the fields, towards the sound of the teenagers kicking their football and laughing as their rap music blares out when I see something.

A glint of something, over on the ground.

My heart picks up.

My stomach churns.

It can't be what I think it is.

Not here.

Surely not?

I walk over to it. Slowly. My whole body tense. My heart pumping so fast I can feel my skull vibrating.

I walk over to the tree. Crouch down to pick it up. Hardly wanting to touch it. Because touching it makes it real.

But then I pick it up, and I see what it is.

Exactly what it is.

Exactly what I feared.

I stand there holding it in my hand when I hear rustling behind me.

I spin around. Let out a little cry.

A man stands there walking his Golden Retriever. Young man. Mid-twenties, I'd guess.

"Sorry," he says. "Didn't mean to startle you."

I shake my head, my whole body shaking. "It's—it's okay. Sorry."

He looks at me like I'm weird, and then he walks off with his dog, back out into the sun.

And there I stand in the darkness.

Shaking.

Cold to the bone.

Holding the item I've discovered in my hand.

Wondering how the hell I've found it here.

But knowing one thing.

This can't be a coincidence.

This can't be all in my head.

Someone is doing this to me.

CHAPTER FOURTEEN

It's late, and I'm sitting at the dinner table, and even though I have barely eaten a thing all day, I have no appetite whatsoever.

I stare down at the arrabbiata pasta dish Freddie has cooked for the pair of us. Another one of his classics. Simple dish, really. Garlic, tomatoes, shallots, Birds Eye chillies. Covered with a hefty helping of grated parmesan.

But sometimes, it's the simple things in life that pack the biggest punch.

I know this too well.

I smell the garlic in the air. The shallots. The heady aroma of the warmed crusty bread smothered in butter. The glass of Merlot.

But I cannot even entertain eating a thing.

I glance up. See Freddie looking across the table at me. Wide-eyed. Half of his bowl already finished. And I know he's concerned.

And he has every right to be.

But really, how am I supposed to act?

I ran into Glynn, which shook me up.

But that's nothing compared to what I found in the woods, right by the school field.

He puts his knife and fork down. Reaches over the table and takes my hands in his. "Sarah, talk to me."

I look up at him. Look up at my gorgeous, doting boyfriend. And I see that lost puppy look to his eyes again. That sense he wants to help me. That he just wants to reach inside my head and see what I'm hiding from him.

I can't even begin to start.

Especially not when it comes to what I found in the woods today.

I've tried not thinking about it. Tried pushing it into a compartment, deep in my mind. But I know as much as I push it away, as much as I try to resist it taking over my thoughts, it'll creep up on me.

Probably when I'm in bed, trying to sleep.

Or when Freddie is fucking me.

I see myself like I am outside my body. My eyes are dead. I'm staring up, and I'm doing all the right things and making all the right noises.

But inside, I am somewhere else.

I may be here physically.

But mentally, I am absent.

I am elsewhere.

I.

Am.

Not.

Here.

"You've barely said a word all night," Freddie says. "You've barely touched your food. And it's my arrabbiata, too. You love my arrabbiata. That's how I know something's wrong."

He tries to joke, bless him. Tries to lighten the atmosphere, lift the mood.

There are things I want to tell Freddie.

There are so many things I want to tell him.

Things he won't believe.

Things I barely believe myself.

But I fear telling him everything. Because as patient as he is, as much as he insists he won't judge me for anything, I know he will see me differently if he knows the truth.

The same way the doctor looked at me differently earlier when she consulted my medical records.

And I am tired of being looked at differently.

That's what I love most about Freddie. I am a blank canvas to him. I am something new to him, even though we have been together for eighteen months.

I do not have the muddy grime of the past dripping from my skin.

And it makes me feel like maybe I can be a new person again because of it.

"I'm sorry," I say. "It's—it's just been a tiring few days, to be honest. The move. All the stuff with Charlie's anniversary around that time. And... And yesterday."

I glance up at him. Hope to catch his eye. I'm torn between wanting to talk about Calvin and not wanting to go into it at all because I know he'll just look at me like I'm crazy.

But he just nods. Half-smiles. "I get it. Sorry. I don't mean to be so pig-headed. I just... sometimes I find it hard to get through to you. Like, it's like you want to talk to me or want to say something. Or you're keeping something to yourself. But as much as I try to find out... I feel like you're getting further away. Slipping between my fingers."

I nod. I can't take that too personally. I know he's right. But it's for his protection. He might not realise it, but it's for his protection.

He can't know everything. He simply cannot.

Some things in life are choices. Others are immovable. Unchangeable.

This is one of those things.

"To be honest," I say. "I think... I think it'll help when I get started back with work." It's a lie, of course. How am I supposed to let what I found go? How am I supposed to let the whole Calvin thing go?

But how am I supposed to tell Freddie any of this without him thinking I am insane?

I think about what I found in the woods.

I think about showing him.

Showing him and showing him that I'm not crazy.

He smiles at me again. Sips his wine. "You know, I think it's good you're thinking about work."

"I sense a 'but' coming."

"Just... hear me out. Your mum and dad. They haven't even been round to see this place yet."

I think on my feet. "They'll be around in no time. It's just their way. Never in a rush."

"Don't you think..."

"What?"

"Nothing."

"No, go on."

"It doesn't matter, Sarah."

"It sounds like it does matter."

"I just... Don't you think it's weird that I've been seeing you for eighteen months, we've moved in together, and I still haven't met your parents? Met anyone to do with you, for what it's worth? Any friends? Family? Anything?"

I hesitate for a second. He's right. It is weird he hasn't met my mum or dad. Or Cindy. My sister, Elana? Not so much. Lives over in Sweden, after all.

Or is it Norway?

I forget sometimes.

"I'm sorry. I know it seems weird. I just... I guess after what happened with Charlie, I've sort of learned to compartmentalise different aspects of my life."

"What's that supposed to mean?" Freddie asks. Tomato juice dribbling down his slightly stubbly chin.

"I just... I don't know. My mum and dad. They were a bit weird about what happened between, erm. Between me and Gregg."

He looks up at me. Narrows his eyes. "What about it?"

I realise I'm stepping into treacherous waters now. Freddie is lovely, but he has a jealous streak when it comes to other men. As much as he is so far out of the picture, my ex-husband is a particular bone of contention. "It doesn't really matter."

"It sounds like it matters."

"Look, Freddie. I've had a rough day."

"And I've had a rough day too," he says, raising his voice slightly. "I've got clients complaining because I'm leaving work in a hurry. Or not quite getting my work done up to standards. All because I'm worried sick about you. Texting you. Checking up on you. And it just feels like... Oh, I don't know."

I swallow a lump in my dry throat. "No, go on. Say it."

He leans back. Looks beyond me. "I just feel like... I feel like even though we're close, there's an aspect of you I barely know. Like I... It's like I barely know you sometimes. I know *about* you. And I feel close to you. I love you. But I don't *know* you."

My throat tightens. My heart starts to pick up. I can feel tears burning behind my eyes.

He looks at me. Right into my eyes. "Your mum. Your dad. Your friend, Cindy. It's like... I don't know. Sometimes it just feels like I have this idea of you and your life and the life you used to live. But I feel like I'm only getting... a version of it. A surface-level version of it. And I guess I want to know what's under the water. I want to see the rest of the iceberg. Dodgy, lumpy icy bits and all."

He smiles again. An attempt to crack a joke. To inject some humour into this conversation.

And I can only smile back.

Even though I feel like shit inside.

I take a deep breath, and I think about what I found in the woods.

And then I sink my fork into the pasta and force a cheese-drenched lump of it into my mouth.

"I'm trying," I say. "I'm doing my best. And I'll do better. I promise."

I say these things to Freddie, but I see the way he looks at me.

I see I am proving the point he just made.

I see I am an iceberg.

I see the mass of ice beneath the surface.

And I push it back down.

Because nobody wants to see that.

Nobody.

Especially not me.

But you're going to see it. Because it's surfacing. Whether you like it or not.

CHAPTER FIFTEEN

I know I cannot hide from the truth any longer.

I am lying awake in bed, Freddie snoring beside me. His snores don't annoy me like snores usually annoy people. They reassure me. Calm me. Remind me that no matter what, despite everything, I am not alone.

I stare up at the ceiling. I swear I can see something moving up there. A spider. Or something else. Sometimes, it's like the whole ceiling is moving with footsteps when I'm drifting in and out of sleep. Sometimes, I swear I hear things up there. And sometimes, I swear I wake up and see eyes staring down at me from the darkness above. Feel breath on my skin. Hear talking. Whispering.

But I know it's all in my head. I've felt like I'm being watched for years. Even when I was with Gregg. That night on the sofa with Glynn. I thought I saw something moving in the corners of my eyes then, too.

And there's been other times. Times I'm alone. I'll look up, and I'll see something hovering there, just for a moment. And before I can even focus on it properly, it's gone. Zap. Just like that.

I told Gregg about it once. He didn't even look at me when I mentioned it. "Eye floaters," he said. "Want to get yourself a pair of glasses."

Dismissed. Shot down, just like that.

Yet another reason mine and Gregg's marriage fell apart so drastically.

But now I'm here with Freddie, and just as I see the movement above, it disappears again. I blink a few times. Nothing there. Gone. Eye floaters. That's all it is. It annoys me that Gregg was right all those years ago. It annoys me that he was right about a lot of things.

I'm lying here awake, listening to Freddie's snoring. I can hear something outside. It sounds like teenagers laughing. Again, as much as I know it will bother the neighbours, I don't mind the outside noise. Reminds me that I'm not alone.

I look at the streetlamp outside our window. It's flickering again. Freddie rang someone from the council about it yesterday, and someone came to take a look at it. It looks like whatever they've done, it hasn't done much.

But again. I don't mind. The light comforts me.

And I know I won't be sleeping tonight anyway.

I look over at Freddie. Look at his muscular outline lying there in bed beside me. And I want to lean over and wrap my arms around him. Hold him tight.

Instead, I lean over. Whisper into his ear the most sincere words inside me right now.

"I love you. So, so much."

He grunts a little. Stirs. I want him to turn around. To tell me he loves me too. To distract me from what I know I'm going to have to do.

But then he rolls back into a comfy position and starts snoring again.

I smile, my eyes welling up with tears. Of course, I can't hide from it any longer. I can't put it off any longer. I need to face reality, to face the truth.

My gorgeous, caring boyfriend cannot delay the inevitable for much longer.

I step out of bed. Quietly as I can. I walk across the bedroom floor. The house isn't a new build, but it's robust. Well, for the most part. Not like the old cottage I used to live in. I learned where every creaky floorboard was in that place. Spent so many nights climbing slowly up the stairs to avoid waking Charlie up. Stepping into his room. Leaning down and kissing him on the head and telling him how much I loved him and how grateful I was for him and how I didn't deserve him—

"Sarah?"

I stop.

Turn around.

Freddie is staring at me in the darkness with tired eyes.

"It's okay, love," I say. "Just need to pee."

He nods. Rolls back over. "I love you," he mumbles.

I smile and feel a tear roll down my face. I want to go back to bed with him. I want to close my eyes and let him wrap his arms around me and forget everything.

I want to ignore the truth. I want to run from reality.

But I know I can't run from this much longer.

So I step out of the bedroom. I walk into the bathroom. Lock the door. Check it's locked. Then check again.

And then I turn around to face this room that still barely feels like my own. I see the hole leading to the attic, right above the toilet, and I hear the creaking up there of the wind.

And then I stare at the cistern at the back of the toilet.

I walk over to it. Stand in front of it. My heart is thumping. My hands are shaking. And as I stand here, I have the horrible sense that Freddie might've already been in here. That he might've found it.

But no. If he found it, he'd have questions.

A lot of questions.

I put my hands on the side of the cistern lid. I lift it. Slowly. I have visions of dropping it. Of the immense bang. Waking Freddie up. Making him worry.

And having nowhere to hide what I found in the woods near Charlie's old school today.

I lift it slower.

Place it down on the floor, being careful to stay super quiet.

And then I look down and see the plastic bag I placed in there staring back up at me.

I swallow a lump in my dry throat. My stomach does somersaults. I'm not sure I can do this. Not sure I can handle this.

But I reach inside the cistern.

The icy water wraps around my hands.

I lift that plastic bag out, and I stare at what's inside it.

My heart beats faster. I swear I hear movement from mine and Freddie's room, but it's just those kids outside. A glass smashing somewhere.

I hold the plastic bag with my shaking hands, and I stare at what's inside.

The thing I found in the woods today.

The very same thing I found in that parcel Calvin handed me yesterday.

The parcel I swore was real.

The parcel that went missing when I passed out.

The parcel Freddie claimed never to have seen at all.

I stare at it, heart pounding, wanting to vomit, and I read the words staring back at me.

I KNOW EVERYTHING

Written in red ink.

And beside that written note...

I see it, the other thing from the parcel, and my head starts to spin.

Then I fall to my knees and vomit into the toilet.

CHAPTER SIXTEEN

I decide it's best not to tell Freddie about the note I found in the woods—or the rest of the parcel contents, for that matter.

Some things are best kept to ourselves, after all.

Right?

I go back to bed after vomiting into the toilet. I put the note back into the toilet cistern. And I put the other thing in there, too. The other thing I discovered. The thing I can barely even begin to understand how it has appeared after all these years. Why someone would choose to taunt me like this.

All I know is that I'm not insane. I did not imagine Calvin as Freddie suggested. I did not imagine the parcel.

But then that leaves questions of its own.

Because if that parcel was real... then how had it gone from in my hand one second to in the middle of the woods near Charlie's old school a day later?

I swallow a lump in my throat. I'm in bed, and it's early. The bedroom is stuffy. I can hear birdsong, so loud, almost *too* loud. Freddie is downstairs making breakfast. Quorn bacon butties, as usual. Another part of his meat free kick. Disgusting. Look like fucking shoe soles. Smell even worse.

As I lie here, I rub my eyes. I've barely slept a wink. A fog hangs over me, the fog that always comes with a lack of sleep. I spent the whole night awake, tossing and turning, trying to think about everything. Calvin. The parcel. The note: I KNOW EVERYTHING.

The *thing* accompanying the note.

And then how that parcel went missing as I lay there collapsed on the kitchen floor.

Only to turn up when I just so happened to be at Charlie's old school field a day later.

I can't make sense of any of it. Nobody knew I was going to Broughton, for one, and especially not the school fields. I didn't tell Freddie a thing about it. And I didn't speak to anybody else.

But as I lie there, listening to Freddie whistling downstairs, I am met with a realisation that I can't deny.

Somebody moved that parcel from my hand.

Somebody took it from me, and then they took it into the woods for me to find.

And there are only so many people it could be.

I think of Calvin. There at the door one second. Gone, the next.

Could he have sneaked in?

Taken it from me as a part of some game?

I think of him standing beside me at the school field. A memory resurfaced. He was there. That day Charlie went missing, he was there.

I can't see how he wasn't involved.

And yet...

There's another possibility I've tried not to entertain. A possibility that makes me feel sick, right to the core.

What if it was Freddie?

I shake my head as I lie on the plump, sweaty pillow. I love

Freddie. He loves me. He cares about me. He wouldn't do a thing
to hurt me.

And yet, I can't help picturing him walking into the kitchen.

Taking that parcel—and its contents—from my hand.

Hiding it so I can't find it.

I shudder. Maybe he did it innocently. Maybe he saw what I'd
found and wanted to hide it so I wouldn't freak out. Sure, it would
be cruel to make me believe I was going crazy. But maybe in his
twisted logic, it was better that way than to face the truth.

But... no.

If it were innocent, he would've had questions.

Lots of questions.

I know Freddie. He isn't he type to let things go easily.

I think of who else it could be as Freddie clatters around with
the pots in the sink. He's sweet, but he doesn't have the deftest of
touches. I think of the people I've run into. I think of Glynn over
at Broughton. What was he doing there? Did I catch him by
surprise?

Was this something to do with him?

Was Charlie's disappearance something to do with him?

I think of the bruise under his eye that night he came to visit
me. The night we had sex. The questions I wanted to ask him,
and the answers I couldn't give.

I think of all these things.

But I draw a blank.

All I know is a man called Calvin came to my door, gave me
the parcel, vanished without a trace. And I'm pretty sure that
same man was there on the day Charlie went missing.

I think about going to the police. About telling them
everything.

And then I feel a knot in my stomach.

Resistance.

One thing is for sure now, as I lie here in bed. Somebody

knows something about my past. And I can't help wondering if they know something about Charlie, too. If it links, somehow.

If maybe my hope, deep down, that he's still out there, may not be in vain after all.

But then why do this?

Why do any of this?

And just what doors in my mind are going to be opened, all in aid of finding out the truth about what is happening to me?

I hear the front door close, and I know I am alone.

I yawn, but I figure there's no point staying in bed. Today, I'm going to investigate. Maybe I'll tell Freddie about what's going on in time. But for now, I need to keep this to myself. Especially when I cannot rule out who is stalking me. Who is doing this to me.

I have to keep my cards close to my chest.

I walk into the bathroom. Use the toilet. And as I sit there, I can't help lifting the lid and checking if the note is still there.

As I lift the lid, I have a horrible feeling that the parcel might be gone. That Freddie might've found it and moved it.

But when I lift the lid, I see it's still there.

I pull it out, somewhat relieved. Well, as relieved as anyone with a note etched in red ink with I KNOW EVERYTHING scrawled across it staring back at them can be.

I decide I can't keep it here. The toilet's making an annoying squeaking noise, and if Freddie does his usual thing of fixing any problem before I even *know* it's a problem, he'll be in this toilet in no time.

I try to figure out where I can put it so he won't find it. Our bedside cabinets are a bad idea. The attic, also a bad idea, especially after hearing about the state of that place.

But then maybe if I put it up there, it'll be out of the way at least. And at least that way I can explain it easily. There has to be plenty of spaces up there to hide it, right?

I go to pull the hatch open to the attic when I hear a knock on the door.

I freeze. My heart starts pounding. Flashbacks to Calvin the other day.

But he wouldn't come again, would he?

He wouldn't risk it.

Surely not.

I head downstairs slowly. I stuff the contents of the parcel in my jacket pocket. My legs are weak. My whole body feels numb. I take deep breaths as I approach the door.

I can see someone through the glass standing at the other side.

Dressed in red.

A momentary sense of fear.

And then I hear a cough.

"Postie," he says. "Got a parcel for you. You alright to sign for it?"

I sigh a breath of relief. The postman. Of fucking course. I need to pull myself together. Need to get a grip.

"Sorry," I say, turning the lock, lowering the handle.

When I open the door, I see the postman standing there. He's wearing thin-rimmed glasses, is in his early fifties, I'd guess, balding slightly on top. He smiles at me as he stands there in his grey shorts—why do postmen always wear shorts?

"Hi, Miss," he says. "Not had the pleasure of meeting you or your fella yet."

I nod. "Sarah," I say. "Sarah Evatt. As you'll probably know from the post."

He chuckles back at me. "Sarah Evatt. Right. I'm Yuri. Nice to meet you."

I nod, and I sign the electronic device he hovers before me. It's a parcel for Freddie, much to my relief. Not sure my ticker can quite handle another mystery parcel just yet.

"Nice house you got yourselves here," he says.

I nod. "Thank you."

"Settled in?"

"Just about," I say. And I sense he can tell I'm lying. Postmen must be excellent judges of character, the number of people they run into every day. Detecting sincerity and false sincerity must be an absolute boon for them.

He takes the little signing device away. Nods. "Well, I guess it can take time, huh? Never easy settlin' into a new place. Anyway. I'd better be off. But it's been a pleasure meeting you, Sarah."

He turns around to walk down the pathway when I sense an opportunity.

"Is there a road called Fairhawk Avenue on your route, by any chance?"

He stops. Frowns. "Fairhawk? Doesn't ring a bell. Let me guess. Got some mail for 'um?"

"Something... something like that. A bloke. Calvin. Can't remember his surname. He came by here a couple of days ago with some mail for me. Said he was always receiving post for the couple who used to live here. Sort of... implied it was a common occurrence."

The postman smiles. "I know what you're trying to imply here, trouble. But believe me. I'm the best bloody postman in Preston I'll have you know! I wouldn't drop a clanger like that. Not a chance."

He laughs, clearly messing around. And I smile too. Even though I'm disappointed not to find anything else out about Calvin.

"Sorry," he says. "I wish I could be more help. If it happens again, get a surname and a full address, and I'll look into it. But I'm pretty sure it ain't me. It'll be one of them Hartley's Mail guys. Hartley's are always screwing their deliveries up, pardon my French."

"Yeah." I laugh, trying to dismiss it. "I know how they can be."

"Anyway," he says, raising a hand. "It's been a pleasure."

I catch a glimpse of the mole on his Adam's apple, and I freeze.

My mouth goes dry.

And I'm back there.

The burning sun.

The maize all around me.

Whispering in my ears.

A softness right through my body.

My heart beating faster and faster and his hands hitting my back and—

"Mrs Evatt?" he says.

I'm here again.

In my doorway again.

"You okay there?" the postman asks. "Looked a little unsteady on your feet there."

I nod. I swallow a lump in my throat, my mouth so dry it's crying out for water, and I go to shut the door. "Sorry. Thanks for the parcel. I'll... I'll see you soon."

He nods. Doesn't look entirely convinced I'm okay. But then I guess he'll deal with a lot of weirdos in his line of work.

I go to step inside, face flushed, wanting to douse my skin in cold water when I notice something.

The neighbour's house.

Next door, to the right. An old woman lives there who keeps herself to herself. Moira, I think Freddie said she's called. Always smoking. Never seen her without a cigarette between her lips.

But it's what's above her front door that catches my eye.

A CCTV camera.

I look up at that camera, and an idea sparks inside me.

I smile.

CHAPTER SEVENTEEN

I press Moira's doorbell and wait for a response.

It's another scorching, beautiful summer's day. A group of kids keeps biking around the neighbourhood, clearly playing some kind of bicycle-aided game of hide and seek. A grey-haired bloke walks with his little daughter on her pink scooter beside him. It's all smiles. All happiness. Even the birds sound elated.

But there's this sense of claustrophobia circling me. I feel suffocated. Like the events of the last couple of weeks and the summer heat are all conspiring to make me feel more and more ill at ease.

But Moira, my next-door neighbour, will mark a start.

A start of figuring out what the hell is happening to me.

And proving to Freddie that I was right about Calvin after all.

I push the doorbell again. Moira's house is much like ours, only it looks a lot less well maintained, more run-down. There are garden gnomes everywhere. I've got to watch where I step so I don't knock any over. In the window, I see a black cat staring out at me with bright green eyes. The windows look dusty. Dirty. I can almost picture the damp, mouldy smell inside there from outside.

I hear no footsteps. No movements.

I push the doorbell again when I see movement through the frosted glass.

"Just a second. I'm an old lady, for heaven's sakes. Not as sprightly as I used to be."

I step back, feeling a little guilty. Maybe I have been hasty. But it's all with good reason.

Moira's CCTV camera.

If she has footage of the other day when Calvin came to drop off the parcel, maybe I can get some answers.

Maybe I can prove to Freddie that I'm not insane.

And maybe, just maybe, I can find out exactly who this man is and what he had to do with my son's disappearance three years ago.

The door opens.

A little woman stands there. And when I say little, I mean fucking tiny. She leans on her Zimmer. Her back is hunched right over. She wears thick glasses and has long grey hair, right down her hunched back. Her face is covered in moles and whiskers. I want to say she's weirdly familiar, but then all old people look pretty much the same at the end of the day, don't they?

She squints at me. "Yes, dear? Can I help?"

I clear my throat and smile, wanting to make as good a first impression as possible. "Hello. It's Moira, isn't it?"

"It's Ms Grimshaw to you," she says, puffing cigarette smoke into my face.

"Ms Grimshaw. Sorry. I... My name's Sarah. I'm your next-door neighbour. We haven't met yet."

She looks up at me through narrowed, twitching eyes. "So you're the new ones. The ones who have the washing machine on all the time. Noisy thing that is. Hear it right through the walls."

I gulp. Fuck. This isn't going to be as easy as I hoped. She's difficult, that's for sure. "I don't mean to bother you. I was wondering—"

"Do you want a cup of tea? Or are you going to just stand there looking awkward all the time?"

I want to refuse. I want to say no.

But I sense Moira Grimshaw isn't going to be one to take nicely to rejection like that.

I sense I'm going to have to play her game for as long as she wants me to play it if I'm going to get any information from her.

"I'd love one. But only if it's no trouble to you."

She smirks. "It's no trouble to me at all. Kettle's in the kitchen. Teabags are right beside it. I take two sugars."

She smiles at me.

What remain of her teeth are black and rotting.

Two sugars.

That much is very bloody obvious.

I SIT in Moira Grimshaw's kitchen/dining room with a cup of tea in hand and do everything I can to resist sipping it.

The house is a tip. The entire lounge area, which I walked through to get to this back room, is full of all sorts of junk. Cardboard stacked in front of a dusty old television. A mirror, smeared with grease and grime. Old clothes spilling out of a bin bag in the corner of the room. And a load of old electronics, too. Old CRT television sets. Radios. Microwaves. And all their boxes.

The kitchen/dining area isn't much better. It looks like the cups and pots haven't been washed in a lifetime. Flies buzz around, and one particularly stubborn bugger keeps landing on me. The cup I'm drinking from has a lipstick stain on the rim, but it's the best I could find.

This place stinks, too. Body odour. Cigarette smoke. A slight hint of urine. There's a stairlift leading upstairs. But despite being mildly disgusted, I can't help feeling sorry for Moira. This place is too big for her. Far too big for her.

It's warm in here, so I've hung my jacket over the chair. But I'm not sure how keen I am on my jacket coming into contact with *anything* in this filthy house.

"So what brought you to Cottam?" she asks, holding her own cracked brew cup. Clearly just delighted for the company now, as we sit at the dining table.

"A fresh start," I say. "My boyfriend and I, we—"

"You're not married?"

"I... I was."

"Oh," she says. And I realise it's the worst combination of facts I could've told her. "Living with a man unmarried. A divorcee. Don't tell me. The pair of you have a kid, too? Just to upset our dear Lord even more?"

"I did. But he... he went missing three years ago."

Moira's eyes widen. I've caught her off guard. "Went missing? I... I am sorry, dear. I didn't mean... Can I get you a biscuit?"

I shake my head. There's no way I'm going near anything edible in here. But I appreciate the sweetness of the gesture. She's only trying to make it up to me for being a little rude. "It's fine. Honestly."

"A missing child. Three years ago, you say? I... I don't know what to say."

"There's nothing to say. But I guess I moved here for a fresh start. A fresh start away from everything."

"I can understand that. But it's hard, isn't it? Trying to start again when the very thing you want to move on from feels like it's still out there. Like there's still a chance."

I nod. I see her staring into space. And despite getting off on the wrong footing, I realise I like this woman. I think her house is disgusting, sure. But I feel safe here. Comfortable, somehow.

"You speak like you know a thing or two about loss," I say.

She glances up at me then. "My husband. We married when we

were twenty. Had the best twelve years. And then, one day, he just took off and left. No goodbyes. Nothing like that. I was worried. Worried sick. Until I heard news he'd moved to Wales. Met another woman three years earlier. Already started a family with her. I could never have children, so that was always a bone of contention with 'him. But anyway. I'm better alone. Stronger alone. It's the way I like it."

She takes a sip of her brew. I can hear the defiance in her voice, and I know she desperately wants me to believe this strong exterior she's putting across. But I can hear sadness in her tone.

"How long have you lived here?" I ask.

"Only two years. My nephew, Kent. He works in property, and he sorted this place for me. Got it fit with a stairlift. Got it all in gear for me."

"It's a... nice place."

"It's a shithole," Moira says, her tone suddenly shifting into language I didn't expect her to be capable of. "But I'm old, and I'm disabled. And what else can an old disabled person on her own in a big house do, really? I can't clean. I can barely cook. Kent drops by every now and then, but usually just to dump whatever old gadgets he's got in the lounge. Always says he'll clean it out every time. Always. Lazy git. That's what he is. Lazy."

I clear my throat and sense an opportunity. "Kent. I'm guessing he's the one who set the CCTV up?"

"The TV? Barely works. Nothing on anyway. Can't be doing with it."

"No, the CCTV."

"The CC what now?"

"CCTV. Security camera. The one outside, above your door."

Moria narrows her eyes, strains to think for a few seconds. Then she laughs. "Oh. That. Yes, another one of Kent's genius additions to my house."

Excitement kicks in. I sense myself getting closer. "I was wondering if I could ask you something about that, actually. My boyfriend and I. We... we had some trouble the other day. And I think your CCTV might come in handy at finding who was responsible."

"Trouble, you say? Like boisterous kids?"

"Not quite kids."

"Burglars?"

"More... an unwelcome visitor."

Moira puffs her lips out. "Hmph. Whatever the case, it's pointless anyway. The camera thingy is a dummy."

"A dummy?"

"Yes. A dummy. It doesn't work. Kent put it in to scare people off. Stop people wanting to burgle me. Same reason he got the cat. Told me she was a 'guard cat'. Only thing she guards is her bloody litter tray when I'm trying to clear it out. Dirty bugger."

I see this black cat slinking around the kitchen work surfaces, and I feel a sneeze coming on. I smell sourness in the air, and I'm in no doubt that tons of unemptied cat shit sit in that litter tray in the corner of the kitchen.

"So the CCTV," I say. "It doesn't... it doesn't work?"

"About as useful as a camera without a lens."

My stomach sinks. Fuck. I was so convinced I was onto something here. If I could just find some evidence that a bloke dropped a parcel off two days ago, I could begin figuring out what all of this weird shit meant.

I could start figuring out what he had to do with Charlie three years ago.

"Well," I say, putting my untouched brew cup down on the side. "I'm going to shoot. But I really appreciate the brew."

"You'll be round again, won't you?"

I smile at her. Nod. I don't know if I will. But I pity her. And strangely, I like her.

"Of course, Ms Grimshaw."

"Oh, please," she says. "You can call me Moira."

She smiles at me. And I smile back at her. It's Moira's game, and she's winning.

But I sense I've got myself in the good books with her, which counts for something.

I turn to the front door and go to step outside.

"I do remember someone hanging about out front, actually."

I stop. My body freezes. I feel cold.

I turn around and look right at her. "You—you do?"

"Yeah," she says. "I didn't think anything of it. But now you mention it; they were definitely hovering. Thought it was a mailman at first. Now, I'm not so sure."

My heart rate picks up. This is him. She's seen him. She's seen Calvin, and she can provide an alibi.

"What did he look like?"

"I didn't get a good look at him."

"But this—this was two days ago, right? Two days ago, about midday?"

She opens her mouth to speak, and then she stops.

Stares at me.

"No," she says.

I frown. "What?"

"It... It can't've been two days ago. That's when Kent came round for lunch. No, this was... this was yesterday, my love. Someone was outside your house yesterday. And they were standing right out front. Staring right up at your house. For ages."

I feel the shiver creep up my spine.

I feel nauseous.

I feel sick.

"Did they... Did you see them do anything?"

Moira shook her head. "My eyes aren't the best. But... actually, yes. Yes, I did."

"What? What did you see?"

She looks me right in the eye. She looks concerned. But I wonder if that's just because of the way I'm looking at her.

"Moira?" I say. "What did you see?"

"I only remember one thing."

"What was it?"

"He had a boy with him. A little boy. And they were both staring right at your house."

CHAPTER EIGHTEEN

I'm sitting at the dinner table staring at my food again.

Freddie is opposite me. He's not even making any efforts to be subtle anymore. I can see he's worried. Concerned. And maybe slightly pissed off, too.

Because I'm not being straight with him.

I'm not being totally honest.

And he knows it.

I'm shaking. I can feel my whole body vibrating. I don't know whether it's lack of sleep or adrenaline or fear or a mixture of all of it.

I just know what Moira told me.

Yesterday. A man and a child standing outside my home. Staring up at it.

I feel sweat pour down my face. I know I'm probably thinking too much into it. After all, there are loads of kids around this area. It's the summer holidays. Loads of parents walking them around here.

But with all that is happening, I can't help wondering.

"You don't look well."

I look up. See Freddie staring across the table at me. He isn't touching his food, either. It's takeaway. Chinese. My usual favourite, king prawns and green peppers in black bean sauce.

But the sauce looks like tar. The king prawns are rubbery and unappetising.

Neither of us is even pretending to eat.

"I'm sorry," I say, closing my burning eyes and shaking my head. I just want to go to bed. Curl up in bed and go to sleep.

But I know I won't sleep a wink.

Not after today.

Not after what happened at Moira's.

"I've heard enough of your apologies, to be honest, Sarah."

I open my eyes. Frown at him. Wasn't expecting that. "What?"

Freddie stares at the plate of food. I see he looks tired, too. Pale. "I said... I said I've had enough of it. I thought you were turning a corner, going for your blood taken. Going to the doctors'. But you're worse now than you were then."

"I'm tired, and I'm not quite feeling myself, okay?"

"Not quite feeling yourself? You're telling me that."

"Well, if I'm too much to handle, why don't you just fuck off for the night?"

I regret it the second I say it. And I see it hurts Freddie. I see it from the look in his wide eyes. We argue sometimes, sure. But this is serious. He's impatient because he's trying to help me. Trying to be there for me.

And I'm doing nothing to reassure him that I'm merely tired.

"I... I'm sorry, Freddie."

He shrugs. Looks away. "Whatever."

I'm cornered. I'm trapped. I want to speak to him. I want to tell him everything.

I am at bursting point.

But what will he think of me if he knows everything?

What will he think if he knows the truth?

"What happened," I say. "With Calvin."

"Calvin?"

"The man. The man who— "

"Oh," he says, nodding. "The man who dropped the mail off. The mystery man who lives on the mystery road who doesn't exist."

I feel my cheeks burning. Tears building in my eyes. "Take that back."

Freddie pushes his food across the table. Drags his chair against the floor. "You need help, Sarah. Seriously."

He gets up from the table and grabs my plate full of food and his. And then he turns around, walks over to the bin. Pours it all in there.

And I know I am being difficult lately. I know how hard it must be for him, wanting me to be honest with him but seeing I'm hiding something.

But anger gets the better of me.

"I'm the one who needs help?"

He looks around at me. Frowns. "What the hell are you implying?"

I know I should stop because it will open a can of worms. But I can't. "I'm the one who needs help? I think maybe it's you who needs help. Because the way I see it, you must've—you must've taken that parcel. Because it's real. It's fucking real, Freddie. And I know it's real because it's..."

I stop.

Wait.

Where is it?

"What the hell are you talking about, Sarah? Seriously. You're scaring me."

And then it hits me.

My jacket.

I went around to Moira's in my jacket earlier.

Stuffed Freddie's parcel, and the contents of *my* parcel, into my pocket.

And I must've left that jacket round there. On the back of her dining room chair.

Shit.

"Sarah," he says. "Speak to me."

I turn around and walk through the kitchen. Walk into the lounge.

"Where the fuck are you going?"

"I need to get my jacket. And then you'll see. Then you'll see exactly why I'm freaking the fuck out so much lately." I know it's reckless. I know it's haphazard. But I'm at my wits' end. I've given up.

Freddie grabs my arm. "Where the hell do you think you're going?"

"Get off me."

He tightens his grip around my arm.

"I asked you—"

"Get off me!"

I shout. Right in his face. I see specks of my own spit dribbling down his cheeks.

And I see the horror in his eyes as he loosens his grip.

He shakes his head. Stares right at me, like he doesn't recognise me.

"I'm worried about you. That's all. I'm worried about you."

I want to apologise to him. I want to say so many things to him.

But all I can do right now is take deep breaths to try and calm myself the fuck down.

"I left my jacket at Moira's. The neighbour's. I... I went around there today. It's a long story. But I'll just grab it, and I'll be back here. Okay? I'll—I'll explain everything."

He looks at me with wide eyes. Like he fears me.

And maybe he should.

If he knew everything there was to know about me, maybe he *would* fear me.

But then he nods.

"Go. Get it. Then get back here. We really need to talk."

I nod. Turn around. Step out into the cool summer evening air. I see kids playing football up the street. Cheering as one of them kicks the ball between a pair of T-shirts used for goalposts. The air full of the sound of children enjoying themselves. Having fun.

I walk over to Moira's. Knock a garden gnome onto its side, crack its big cheery face. I push the doorbell with my shaking hand. Wait. Wait for her to hear. Wait for her to come to the door.

'Cause I need that jacket.

I need to show Freddie what I found.

What that bloke, Calvin, brought me.

I need him to see. Whether he likes it or not.

I push the doorbell again when the door opens.

Moira stands there.

She's already holding my jacket.

An instant wave of relief crashes over me.

She looks up at me. Smiles. "Didn't expect you back so soon."

I try to keep my composure, fully aware of how flushed I must look. "Thank you. Really."

"It's my pleasure, dear. Although you could've just waited until your next brew trip. I'm not one for people, usually. But I enjoyed today."

I smile at her as I take my jacket. "Me too. Thank you."

"Well, I'll be seeing you."

"Yeah. See you around, Moira."

She closes the door. I regret being so short with her. But right now, I am focused. Solely focused on my jacket. On what's in that pocket.

And showing it to Freddie, once and for all.

I walk back to the front door.

I open it. Step inside.

He's still standing there in the hallway, right where I left him. Staring at me. Like he hasn't budged a muscle.

I rustle around in my jacket pocket. "First, here's a parcel for you." I throw the parcel at him, watch as it tumbles from his chest, and hits the floor. I know I'm being petty, but I'm pissed. I'm pissed at not being believed. I'm pissed at not being taken seriously.

He scrambles to pick it up, his cheeks blushing. "You'd better have a fucking good explanation for this."

"Oh, you'll hear my explanation. Hell, you'll see it. Because it's in here. It's..."

I reach into the pocket even further, and my stomach sinks.

"What..."

I open the pockets.

I search around in there, everywhere.

The inside pocket.

The ones at the sides.

I search them, again and again, and again.

"Well?" Freddie asks.

I don't know what to say.

I don't know what to do.

Because the note.

And the *thing*.

The whole damned parcel.

It is gone.

Again.

CHAPTER NINETEEN

"Well, Sarah? Are you going to explain yourself, or are you going to stand there and keep on treating me like I'm a fucking idiot here?"

I search the jacket pockets again and again and again.

But all searching does is scare me even more.

Because it's not here.

There's nothing in my pockets.

No parcel contents.

No note.

I KNOW EVERYTHING

And no...

No.

I don't want to even think about it.

I don't want even to contemplate somebody else finding it.

"Sarah?" Freddie says. He's standing there with his parcel in his hands. The veins on his temples are up, so I know he's mad.

And can I blame him?

I see things from his perspective. Really. I do.

I've pushed him away. I've buried my head in the sand and tried to handle my problem myself. And I've treated him like shit, isolating him from my problems and just expecting him to tiptoe around me, not to ask any questions.

But I don't know what else I'm supposed to do.

Because I'm afraid.

And I'm afraid now more than ever.

"Moira," I say. "It—it must've slipped out my jacket pocket."

I turn around to rush to the door again.

This time, Freddie grabs me—but gentler, this time. Not as tight.

"Sarah." His voice is softer. Assertive, but soft. Caring. "I don't want you running out there again. I don't want you going next door again. Not now."

"I need to."

"No. What we need right now is... is to sit down with a brew and to chat. Okay?"

I hear his desperation. I hear his love. And I'm sorry. I'm so, so sorry.

Because despite everything, I can hear how much he cares about me.

I can hear how much he loves me.

And how do I repay him?

By keeping him in the dark.

He turns me around. Gently. No malice in his actions at all.

He looks me in my eyes with his big brown eyes.

Holds my shoulders gently with those hard, heavy hands.

"It's okay. We're okay. Both of us are okay."

I shake my head. "But it's not okay—"

"We're going to sit down on the sofa. Both of us. Together. We're going to have a cup of tea. And we're going to talk. You're going to tell me everything that's on your mind. And I'm going to listen. Not judge. Listen. And we're going to get through this. Okay? Both of us are going to get through this."

I shake my head. Because I know I need to go to Moira's. I know I need to search for the note and what I dropped in there.

Because that's the only explanation for it. I must've dropped it all.

"Sit down. On the sofa. I'll put the kettle on. Okay?"

I nod. Take a few deep breaths. They don't do much to stave off the nausea coursing through my body. Nothing will.

But I walk over to the sofa. I sit down. I lean my thumping head back against the sofa, and I close my heavy eyes.

I just want to sleep.

I just want to drift off to a sleep where I don't think of the school, and Charlie's sweaty hand letting go of mine, and the stage, and Charlie's disappearance, and Calvin, and the maize fields and—

"I won't be a sec," Freddie says.

I look around at my boyfriend, who I adore, and smile as he disappears into the kitchen.

But I feel so sad.

Because I'm about to betray him again.

I wait until I hear the kettle click when I get up and run towards the front door.

"Sarah!"

I'm out of the door before he can stop me.

I'm running over the flowers, knocking more of Moira's garden gnomes over.

I'm banging on her door. Hammering her doorbell.

"Moira?" I shout through the letterbox. "It's Sarah. Please. Let me in. Please."

I see people looking at me. Neighbours. Kids in the street. A man walking his dog, muttering something to the woman beside him.

I see their eyes on me, and I feel like I did back then.

Not *just* then but the other time, too.

The time when they judged me.

The time when they—

"Moira!"

I hear no movement, see no movement inside.

So I turn the handle.

It lowers.

I stagger inside Moira's house just as Freddie steps through our front door.

I rush through the lounge. Scouring every inch of the floor.

I barge into the kitchen and search the floor. Every inch of it.

But there's nothing.

Nothing at all.

I turn around to check the lounge again when I hear movement upstairs.

I look up the stairway.

Moira is standing at the top of the stairs.

She isn't on her Zimmer.

And I can't help noticing the stairlift is right here, right at the bottom.

"Where are they?" I say.

"Sarah? What—"

"Tell me where my things are!"

"I gave you your jacket back. You're—you're scaring me, love."

She grabs her Zimmer, now. And she pushes something in her hand, too. A button. A button that brings the stairlift right back to the top of the stairs for her.

And I can't help feeling stupid at that moment for suspecting Moira of any wrongdoing.

But then what am I supposed to think?

That's when I swear I hear a voice.

"Who—who are you speaking to?"

"I—I'm not speaking to anybody," Moira says.

"I heard—I heard movement up there. Is there somebody up there?"

She looks at me like they do when they think you're crazy.

She shakes her head as she settles into her stairlift, keeping her eyes on me. "I—I'm sorry, Sarah. But you didn't hear a thing.

Now, can you—can you leave my house, please? Before I... before I phone the police."

Before I phone the police...

I hear those words then see myself standing here, almost as if I'm above myself, looking down.

And I realise how this looks.

I realise exactly how it looks.

"I... I'm sorry," I say. It's all I can say. All I can manage.

And then, before I can do anything else, I bolt out of Moira's house, out to the onlooking eyes of the neighbourhood...

CHAPTER TWENTY

I think of my life in two distinct segments.
The days before Charlie went missing.
And the days after he went missing.

* * *

I LIE IN BED. The sheets are wrapped around me. Freddie is by my side, stroking my hair, my back. Whispering in my ear. Telling me everything is going to be okay.

But I am not here.

I am elsewhere.

All the bricks of my life have tumbled out of place. All the carefully organised compartments have burst at the seams, their contents spilling out, mixing up with each other. Infecting each other. Polluting each other.

I am in so many places right now. So many places, other than where I really, truly am.

I am on the school field at the fete, Charlie's hand in mine.

I am standing opposite Calvin as he smiles at me with those yellow teeth, with that onion breath.

I am in Glynn's arms.

I am arguing with Gregg.

I am begging the police not to give up searching for my son because he's alive out there, he's alive and he's still out there and he's—

I am in the maize field again.

The summer heat burning down on me.

The weight on top of me.

The neck mole pushing against my mouth.

"Everything will be okay, my angel. Everything will be okay..."

I feel a burning pain on my wrists where he holds me.

And then I hear a baby crying as I hold it close to my chest, part elated, part terrified.

I hear cries and tears and feel pain, and I want to run away; I want to escape.

But I don't know where to run to anymore.

Freddie is holding onto me. I wonder why he's shaking; then I realise it's me. He whispers things in my ears. Sweet things. Reassuring things. Things I want to hear.

And I am so grateful to have him here beside me.

I am so thankful that he is so loving.

So loyal.

I let him hold me, let him comfort me. And I hope we can move on from this. I hope all the bad stuff of the last couple of weeks since moving here can just disappear.

I want to sink into his arms and let him take all my worries and fears away.

And I feel ashamed. I feel pitied. I am not a pitiful woman. I am a strong woman. I am a fighter. I am so, so much stronger than this.

I am not this pathetic, wailing mess.

I have been through hell.

I have been through worse than this.

But I am tired. And I feel destabilised.

And I don't know what the fuck's going on anymore.

He holds me. Strokes me. Softly. And I know he wants to talk. I know he wants to understand. I know he wants to help me so much, and I wish I could let him. I really do.

And I wonder whether perhaps the items being lost might not be such a bad thing after all. Even though I can't understand it. Even though I can't make sense of it. How does it go missing from my house?

How does it go missing and then turn up right by where I lost Charlie?

And how does it go missing from my pocket when I swear it's there?

I entertain the most logical explanation.

A man who lives on a road that doesn't exist.

A man who nobody knows.

Delivering a parcel nobody has seen.

Nobody but me.

My stomach knots.

I don't want to think about the likeliest option here.

I don't want to entertain it.

"You don't think I'm crazy," I say. "Do you?"

Freddie doesn't respond. He just strokes his fingers against my back. Softly. Gently.

"Babe?" I say.

"I... I don't think you're crazy, no."

"But..."

He sighs. And that sigh is enough to tell me all I need to know. "Let's just say there's some inconsistencies. Even you see that."

"I get it. I know what it looks like, and I get it—"

"There are some inconsistencies," he continues. Calmly. "But I don't for a minute think you're crazy. I think... I think you fully believe what you are seeing. I don't think you're lying. I don't think you're being deceitful. I think you're telling the truth. But it's… it's your truth."

There's nothing I can say. He puts it as sweetly and sensitively as he possibly can, in that sweet and sensitive way that is so typical of him.

But he says what he says, and I hear him loud and clear.

"Which means you don't believe me," I say.

He takes a deep breath. Sighs. "It would help if you actually told me what it is we're supposed to be looking for."

And there he has me, again. He has me caught.

I KNOW EVERYTHING

And the other thing.

The questions they will prompt…

No. I can't go there.

I just can't.

I wonder if maybe I am going insane. If I am losing my grip on reality.

But no.

I am certain.

I am convinced.

I am—

"I didn't want to show you this. And I wasn't going to. I'm still not sure it's a good idea. But I think I should probably be honest with you."

My stomach lurches.

He knows.

He's found it, and he knows.

He gets up. Walks to the other side of the bedroom.

And all I can do is lie there.

All I can do is stay totally still as he goes to his top drawer.

As he pulls something out of there.

A box.

A little blue plastic box.

Not what I'm expecting.

He turns around. Doesn't look at me. But looks into this box.

And then he walks over to me.

Holds the box out to me.

"I'm not doing this to make you suffer. I didn't want to do it at all. But... Sarah. You need to look at what's in this box. And when you do, I think you'll realise why I'm so concerned about you. I think... I think you'll agree with me. About what needs to happen next."

I am frozen solid.

I don't want to look.

I don't want to see.

But I know I have to.

I reach for the box with my shaking hand.

I look inside it.

I don't understand. Not at first.

But then I *see*.

I see what is staring up at me—at what it means—and I understand.

"I think you'll agree it's probably wise we get the doctor called tomorrow," Freddie says. "Don't you?"

And the hardest thing to swallow of all?

I can't even disagree anymore.

PART TWO

CHAPTER TWENTY-ONE

I am standing outside the doctor's surgery, and I want to be anywhere but here.

It's nice. Bright. Sunny. Warm. Too warm. I'm over-dressed for the occasion, in a nice skirt, a black T-shirt, a little cardigan over my shoulders. It's weird, though. Firstly, the idea of getting dressed up to go to the doctor's. Grandma used always to be the same. She was in and out of hospital, and she was always adamant that no doctor or nurse could see her without her makeup on.

She died putting her lipstick on in the bathroom mirror one morning. Fell over, cracked her skull on the sink. Massive aneurysm. But nobody was quite sure whether it was the fall or the aneurysm that killed her.

Kind of poetic in a sinister way.

Or at least, that's how I remember it.

Sometimes my memory isn't so good.

But regardless, I've got this weird way of always needing to get dressed whenever I feel rough. Even when I was absolutely wiped out with COVID last year. My head ached. My muscles felt like little knives were stabbing into them repeatedly.

But still, I got up.

Still, I took a walk.

That's exactly why I'm here today. Dressed so nice.

Because even though I feel deep down like I'm completely well, completely okay, I know I am not well.

I can't even deny it anymore.

I can't even run from it anymore.

Not after what Freddie showed me in the little blue box last night.

I wince at the thought. My stomach turns. My skin crawls. Because at that moment, I knew I must be losing my mind. Much as I've tried to insist I'm not. Much as I'm convinced someone is after me, someone is following me, someone knows something about my past... and that someone knows something about Charlie.

As much as I am certain of all these things, I can't deny what Freddie showed me in that blue box.

I stand at the door to the doctor's surgery. Heart beating faster. I don't want to go in. Don't want to step inside. I want to turn around. Walk away. I want to step on the bus and go to Broughton. Or just anywhere, really. Somewhere that isn't *here*. A day to myself to really think things through. To really mull things over.

But I know how pissed Freddie will be if I go down that road.

I know how adamant he is for me to go to the doctor's.

To get myself "sorted out."

Poor Freddie doesn't know a thing.

I scratch my arm without even realising I'm doing it when I feel a sharp pain under my nails. I look down and see it is bleeding.

And seeing the blood there, feeling the sharp pain there, it brings it all back.

The tight pain around my wrists.

Trying to fight free. Trying to scream.

The hand over my mouth.

"Quiet. It'll be over soon. It'll be all..."

And then running through the maize fields.

And then...

No.

The place I don't want to revisit.

The place I don't want to return to.

I shake my head as my heart starts racing, and I hear footsteps behind me.

"Scuse me. You waiting to go in?"

I jump. Turn around. An Asian man, nice smile, standing there behind me.

I open my mouth to apologise. I must've drifted off. Must've got lost in my thoughts. "Sorry," I say. "I..."

I want to tell him I'm going inside. I want to do the right thing for Freddie. He dropped me off here and told me he was just nipping off for some decorating supplies from Anji's Emporium at the top of the road. He offered to drive me home, but I can text him. Tell him I'm meeting Cindy. Anything to get him off my case.

I am torn.

I don't want to let him down. I don't want to disappoint him.

But at the same time...

I don't want to enter this doctor's surgery.

I don't want to be reminded of the past.

"No," I say. "I'm... I was just waiting for someone. After you."

This man looks at me, clearly a little bemused. Nods. "If you say so. Have a good day, miss."

I smile at his blatant politeness. "Thank you. Same to you."

I watch him walk past me. Watch him enter the doctor's surgery.

And as I stand there, head spinning, I know where I need to go.

It's sudden. Very sudden.

And I'm not even sure how practical it is. I'm not even sure of the logistics of what I'm facing.

But I know what has been happening to me lately.

And those events are real.

Calvin delivering the note and the parcel.

I KNOW EVERYTHING.

Losing it in my kitchen.

Finding it in the woods, right by the school field.

Finding it, taking it home and it going missing again.

I know I haven't imagined these things.

I know these things are real.

But Freddie doesn't believe me. Sweet as he is, he doesn't believe me.

So I need to investigate myself.

And that does not start with facing my past here at the doctor's surgery.

I take a few deep breaths. My heart thumping like mad.

Sweat trickling down my face.

I know where I need to go.

I swallow a lump in my throat.

And as wrong as it is, as wrong as I know it is, I walk away from the doctor's surgery.

I get the sense that I am being watched.

CHAPTER TWENTY-TWO

I am back at home, and I know Freddie knows something.

I've tried not to draw too much attention to myself. I mean, in Freddie's mind, I've been to the doctor's, after all. It stands to reason that we've been discussing some pretty personal things. Things he should not be expected to probe me over for a little while.

All in your own time, love. I can almost hear him saying the words to me right now. *Talk to me when you're ready to talk to me.*

But there's none of that.

There's a silence.

There's a coldness.

And I know he knows something.

We're sitting on the sofa. Usually, if I'm feeling rough, or if he's feeling rough, we'll have an arm around each other. He'll be stroking my back with those big fingers, so gentle, so caring. He has a way of putting me into a weird trance like that. Making me feel so calm. So relaxed. So comforted. So at ease.

But this afternoon, there is none of that.

He's sitting beside me, hands glued to his knees. He's staring at the television. A Place in the Sun is on. One of those shows we usually have on in the background. Commenting on the idiots wanting everything from their house but on a ridiculously low budget. Sea view. Pool. Buzzing location. All for fifty thousand pounds, please.

Really? Get a grip.

But we're never usually watching it intensely in any way. We're usually chatting. Doing other things while watching it.

But right now, he's not saying a thing. He looks focused on it. I can see his jaw twitching. Hear his teeth tapping against one another like he's grinding them together. I can see how closely he's watching it. And it concerns me. It bothers me.

Especially because I didn't go to the doctor's today as I'd promised.

Especially because I...

I swallow a lump in my throat.

I'd told Freddie I was going to go for a bit of a walk after my appointment. That I was going to just take the morning for myself. And that wasn't a lie. It was true.

I just wasn't being completely honest about what I was actually doing.

I wonder if he knows. But how can he know? It's not like he's stalking me or anything.

Or is it?

I don't know what to say. I just know that he's quite clearly not in a good mood. Not in a talking mood.

And I don't know how that makes me feel.

Especially when he's usually so caring if I'm not feeling myself.

"Are you okay?" I ask.

He looks around at me. And for a moment, I see that look in his eyes that I dread. A twitch to his eyelids. Disdain. Pure disdain.

He knows.

He knows and he hates me and...

And then he breaks into a warm smile. "Course. Sorry. Just feeling a little tired. Work's getting to me lately."

He puts an arm around my shoulder. Strokes my back, but a little less lovingly than usual.

But he seems okay, though he does look a bit tired. I can believe the work thing.

But still. As much as I'm happy he hasn't quizzed me about my trip to the doctor's... the sheer lack of questions about it has me worried, not gonna lie.

"Aren't you..."

"What?" he asks.

"Nothing."

"Are *you* okay?"

"I just... I don't know. You haven't asked me how today went at all. I guess I'm just checking you're alright."

He looks at me again. Stares deeply into my eyes.

"Sorry," he says. "I just figured it wasn't something you'd want to talk about much. Figured you'd come to me in your own time. This stuff is personal. Right?"

I search his face for a sign that he's mad. He's saying all the right things, but I'm not *feeling* them at all.

But I smile back at him. What else can I do? Make a meal about a doctor's appointment that didn't actually happen?

"How was it, anyway?"

I feel relieved he has finally asked me. It gives me an opportunity to lie. As guilty as I feel... if he finds out the truth, I don't know how I will explain it to him.

There are so many things I don't know how I'm going to explain to him.

So I have to keep weaving the lie as elaborately as I can and just hope he doesn't see through it.

And of course, I'm only doing it because it's the right thing to do.

To protect him.

That might be hard to get your head around. Just how deep this lie goes. But how rooted in protecting him, it actually is.

In protecting myself, too.

"It was... difficult," I say.

Freddie's eyes widen. "Difficult? How so?"

I look away. Swallow a big lump in my throat. I'm starting to feel upset. Mostly through guilt. "I just... Well, it wasn't easy. Accepting... accepting what I went about."

"The papers?"

I nod. Feel a sickly twinge in my stomach. "The papers."

Freddie stares at me a little longer than I'm comfortable with. "And what did the doctor have to say?"

"She... she referred me to speak with someone. Told me it's likely I'm just experiencing some trauma because of it being summer and all that comes with summer. After Charlie, you know. And the move. Struggling to sleep. All these things. But she... she said she was going to up my anxiety meds, too. That they might help."

Freddie looks at me. Right in the eyes. His smile is gone, and I know something is wrong.

"Freddie?"

He looks away. Looks at A Place in the Sun. At this idiot couple wanting far more than their money can afford.

And he sighs.

"That would be a very believable story, Sarah. If it wasn't a complete and utter fucking lie."

My stomach sinks.

He knows.

I don't know how he knows, but he knows.

"What—"

"Don't sit there and play dumb. Don't sit there and lie to me. I watched you. I watched you stand by the entrance to the doctors. I watched you stand there for an uncomfortably long time. And then I watched you walk away to God knows where."

I can't even think up an excuse anymore. "I ... You watched me?"

"Don't flip this onto me," Freddie barks. He stands from the sofa now. "Don't you *dare* suggest for one minute I'm in the wrong in any way here."

"I—I—"

"You didn't go, did you?"

"Freddie."

"Did you?"

"No," I say.

It's almost a relief to admit it. Almost a relief to get it off my chest.

But only for a moment. Because when I look up at Freddie, when I see the look on his face, I know how upset he is.

"You promised," he says. "This was supposed to be the beginning. This was supposed to be the start. Of you getting better. You promised, Sarah. So why didn't you go?"

I move my mouth, but no words come out.

"Why didn't you go, Sarah?"

"Because—because I don't know what to believe," I say.

Freddie narrows his eyes. "You don't know what to believe? Then where *did* you go?"

I look up at him. Heart racing. And as much as I know it'll infuriate him, I know there's only one thing I can do right now.

Tell the truth.

"I... I don't think I'm mad. I don't think I'm insane. I don't think this is all in my head. I think... I think someone is following me, Freddie. Someone is taunting me. About—about the past. About Charlie. And I'm not sure how it all links together. I don't even... I don't even know what it *means*. But I need to solve this."

He stands there. Stares right at me. Silent.

And for a moment, I wonder if he's about to come around. If he's about to see things from my perspective.

"Where did you go, Sarah?"

I open my mouth. For a moment, I consider telling the truth.

"I went... I met Cindy."

But it's obviously a lie. Obvious to anyone.

He stands there a few seconds. He looks like he's about to say something. Like he's really considering it.

But then he storms off out of the lounge.

"It's not in your head, hmm?"

"Freddie?"

He races upstairs.

"Not in your head," he mutters. "We'll see about that. We'll remind you again, should we?"

I hear him going upstairs, and I hear him rustling around the bedroom, and I want to run away.

I want to escape.

But I know I'm going to face the truth.

I know I'm going to face it all over again.

I hear him stomping down the stairs and scratch my arm and feel hands wrapped around my wrists and hear screaming and I'm standing in the maize fields again and—

Water.

Water on my hands.

The sound of crying.

Of something cracking.

And then blood and—

And then Freddie is back opposite me, and I'm back in the room.

He stands opposite me.

That little blue box in hand.

The box he showed me the contents of last night.

The box that prompted my trip to the doctor.

He pours out all the contents onto the floor.

Throws the blue box against the wall.

"Look at that," he says. "Look at that and tell me you're not making this up. Look at that and tell me it's not all in your fucking head."

I don't want to look.

I don't want to see.

"Look!"

I look down at the floor.

Look at the cream carpet.

And I see them, just like I saw them last night.

The pieces of newspaper I tore up two weeks ago.

The ones with Charlie's face on.

The ones with the story about Charlie going missing.

The ones he was so apologetic about.

"Don't you see?" he shouts. "Don't you fucking see?"

Staring up at me, from these torn newspaper pieces, there is nothing about Charlie.

No headline.

No pictures.

There is absolutely nothing Charlie related on these pieces of old newspaper I tore to pieces—at all.

CHAPTER TWENTY-THREE

I think about my life in two very distinct segments.
The days before Charlie went missing, and the...

* * *

OKAY. You get the idea now. My life went tits up when Charlie went missing.

But if you thought it was all rosy and dandy before he went missing, you haven't been paying attention.

* * *

I LIE IN BED AGAIN. I'm feeling more at home in bed lately. I ran upstairs after Freddie threw the newspaper cuttings down on the floor. I didn't want to face the truth. Didn't want to accept the reality before me.

So I ran away. Slammed the bedroom door shut. Squeezed my eyes together and tried not to think of the pain in my arm, of the thoughts of that blistering hot day on the school field.

Of Charlie letting go.

Disappearing.

Calvin beside me.

"Lovely day for it, in't it?"

Of...

Do I see something else now?

Something I've never seen before?

Over by the stage. Right in the corner of my eyes, I think I see something.

Movement.

Movement in the maize fields.

Maize fields.

I think of childhood. I think of how happy I felt on those sunny days. The days in the tall grass. The days with all the other children, like me. How happy we were. How perfect everything seemed. How *sunny* my memories were.

I think of those times, and I feel a warmth inside. Not like the sickly warmth of the day Charlie went missing. Not like the incessant heat of this summer. Of mornings waking up, the bedroom boiling, the windows closed.

I think of a different kind of warmth.

A warmth *within*.

I am laughing.

I am smiling.

And she is standing opposite me.

She is standing opposite me and—

The pain around my wrists.

The screaming.

"Everything will be okay, my angel. Everything will be okay..."

And then Charlie is missing and—

I KNOW EVERYTHING

And the other thing in the parcel.

I open my eyes.

Freddie is by my side. He's got his arms around me. He apologised for flipping at me earlier. Told me it's only because he cares. Only because he loves me. That he wants me to get better.

I want to tell him the truth.

The truth that I won't get better.

I won't *ever* get better.

Because you can't fix *this*.

I feel his arms around me. I hear him saying things to me occasionally. I hear his words of comfort. His words of reassurance. I hear them all, but I know the truth.

There is no emotion to them anymore.

There is no deep sincerity to them anymore.

I am not the woman he thought he moved in with.

He always knew I was damaged. Always knew I was broken by what happened to Charlie. He always knew I was different.

But he had no idea about the depths of just how damaged I am.

And he's starting to tire of me.

I lie there with my eyes open, burning. It's late now. I want to get up and move around. But I know getting up will only provoke questions. I know I'll have to go to the doctor and promise it for real this time. I know I'll have to address my mental problems. I know I'll have to play along.

But while I cannot argue against the newspaper cuttings and the evidence I saw right before my eyes... I am adamant about one thing.

I am not going insane.

I am not losing my mind.

Someone is following me.

Someone is doing all this to me.

I see the streetlight right outside our bedroom flicker and watch it descend to darkness.

I shiver. I don't like the darkness. It reminds me of the darkness that crept into those sunny days when I was a child.

That sense that there was something beneath the surface.

Something I didn't want to look in the eye.

But something I couldn't hide from.

I climb out of bed. Freddie is snoring now, so I'm not so worried. I walk across the bedroom floor, the carpet cool against my bare toes. I walk up to the window. Pull it aside.

The streetlamp has gone out. The street is dark. I can see the lights from televisions in the houses. I can hear laughter somewhere in the distance. I can—

A car door slams shut. I jump. Look down.

It's someone at Moira's. Her nephew, Kent, probably. I can smell cigarette smoke in the air. She's always smoking. One of these days, she's going to burn the pair of bloody houses down.

She speaks to the man in hushed tones, then turns around and looks right at me. I swear we make eye contact. Then she turns away and walks back to her home.

I go to close the curtain when I notice something that makes my stomach turn.

First, I see him standing there.

A silhouette of a man.

Doused in black.

I can't make him out properly, but he's looking up at the house.

Right up into the bedroom window.

I want to shout for Freddie. Want to tell him to come over here. But I can't say a thing. No sounds escape my lips.

I stare at that silhouette standing there. Still staring up at me. Dread filling me, threatening to burst to the surface.

And then the streetlight flickers back to life.

The light blinds me.

I step back, let go of the curtain.

It's then that I swear I hear movement.

Footsteps.

It's then that my stomach hits the floor.

Because someone is in the house.

CHAPTER TWENTY-FOUR

I hear the footsteps downstairs, and I know I am not alone.

I can't move. I'm standing at the window, right at the foot of the bed. The room is light again, the streetlamp outside flickering back to life, filling the room with this nice soft glow that's usually so comforting, usually so reassuring.

But I'm not reassured right now.

I'm fucking terrified.

I can't move a muscle.

Because that person standing outside. Staring through the window at me.

The man.

What the hell is he doing out there in the middle of the night?

Where the hell did he go?

And then...

Another footstep.

And I can't help fearing it's coming from the stairs.

Someone is coming up the stairs.

Someone is coming up the stairs and they are going to find me and they are going to come in this room and—

"Freddie?" I say.

I barely even think before I speak as I stand there, shaking, sweating. I am literally shivering on the spot. Sweat pools down my face. I don't know whether I am stiflingly hot or freezing cold, only that I cannot move a muscle.

Someone is here.

Someone is downstairs.

Or are those footsteps coming from next door?

Or in the attic?

Or outside?

I can't even tell anymore.

I just know it sounds like someone is in my home.

And it sounds like they are downstairs.

"Freddie?" I say again. Turning around to the bed. My boyfriend lies there, snoring away. He is fast asleep.

I want to scream. Want to cry out.

But at the same time, as I stand there in the darkness, I wonder whether waking Freddie is the right thing to do at all.

Because what if this is something to do with the parcel?

With the disappearing parcel?

With all the weird shit happening lately?

Because it has to be. There can be no other explanation for it. Right?

I stand there. Unable to move a muscle. And for some reason, all I can think of is that stiflingly hot day on the school field. My hand in Charlie's. Charlie's disappointment with me. Like there is something unspoken between us.

And the baby growing inside me.

The product of mine and Glynn's brief fling.

And I wonder if Charlie knew. I wonder if my son saw something. And I wonder if that's what led him to be so off with me.

Or if there's something else.

I stand there, heart racing, staring at the bedroom door when I hear shuffling to my left.

"Sarah?"

I turn around. Freddie is sitting up in bed. He's looking over at me with narrowed, bloodshot eyes.

"What's... What's wrong, Sarah?"

I open my mouth to speak, but no words come out. My mouth is so dry. I can't speak.

But despite all my fears about him knowing everything, I am just so happy not to be alone.

Because at least now I have an opportunity to prove to him I'm not insane.

I have a chance to convince him something weird is happening once and for all.

"The man," I mutter. "Outside—outside the window. And then..."

I hear creaking downstairs. It sounds like the kitchen, now.

"Sarah? What's up? Come back to bed."

"Didn't you hear that?"

"Hear what?"

"The—the footsteps."

"What footsteps?"

"There's someone here, Freddie."

"I don't know what you're—"

"There's—there's someone here. I saw someone outside, and then I heard someone inside. Come on. I'll show you. Please."

I walk towards the door, my legs all tingly. I don't want to leave the room. I feel like I'm stepping into a dark, hellish void that I'll never return from.

And then suddenly, Freddie is at my side. Holding my hand. Standing right there with me.

He's tired. His breath smells a little. He seems a bit sleepy.

But he's calm. And he's here.

"Come on," he says. "I'll come downstairs with you. We'll see. We'll both see."

I know he still doesn't trust me. Still doesn't believe me. Especially after the Calvin incident. Especially after the newspaper incident. I know he thinks I'm crazy. I know he thinks I need help.

And I *do* need help. There's no denying that.

But I know what I saw outside.

And I know what I heard downstairs.

"I'm here with you," Freddie says. "Every step of the way."

We step out of the bedroom, out into the darkness of the landing. I switch the light on, and it disorients me. Blinds me. There's something so invasive about a bright light at night. Something so unwelcoming about home in the darkness. It's like it is sleeping too, and it knows when you are awake. Knows you aren't supposed to be awake.

And if you stir too much, it might just wake up itself.

Like a living being.

I approach the top of the stairs slowly. I know what I heard. And as I stand by the bathroom door, I wonder if someone might be behind there. Already up here.

"It's okay," Freddie says, squeezing my hand lightly. "We're okay."

I nod. I want to believe him, want to tell him his presence reassures me. But I'm terrified.

I stare at the top of the stairs.

And as I move towards them, I expect to see someone waiting down there, staring up at me.

There is nobody there.

I stand there a few seconds. Part of me is relieved.

But another part of me is terrified.

Because what if Freddie is right?

What if this is all in my head, all over again?

"Come on," he says. "Let's go see."

We move slowly down the stairs. Step by step. I didn't think the floor creaked here, but it's really going for it now. Waking up the beast. The beast was sleeping, and now it is awake.

And it is unhappy.

I reach the bottom of the stairs. I'm not sure how much further I can go. Not sure I want to see what's in here—or what *isn't* in here.

Not sure what's worse.

"Sarah?" Freddie says.

He looks at me with those calm, collected eyes. Smiles.

"It's okay. I promise. Everything is okay."

I look back at him.

Stare into his eyes.

And I love him.

I love him and his loyal, patient ways so so much.

I nod back at him.

And then we step into the kitchen.

I hit the light right away. And I regret it. I wish I'd just walked in here in the dark and tried to see if I could see anything, but the light blinds me for a moment, renders me useless.

Vulnerable.

But as my tired eyes adjust, I realise there is nothing in here.

The back door is locked.

The windows are intact.

There is nothing out of the ordinary here.

And that concerns me more than I expected.

I look around at Freddie and see him staring at me in *that* way already, and I hate it.

I push past him.

"Sarah—"

"The lounge."

"But—"

"The lounge. I heard someone, Freddie. I heard someone. I know what I heard."

"Don't you think maybe you were just—"

"What? Dreaming? Making it up? Like everything else?"

"No," he says. But I can tell he is desperate. I can tell he is torn.

"Then what?"

"I... I just... I just don't know what to say. Only that we need to go back to bed. Come on, gorgeous."

I stand there. Stare at him. Heart racing. Feeling betrayed, but also understanding. Because I know how hard this must be to him. I know how this must look to him.

"I'll check the lounge first," I say.

I step in there. Search it in the darkness, first. The dark leather of our two-piece sofa. The television screen in the corner, jet black. The two glasses of wine sitting atop the fireplace, one of them only half-empty. There for days now.

I look towards the front door. See nothing at the letterbox. See nothing on the doormat.

I walk to the door.

Check the lock.

Locked.

I stand there. Put my head against the wood. And then I open my eyes and I turn the key and open the door.

I am standing at the door. Above, the streetlamp flickers. I can hear a dog barking in the distance. A car door slamming somewhere. A faint scent of weed in the air from somewhere up the street.

I see nobody where the man stood.

Nobody at all.

I just feel the cool air against my skin, and I ask myself the question again.

Are you insane?

Are you losing your mind after all?

I take a long, deep breath, feel that cool air against my burning, shivering skin, and then I turn around.

That's when I see Freddie standing there.

His eyes are wide.

He looks concerned by something.

Alarmed by something.

A new shade of pale.

"Is—is everything okay?" I ask.

He moves his hands behind his back.

Fast.

He looks at me with those wide eyes.

With that pale face.

"Freddie? What is it?"

He stares at me for just a moment longer than is comfortable.

Then, he breaks out in a smile.

"Nothing. It's okay. Everything's okay. Come on. Let's go to bed, Sarah. Let's go to bed."

I stand there.

I stare at him.

And against my better judgement, I nod.

But as I walk towards my beloved boyfriend, I feel uneasy.

Because I know he is lying.

CHAPTER TWENTY-FIVE

I'm at the doctor's again. Only today, I don't have a choice about going in. Because Freddie is sitting beside me.

I hate the waiting room at the surgery. Hate the way little kids run around like it's their playroom. Hate how stuffy and hot it is. Can't possibly be hygienic, especially with everyone in here already harbouring whatever illness or other.

The ventilation here could be a lot better, especially post-COVID, and since the face mask mandates had been lifted. I'm sweating. The air conditioning pumps away above, but it looks like it could do with a good clean.

Freddie holds my hand. Slightly looser than usual. Like he's not completely here.

And it makes me wonder if something is wrong.

No.

Not just "wonder."

I *know* something is wrong.

He has been off ever since last night. Ever since I heard the footsteps downstairs. Ever since I went to the lounge door and looked outside, fully convinced I was losing my mind.

I turned around and saw him standing there. Wide eyes. Hands behind his back.

His face a little paler than before.

Was he hiding something from me?

Especially when he told me everything was okay.

What is he keeping from me?

I asked if he was okay, and he insisted he was. Told me to get back to bed. But then he disappeared to the bathroom for a little while. I heard the tap running. Then I heard him head back downstairs. Outside.

I wanted to go down there. To follow him. To see what he was doing.

But he just came to bed and told me he couldn't sleep, so he'd had a wash and a hot chocolate. Not too far beyond the realms of possibility. It was something he'd done before.

But ever since I woke up this morning, I've felt something off with Freddie. Something wrong with him.

I wonder if maybe he's just worried about me. Maybe he's concerned. Maybe it's just the shock of everything finally catching up with him. The realisation that I am not the woman he moved in with. I am not the woman he wants me to be.

Damaged, sure. But not permanently broken. Fixable. He knew I had my baggage. What mother who lost their son *didn't* have their baggage?

But this. This was surely beyond what he expected. What he'd signed up for.

And the most painful part of it all is I still feel so, so terrified about being completely honest.

"Sarah Evatt?"

I flinch. Look around.

The doctor is standing there again. My stomach sinks. It's that doll again. Doctor Murray. The pretty one with the blonde hair and the eyelash extensions and nails far longer than a professional doctor should have.

I want to shake my head. To tell her I'm okay. That this is all a mistake.

I want to disappear again. Just like yesterday.

Only I know I can't go where I went yesterday.

Not with Freddie so on my scent.

Because he'll have questions.

So many questions.

I sit there and look at Freddie. And in my eyes, I know I am begging him not to make me do this. Not to face her. Not again.

But I realise, as he squeezes my hand gently, that I do not have a choice anymore.

I nod.

He leans over. Kisses me.

An old man sitting opposite tuts and rolls his eyes. "We're all waiting here," he mutters.

And that alone convinces me to go a little bit slower, just to piss him off.

"Don't worry, Sarah. Everything will be okay."

I frown. "What—what are you—"

"I'm coming in with you," he says.

"What... That wasn't the plan."

"I want you to tell the doctor everything, Sarah. Everything you've told me. And I want to hear you tell her, too. So we can get to the bottom of this. So we can get better. Once and for all."

I'm standing and staring at Freddie in the middle of this waiting room, and I can't believe he is doing this.

Suddenly, I am trapped. I am stuck. And I don't know how to get out. I don't know how to free myself.

"Um... is there a problem?" the pretty doctor asks.

I look at Freddie. Stare into his eyes.

"Please, Sarah," he says. "For us."

I want to tell him he can come with me.

That he can join me.

I want to tell him he can hear everything.

Every.

Thing.

But as I stand there, shaking, like a rabbit caught in the head-lights, I can't speak.

The doctor is here now. Standing beside us. Looking at me like I'm some kind of freak.

And that's because she *knows*.

She saw it on my record, and she *knows*.

"Is everything okay?" she asks.

"My girlfriend would like me to join her for today's consultation. Isn't that right, Sarah?"

I look at Freddie.

I look at Doctor Murray.

I look at the rest of the patients glancing over, staring at this rare waiting room drama.

I look at the little boy in the corner of the room running around, toy airplane in hand.

I take it all in, and I feel trapped.

Tight fingers around my wrist.

Someone pressing me down.

"My angel..."

"Sarah?" Freddie says. "That's okay. That's what we want. To help you. Isn't it?"

I look Freddie in the eyes.

And then I hear Doctor Murray clear her throat beside me.

"It's entirely up to the patient," she says. "Do you want your partner with you for this, lovely?"

I look at her.

I look at Freddie.

And then I say something that I know will have ramifications for weeks to come.

"No," I say.

CHAPTER TWENTY-SIX

I see him waiting in the van for me, and I know already he isn't happy.

I walk over to the van. Get inside. It's cooler outside now. Cloudier too, and quite a bit breezier here. I've only come out in a thin cardigan, so I'm somewhat relieved to get out of the cool and into the heat of Freddie's van. Even though I've been banging on all summer about how hot it is outside. Never satisfied. That's what my mum and dad used to always say. *You're never satisfied, Sarah. We could give you the world, and you'd want the galaxy. Ungrateful, that's what you are.*

I sit in the passenger seat without saying a word, and I wait for Freddie to explode.

He doesn't say anything. Just turns the key, reverses out of the parking spot, and drives out of the doctor's car park as calm as can be. And in a way, I find this worse. I find it more difficult to deal with. Because I *want* him to grill me. I *want* him to lambast me for what I've done.

Because I deserve it.

But this silence, this is even worse.

I know he's pissed with me.

I know he's at his wits' end with me.

And I know he's hurt by me, too.

I know he feels betrayed.

And can I blame him, really?

He stood there in the doctor's surgery and told me he would go into the GP's office with me. He told me he was going to support me. That we were both going to tackle this. Together.

And what did I go and do?

Turn him away.

Stand there, look him in the eyes and tell him I didn't want him there.

I know why that is. Deep down. Of course, I know why.

Because I don't want him knowing everything about me.

I don't want him knowing the truth.

But I know he will feel even more hurt and betrayed by my lack of willingness to have him there.

"It went okay," I say, growing agitated by his silence as we drive through Longridge. "In case you were wondering."

"You sure about that?" he asks.

"What's that supposed to mean?"

"You didn't sneak off on a little adventure behind my back while the doctor wasn't looking today, did you?"

I roll my eyes. "You shouldn't have put me on the spot like you did."

"*I* shouldn't have put *you* on the spot?"

"No. It was wrong. A doctor's appointment is private."

"We're supposed to be working through this *together*, Sarah," he shouts.

"Then the next time you plan on pulling a little trick like that, can you at least give me a heads up, so I have more than enough time to let you down gently? And not embarrass myself and everyone else in the middle of the fucking doctor's surgery?"

He swings the van to the pavement in a sudden jolt. So unexpected, I almost bang my head against the window. The vein on his temple is pulsating. Sweat trickles down his face. His eyes are wide. I can see he is pissed off. I can smell the sweat in the air. This isn't good. Not at all.

We've argued before. But I've never seen him get truly mad. Nothing we can't solve with a nice dinner and some passionate sex, anyway.

But this. This is different. And it upsets me.

"How dare you," he says. And he sounds more upset than annoyed. And that hurts me so, so much. "I stand by you. I stand by you when you're up in the night, claiming you're hearing people in the house. I stand by you when you're tearing up the newspaper sheets claiming Charlie's staring back at you. And I stand by you when you disappear to fucking who-knows-where instead of the doctors'?"

"I—I met Cindy—"

"Cindy? Cindy, your best friend who I've never fucking met myself?"

"She's... I..."

"I don't know you, Sarah," he shouts.

And it hurts me. It cuts me. Really, really deeply.

Because he's right.

He doesn't know me.

The one thing he's wanted from me is the exact same thing I've wanted to hide from him.

And it's only now I begin to see it's tearing us apart.

"This move was supposed to be a fresh start," he says, looking away from me now. Hands clenching the steering wheel. Tears in his eyes.

"What do you mean by that?"

"You know exactly what I mean by that, Sarah. You've been getting distant for the last few months. Even before we moved in together."

"That's... that's not true."

"Don't give me that. Don't—don't give me that bullshit. You

know, I wasn't even going to tell you about the rat last night. I didn't want to fucking freak you out. But you know what? Fuck it."

I frown. First, confused. Because all this talk of me drifting from him for months. It isn't true. Is it?

But then tension wells in my throat about the second thing he said.

"The—the rat?"

"Yeah," he says. "The rat. The one I found on the kitchen floor when you went to the front door."

It hits me like a punch to the gut.

The way he was acting so weird last night.

Like he'd seen a ghost.

"What?"

He looks at me with tired, bloodshot eyes, and he sighs. "I found a rat. Only it wasn't in a good way. Bleeding. Right in the corner of the kitchen. Bleeding out of its mouth and its ears. Tail gnawed down. Had to put the poor thing out of its misery. That's why I was a while last night. Didn't want to upset you. And I guess that's why I'm even more tetchy today. It shook me up. Can't get it out of my head. But... but the weirdest thing was its eyes."

I hear his words, and I already know what he's going to say, and it fills me with complete and utter dread.

"Its eyes," he says. Sounding a little bothered again. A little panicked. Like this was what had been bothering him all along, right since last night. "They... they were gone. Gouged away. Like —like someone had done it to the poor thing."

I hear Freddie's words.

I see myself in those maize fields again.

A teenage girl again.

And I know, for a fact, once again, that this is not in my head now.

Someone is after me.

CHAPTER TWENTY-SEVEN

I am thirteen years old, and I am staring down at the bloodied, mutilated body of a rat.

It spins around on the spot. Chases its tail. And I remember feeling sad for it. Because it's in such a horrible state. Its fur is all tufted, all matted. Blood trickles from its ears.

But its eyes.

Its eyes are what stick with me the most.

Or rather the place where its eyes should be.

Those blank spaces, swollen and red.

I am in the middle of the maize fields, and someone has their hand to my back.

He has his hand to my back.

"It's suffering, Sarah," he says. "Look at it. The longer you leave it suffering like that, the longer you deny it the chance for peace."

I look down at it, and I feel sad. Because I don't *want* it to suffer. I don't *want* it to feel pain. I want it to be okay. Because it looks like it's in pain. Like it's in so much pain.

But at the same time, I don't want to hurt it even more.

I don't want to harm it.

He pats the back of my hand, and I notice the shovel between my fingers.

"Go on," he says. Father, we call him, but he isn't my dad. He smells fresh. Like flowers. Like he always does. So fresh. So comforting. So... nice. "One strike, over the head. That's all it'll take. One strike, then it's done."

I sense them looking at me, the rest of them. The ones who think I'm weak. The ones who tease me for being a scaredy-cat. I sense them snickering at me as they stand there, dressed all in white in the searing heat of the mid-afternoon sun.

I am hot. Sweaty. So, so sweaty.

And I just want to walk away from here. I just want to go home.

But I can't.

I can't, because this *is* home.

I hear *her* laughing, and it makes me feel even worse about the whole thing.

I look up. See her standing there, blonde and beautiful, and I know I'm the ugly one of the two of us. The ugly duckling. The sister who is never quite good enough.

I know she's going to go far. I know Mum and Dad expect the best of her. Dad says she reminds him more and more of Mum every day.

And Father, well... he's got high, high hopes for her.

But they never say that stuff to me.

They say I'm sweet and that I'm cute and that I've got a heart of gold, but never anything like that.

Mostly bad things, actually.

Like I'm trouble.

I look down again. Stare at the rat. Scurrying around, hobbling from side to side. I see now that chunks of its fur are missing. Big patches, painful skin underneath.

And I see now, as I stand with this shovel in my hand, that it stares up at me with those blank, empty eyes.

It gazes up at me like it knows.

Like it knows what is coming.

Like it is begging.

"Go on," Father says.

And then I hear the rest of them standing around me. See them in the middle of these high maize fields. Smiles on their faces. Totally unfazed.

I see them chanting.

See them staring at me.

"Go on, go on, go on..."

My heart races.

I just want to go home.

I just want this to be over.

I look down at the rat. Hold my shovel, my hand getting shakier, sweatier.

I look down into its empty eyes, and I swear I hear it squeaking.

Begging.

But is it begging me to put it out of its misery?

Or is it begging me to let it go?

I stand there, and I lift the shovel.

The chants getting louder.

The air getting warmer. Thicker.

Everything around me spinning.

My only focus, this rat.

"Go on, go on, go on..."

I feel his hand on my back. Heavy. Warm. Reassuring.

And then I hear him. Just once more.

"Now, Sarah. Now."

I close my tearful eyes.

Listen to the chanting.

Feel the heat against my skin.

And then I lower the shovel.

The chants slow down.

My heart stops pounding.

Everything seems to stand still, just for a moment.

I open my eyes.

Drop the shovel to the ground.

"I can't," I say. "I—I can't."

He moves his hand from my back.

I sense the disappointment in the air.

The feeling inside of being a disappointment. A failure. Again.

And I look down at that rat staring back up at me, and—

It all happens so fast.

She steps over.

She lifts her foot.

And she stomps it down on the rat.

I hear its neck crack.

I hear it let out one last little, high-pitched squeal.

And then I look up and see her standing over it.

Her.

Of course, it's her.

Who else?

She stands over the rat. Blood splattered over her white dress.

Smile on her face.

So beautiful. So perfect.

Like out of a photograph.

She looks at me as everyone around her laughs and smiles.

And all I feel at that moment is shame.

"Good girl," he says, walking over to her. Putting his hand on her shoulder. "Good, good girl."

I see her, and I see all this praise and adoration she's getting.

I see the cracked skull and the bloody brains and guts of the rat on the ground.

I see all these things.

* * *

AND THEN I see Charlie and hear the crying and see the maize
fields and the water and the blood and—

* * *

"SARAH?"

I open my eyes.

I am in the passenger seat of the van.

I am back home. Sitting on the driveway.

Freddie is beside me.

He looks at me. A little pale. Not smiling. But calmer now,
clearly.

"Are you okay? You zoned out for a good while there."

I look back into his eyes, and then I nod.

"I'm okay," I say.

"Are you sure?"

I want to tell him no. I am not okay.

But I fear telling him the truth is an impossibility at this
stage.

Especially when he is fully convinced I am insane now.

I want to tell him the relevance of the rat.

I want to tell him why it is so important.

What it means.

I want to tell him everything.

I can feel it bursting out of my system.

Trying to crawl its way free.

"I... I haven't been entirely... entirely honest with..."

And then I stop.

Because I see a man walking down the street.

Walking away from us. Off in the distance.

Looking over his shoulder.

And I go cold inside.

Because this man is the man who gave me the parcel.

The note.

I KNOW EVERYTHING

This man is Calvin.

CHAPTER TWENTY-EIGHT

"Sarah? Are you okay?"

"It's him," I say.

"What? It's who?"

"Calvin. The—the man who gave me the parcel. The man from Fairhawk Avenue. It's him. That's him. Right there. He's right there, Freddie. See?"

I am sitting in the passenger seat of Freddie's van, and I cannot move.

All I can do is sit there.

All I can do is stare.

Because the man walking away from us both.

Walking off into the sunny day.

He may be some way away, but it's him.

There's absolutely no doubt about it.

It's Calvin.

The man who gave me the parcel.

The man who gave me the note.

And the man who went on to disappear without a trace.

"Drive," I say.

"Sarah? What the hell are you talking about?"

"You think I'm insane. All this time, you've thought I was insane. But I'm not. And I can prove it. Drive. Drive right this second, and I'll prove to you it's him. I'll prove to you it's Calvin. It's the man."

Freddie stares at me. Hands on the wheel. A startled expression to his face.

"Freddie!"

"Sarah, no."

"What?"

Freddie shakes his head. "I'm putting an end to all this, right here, right now."

"But—"

"Out of the van, Sarah. And into the house."

He holds out his hand.

Up the street, I see Calvin getting further and further away.

"Sarah?"

I look around at Freddie, and I sense he already knows exactly what I'm going to do.

"Come on," he says. "No more of this. We need to get you inside. And you need to rest. You need to focus on getting better. On..."

I don't hear what else he says.

Because before he can say a thing, I'm out of the van and onto the road.

"Sarah!"

I run down the street. I haven't run in years. Not like this. Not out of fear. Not out of terror.

I can think of a time I did.

But I don't want to think about that.

"Sarah!" Freddie calls.

But I'm not looking back.

I have to get to Calvin.

I have to stop him before he gets away.

I need answers.

I run off the road, onto the pavement. It's warm, and I am sweating. But there is something strangely freeing, running like this. Something that reminds me of my childhood. Of my youth.

Of the maize fields.

Of the smell of freshly cut grass.

Of the laughter and the joy and the—

I see the rat explode before my eyes, and my memories turn sour.

I run onto the pavement. A little girl on a white-tired bike appears out of nowhere, and we almost slam into each other.

"What the hell?" her dad shouts.

But I am focused, and I don't give a shit. Frankly, I don't give a shit what anyone on this street thinks of me right now.

The man who came to my door and started all this is here.

The man who was there at the fete that day three years ago is here.

He's right up the street, right ahead of me.

And I am not stopping until I reach him.

"Calvin!" I shout.

The man keeps walking. Doesn't look back. Not once.

I grit my teeth. Clench my jaw. I want to throw myself at this man. I want to wrestle him to the ground and claw his eyes out. I have barely slept in days. I have had my boyfriend suddenly think I'm some nut job. My neighbours think I'm crazy. And my doctor... hell, my doctor knows things about me that I am ashamed to admit.

But all that aside—everything aside—none of it matters.

All that matters is Calvin.

"Wait," I shout.

Calvin looks around. Glances at me. Frowns. And then he turns around and keeps walking. A little quicker now. Like he's trying to get away from me. Trying to escape me.

Not so fast, you fucking prick. You're not going anywhere.

I run further. My feet are sore. I have a nasty stitch already.

Somewhere behind, I can hear a car engine, and I'm convinced Freddie is following me.

But again, I don't care.

I am done caring what people think at this point.

This is the man who taunted me about my past.

And this is the man who I suspect must know something about Charlie.

The man who was there, three years ago.

Who made small talk with me the day Charlie disappeared.

The man who has followed me.

Terrorised me.

He's right here. And I have a chance to prove my sanity, once and for all.

I am metres away from him when he stops and turns around.

I try to slow down in time, but I fail. I slip. Fall to the ground. Graze my palms on the warm tarmac. A small crowd of people are gathered in the park, all of them staring over at the commotion.

I look up at Calvin as he stands there. Rubbing his arms.

His wide eyes.

His slicked back brown hair.

And that onion breath.

That unmistakable onion breath.

"Are—are you okay, miss?"

I push myself to my feet, and I wrap my hands around the collar of his shirt.

"Who the fuck are you, Calvin?" I shout. "Who the fuck are you, and what the fuck do you want with me?"

Calvin's eyes widen. "What—what are you doing?"

"You came to my door," I shout. Tears streaming down my face. My voice cracking, breaking up. "You—you gave me a parcel without an address. You said you'd met my boyfriend. You said all these things. But they weren't true, were they? They weren't true."

I hear people running over. People trying to stop me.

I see my hands around his throat now.

The fear in his eyes.

And it takes me back.

That maize field.

The dirt in my hands.

"No. Please. Don't—"

"Who the fuck are you, Calvin?" I scream. "And what do you know about Charlie? Because you were there that day. I know you were there that—"

"I'm—I'm Cameron," he shouts.

He yanks himself away from me. Rubs his neck. I can see specks of blood from my grazed palms on the collar of his white polo shirt.

He plants his hands on his knees. "I'm Cameron. Not Calvin. I came to service the boiler at yours a few weeks ago. A favour for your boyfriend here."

I shake my head. I don't understand.

I look around and see Freddie climbing out of the van. He is blushing. People around staring. Walking up. Closing in on the commotion.

"No," I say, shaking my head. "That's not true. You said you were called—you said you were called Calvin."

"I said I was called Cameron," he says. Angry now. The adrenaline clearly buzzing. "I came. Serviced the boiler. And I left. I don't know who the hell you think I am, lady. But you need your head checking, love. ASAP."

I can't speak.

I can barely breathe.

All I can do is stand and watch as a small group of people gather around this man who calls himself Cameron, all of them keeping their distance from me.

"Sarah." It's Freddie. He grabs my hand. Squeezes it. Tight. "Come on. It's time to go home now."

I want to argue as I watch the man I know to be Calvin walk away.

I want to fight.

Because he gave me the parcel.

And he was in my memory of the school field that day.

I want to do so many things to protest my innocence.

But in the end, all I can do is follow Freddie into the van, in the eyes of a crowd, and I cry.

CHAPTER TWENTY-NINE

I sit at the kitchen table with my head in my hands, and I know I cannot hide the entire truth from Freddie for much longer.

Or from myself for much longer.

He sits opposite me. He isn't saying anything. I can smell something in the air. Fruit tea. Berry flavour, which is always usually my favourite.

But right now, it smells bad. Sickly sweet. Makes me want to throw up. Makes me want to hurl.

It's floral.

And that floral smell just reminds me too much of childhood and the maize fields and the rats and—

Charlie.

And *his* hand on my back.

And her smile.

And...

I lift my head. Freddie sits opposite me. He looks away the second I glance at him. But I can tell he's been staring at me all this time. Cogs turning. Trying to figure out what to do. What to say.

How to leave me.

I know I'm probably being harsh on myself. Freddie is lovely. But what is he supposed to think at the end of the day?

I'm having a breakdown right before his eyes.

And I'm not even sure I can deny it anymore.

"We need to talk about what happened," he says. "With that man. With Cameron."

I close my eyes. Shake my head. I think back to seeing him walking up the road. Chasing after him. Sliding onto the ground and grazing my hands.

I think of my hands around his throat.

The fear in his eyes.

Screaming at him. Loud.

And then I see the eyes of the rest of the street on me, staring at me. I hear their whispers behind my back, saying how crazy I am, how insane I am.

And I see how close I was to telling Freddie everything just before I saw Calvin—Cameron, whatever he's called.

And just how dangerous that feels.

"I told you," I say. Barely any energy left. "I... He came round. He—"

"Gave you some parcel. Yeah. But that's not how it happened, is it, Sarah?"

I shake my head. I am exhausted. "I don't know what else I can say to make you believe me."

"I'm not sure there is much else you can say, Sarah. I'm sorry to say that. Really. I am. But... but the truth is, this guy's called Cameron. I bumped into him one of the first days we were here. He fixes boilers, all that sort of stuff. I didn't click when you said about the onion breath. Like, I had a weird feeling, but I didn't want to say. But you were here when he serviced the boiler. You let him in, and you made him a brew, and that was that. Do you remember? And answer me honestly. Please."

My head is a mush of memories and imaginings. I'm not even

sure what is real and what isn't real anymore. I vaguely remember a man coming around to take a look at the boiler, but I don't remember much about him. He just came in and out. I didn't make him a brew; I don't think.

But what Freddie is saying. Is it possible? Really? Could it be that I am confusing what happened? Mixing things up?

Could it be that I am converging memory and fantasy all over again?

Because it wouldn't be the first time.

As much as that pains me to admit it, it would not be the first time.

I swallow a lump in my throat. Look away.

"I think... I think it might be time you talked to me about what happened when you lost Charlie."

I glance around at him. My heart picks up.

"Properly. I don't know a thing about you, Sarah. Not really. And I'm starting to feel like if we're going to go anywhere with this... if we're going to make any kind of progress, I need to know. Do you understand?"

I want to tell him to go away. To leave me alone.

I want to scream at him that this isn't any of his business.

That I can't face the truth.

But I see this loyal, loving man opposite me, and I know exactly what I have to do.

"When Charlie went missing... I fell apart. The trauma of it. It... it messed with my head. I needed therapy. I needed medication. Because some days... some days I didn't know what was real and what wasn't. But that's not what this is, Freddie. It's different this time. I swear it's different this time."

He looks at me. And the way he looks at me, I know what he's thinking. It's not different. It's exactly the same. I know how desperate I sound. How ridiculous I sound.

"I promise, Freddie. This—this is different. It has to be. The thing with the rat, that's..."

Freddie frowns. "The thing with the rat? What does that have to do with anything?"

I cover my face with my hands again.

I shake my head.

I feel my skin crawl.

Because as honest as I have been with Freddie, as much as I have opened up to Freddie, I can't go further.

I can't say anything else.

"You wouldn't understand," I mumble.

"And that's the problem," Freddie says, standing, scraping his chair on the tiled kitchen floor. "Right there, that's the problem. Every time we get close, every time we make a breakthrough, it's two steps back. And I'm not sure I can take it. Not anymore."

I look up. My worst fears are playing out right before my eyes. "Freddie?"

He is crying. Shaking his head. "I want to care for you, Sarah. I want to help you. But if this goes on... if this dishonesty goes on... if this... this lack of openness goes on... I'm not sure I can be *with* you. I'm not sure it's fair on either of us. And it absolutely breaks me to say that. So something has to change."

I can't believe what I'm hearing.

"This changes, Sarah. I'll always care for you. I'll always love you. And I'll always look after you. But you need to start being honest with me. You need to start letting me in. Because I can't be with someone who isn't really there. Not anymore."

It sounds like he's breaking up with me.

It sounds like he's offering me an ultimatum.

And the hardest thing?

The hardest thing of all?

I'd rather he left than open up.

And that tears my heart in two.

CHAPTER THIRTY

It's the dream again.

I am there. I am on the field. I can hear the laughter of children, feel the heat of the sun burning against my sweaty face. My mouth is dry. I can taste the remnants of last night's wine right at the back of my throat. My head aches. Am I hungover? I'm not sure.

I just know I feel guilty.

Charlie's hand is in my left hand. And with my right hand, I feel my tummy. I know what is inside me. I know what Glynn and I created.

And right now, as I stand here, I know it didn't quite happen how I remembered it.

I know what happened between Glynn and I was... more complicated than I've made out.

But I push that aside.

It isn't relevant.

Not for now.

I see the band on the stage. I see the mass of children swarming towards that stage. And I see Charlie. only...

Wait.

No.

Charlie is still by my side.

And Calvin isn't here anymore.

Calvin or Cameron or whatever the hell he wants to call himself is not here.

He is gone.

I feel a shiver down my spine. Because things are happening differently now.

I am standing there in the field, and Charlie hasn't let go of my hand.

He's still holding my hand.

"Don't you want to go see the band?" I ask.

He looks up at me. Opens his mouth.

And then he shakes his head.

"I... I'm okay here, Mum."

I hear these words, and I well up.

Because I know he struggles to fit in.

I know he has had problems with his friends.

I know Alan can be a bit harsh on him sometimes.

I know all these things.

And yet, all a mother can do is stand here, hold her son's hand, and nod and smile.

"Are you sure?" I ask. "I think it'd be good. To go see Alan. To get real close to the stage. Don't you?"

And it's these words that hurt me.

These forgotten words—words I've tried to gloss over—that kick me in the stomach.

Because he looks up at me, and I see the disappointment in his eyes.

He sees where I am looking.

He sees why I'm trying to get him to run down to the stage.

"Go on," I say. "Run along. You'll have fun."

He opens his mouth to say something.

"I need to speak to you about... about something."

I glance over his shoulder, and I see Glynn standing there, and I want to be beside him. I want to feel the tension between us. The heat between us.

I want to hear my son out—of course I want that.

But at that moment, it shames me to admit it.

I've suppressed it. So, so much.

But at that moment, I want Glynn more.

"We can speak about it later. Go on. You go watch the band. Enjoy yourself."

He opens his mouth to protest.

And then he lets go of my hand, and as I see this moment, I scream.

I want to stop myself letting go of his hand.

I want to stop him.

But I can't.

Is this the truth?

Or is this a false memory?

I don't even know anymore.

I just know that the next moment, I am in the maize field.

Glynn is deep inside me.

Fucking me.

Fucking me while the band plays behind us.

While the children scream and laugh.

Fucking me while he's already got a child inside me.

And while God knows what happens to Charlie keeps on unfolding, I am moaning out Glynn's name.

Pulling him closer.

"Harder. Harder. Harder."

I'm chanting.

Just like they chanted around me.

"Go on, go on, go on."

"Harder, harder, harder."

And then I am digging my fingernails into his back and

coming hard, and all I can think of is the shame, the pleasure, the guilt, the loss, the ecstasy.

And then it snaps.

All of it snaps.

* * *

I AM NOT the woman you thought I was.

I have my secrets.

And I'm beginning to lose sight of which of those secrets is even true anymore.

I need to see someone.

I need to speak to him.

Desperately.

I just worry what toll it might have on me and my relationship.

But I know what I have to do now.

CHAPTER THIRTY-ONE

I have to wait until Freddie is absolutely certain I'm safe to be left alone before making the move that I know could wreck my already flailing relationship.

A week has passed since the Cameron incident. Since the tense stand-off with Freddie over dinner. Nothing has happened. Nothing of note. No more parcels. No more packages. Nothing out of the ordinary whatsoever.

And I have to admit that it makes me wonder. Everything suddenly going silent, right after that final trip to the doctor's?

Right after the change in my medication?

I know how I sound. Like, I'm fully aware of what you're thinking right now. I'm insane. I'm unreliable. You can't trust me. I get it. Really. Sometimes, I don't even know if I can trust myself.

I snapped after Charlie went missing. I struggled with the fallout of it, mentally. I neglected myself. It took a toll.

And the whole saga put me on medication that helped me get my life back in order.

There is no shame in that.

But right now, I am adamant when I say that I am convinced of what is happening to me. And the talk of the dying rat is what convinced me, more than anything. Because I didn't see that. Freddie saw it. And it just ties in with my memories far too... conveniently.

Unless *that* memory is a false memory too.

No. Don't be insane, Sarah.

You know what's real.

You know there's something going on here.

Even though every fucking thing is starting to suggest otherwise.

I stand at the door. The house I'm at is nice. A big detached, right in the middle of the countryside, just outside of Preston. Fields all around. Barely any houses down here at all. Ivy-covered walls, something that always reminds me of being younger.

Nature.

I stand there at the door and wonder if I really want to do this at all. Whether I really want to go through this exchange. And really, what I'm trying to achieve by it. Am I looking for some kind of confirmation? Some kind of redemption? I'm not even sure myself anymore.

I just know that I need some security. Some stability. Someone from my past, as much as I try to push against it, as much as I try to resist it.

I go to pull the ornate doorbell handle when I hear the door creak open.

I turn away. Instinctively. Fear taking over.

I see a woman standing there.

She is blonde. Older than me. Hair looks bleached like she's trying to hide the fact she's going grey. I make a note to try it myself. Might freshen my image up a bit.

She's holding a bin bag. Staring at me with wide, green eyes.

"Can I help you?" she asks. Smile on her face.

I wonder if this is her. The woman he moved on with. The one he left me for. Because regardless of what I did, that's still how it happened. *He* left *me*.

"I... I'm sorry," I say. "I shouldn't be here. I..."

I turn around. Walk away.

"It's Sarah. Right?"

I stop. Freeze. The hairs on my arms stand on end. She knows. Knows exactly who I am.

I swallow a lump in my throat and turn around. "Look. I'm sorry. I know I shouldn't have come here. I'm just going through a rough time right now, and I guess I was looking for some answers about the past. There's nothing to it. I promise."

She stares at me, somewhat bemused.

"And if... if Gregg asks, please don't tell him about this. Keep it between us. I won't bother you anymore. Sorry."

I go to walk to the gate, burning up, embarrassed. Idiot. Why the hell am I coming here in the first place? What am I hoping to discover? What am I hoping to achieve?

"Who's Gregg?" she asks.

I stop. Turn around.

She is still standing there with that bin bag in her hand. I want to ask her if she's joking, but she looks deadly serious.

"Gregg," I say. "I thought... Sorry. But you're not married to Gregg? Gregg Evatt?"

The woman smiles. "I'm not married to anyone. Is there a problem, Sarah?"

I shake my head. Am I literally losing my mind? If Gregg doesn't live here, then why the hell am I here in the first place?

"Sorry," I say. "I... Who are you? And how do you know me?"

"You really don't remember?" she asks.

I sense I remember.

I sense, deep down somewhere, there is a memory of this woman.

But I have pushed it away.

I have suppressed it.

I have—

And then it clicks.

Hard.

"I thought it was you," she says. "I mean, I know we shouldn't really speak about... about the past. But it's a long time ago. And the past is the past, right? Why don't you come inside? I was just making a brew."

But I am frozen to the spot.

Because this is the house Gregg bought. This is where he moved. I know it was because he told me.

He...

Wait.

"How—how long have you lived here?" I ask. It's the only thing I can say.

"Why don't you come ins—"

"How long have you lived here?"

"I've... I've lived here for ten years, darl. I got away. Just like you did. But whoever you're looking for... he isn't here. I'm sorry."

I stand there.

I stare at this woman.

I see her eyes, and I see a reflection of myself in them, a reflection of the things I've been through myself, the things I've seen.

I see a look of regret.

And a look of shame.

And then, as much as I want to stay, as much as I want to talk, I turn around, race out from behind the gate, and I run.

CHAPTER THIRTY-TWO

I sit in my red Mini Cooper just outside Costa down the road from the cottage, and I try to wrap my head around everything that just happened.

It's the middle of the afternoon. Freddie is on a job today. I told him I'm going to start up my online tutoring again soon, something I've been dragging my feet on for weeks, but really that's all just a lie. I've spent the last week convincing him I'm okay. Taking my new meds. And sure, nothing has happened since then. Everything has been... nice.

But I have no intentions of setting any goals or targets when it comes to my tutoring today.

I told him I was nipping out. That I was just getting some air. Might grab a coffee. And he was so worried about me. So concerned. He even offered to take the day off and join me, but I reassured him I am okay. That I am perfectly capable of taking a day for myself. That I am totally fine.

But how can I even say that anymore?

Especially after what happened at the cottage, with the woman?

I hover over Gregg's number on my phone. I haven't called

him in years. Haven't text him in years. I just know he told me exactly where he was moving to. Nook Cottage. Langford Lane. Grimsargh. The place me and Gregg used to drive past. The place he told me we'd both move into, together.

Only that's not how it happened in the end.

He moved in here after our issues. With his new Mrs, no less.

Only that's not how it happened. The woman there. It was someone from my past. Someone I barely recognised, yet still *her*.

There was no room for mistakes. And this couldn't be a coincidence. It just couldn't.

I can't shake the feeling that the woman from the cottage is involved with all the weird shit that has undeniably been happening to me lately.

Especially with what she knows.

And that makes my stomach turn even more.

Because if the woman is involved... does that mean Gregg is somehow involved, too?

I think of my ex-husband, and I shake my head. Gregg was sweet. Loyal. Reserved. He was as straight as they get. I was the villain in that relationship. I was the enemy. I was the one who slept with Glynn. Who got pregnant. And I was the one he blamed for losing our son.

But I think of the look in the woman's eyes as I stood at her door.

I think of the fact that Gregg gave me that address.

It can be no coincidence.

Preston isn't a massive place, sure. But it's not *that* small. Surely not *that* small.

There's only one thing for it, I realise, as I sit here now.

I need to find Gregg.

I open up my phone. Search 123People for a trace of him. Nothing. Fuck.

Then I try Facebook. But again, no sign of him. Which I find hard to believe because he was always a bit of a nerd.

I hover over his number. Think about just ringing him. Just getting it done with. Telling him I have to speak to him about something; something serious. Something concerning Charlie.

But then if he is involved somehow in all of this... then he isn't exactly going to take nicely to me calling, is he?

I wonder what he knows.

I wonder if there is more to this. To all of it.

I tap on his number and throw caution to the wind.

The line dies in an instant.

Shit. So either he's blocked me, or this number doesn't exist anymore.

I go into WhatsApp. If someone else has his number, I'll be able to see their new photo next to his name. A sure giveaway that someone else has his phone.

But then the line died. It didn't even ring. So where's that going to get me?

I put the phone down. Close my eyes. Take a few deep breaths, in through my nose, out through my mouth. And I think about the ramifications of Gregg knowing the woman from the cottage. Of what that would mean.

But then... Gregg already knew, didn't he?

That's the real thing that came between us.

The truth about my past.

The truth about everything.

I am trying to disappear into the darkness when an idea springs to mind.

The offices down by the docks.

Gregg moved there years ago. He was really proud. Said they were really modern offices, really flash.

I know it's a bit stalkerish. A bit crazy.

But I know how serious this is. How important this is.

For some reason, Gregg gave me the address of that woman from my past.

And I need answers on that front.

I sit in my car. Eyes open. Phone on my lap.

I know where I need to go.

And I know who I need to look for.

I start up the engine.

That's when my phone buzzes.

I jump. Half expect it to be Gregg calling me back, which fills me with fear, just for a moment.

I see it's a Snapchat notification.

I dismiss it. I don't even use bloody Snapchat. And the account looks like a spam one, anyway.

I'll check it later. Forgot I even had the bloody app installed, in all honesty.

I shove my phone in my pocket.

And I start up the car, and I drive towards the docks.

It's time to track down my ex-husband.

And it's time to get some fucking answers.

CHAPTER THIRTY-THREE

I sit in the car park of the Preston Docks Business Park and wait for Gregg to emerge.

It's 5 o'clock. He always used to finish bang on five. He'd rush out of the building, call me right away, tell me what he was going to pick up for dinner on the way back. Or if I were making dinner, he'd always nip out and grab a treat for the pair of us anyway. A bottle of red. A couple of big bars of chocolate. He was always so nice. Always so caring. Always so... grown up.

I have my regrets about how I treated Gregg. Really, as horrible as it is to admit it, he's the man I should've settled down with. Freddie is amazing—truly amazing—but I sense he doesn't truly get me. Truly understand me. Especially now the cracks are showing.

I'm sitting in my car. I stare up at the building where he works. TruCorps Technology. I hope he's still here. If he isn't, I'm on a wild goose chase. I know how happy he was to get this promotion. How content he seemed. How he said he was set for life here.

But then, I know how much life can change, too.

I wonder if he's even still around here. Still around Preston.

It's just over two years since I last saw him. A lot can change in two years.

And I'm beginning to wonder just how much I really knew about Gregg, especially after the whole woman at the cottage thing.

My stomach turns when I think of it.

The maize fields.

The warm weather.

And...

No.

I don't want to think about *her* now.

I don't want to think about *anything* to do with that day when I was sixteen now.

Or what it might mean.

What it might have to do with Charlie.

If it has anything at all to do with Charlie.

I just don't know.

I look around the car park. Stretch my legs. Try to find his car. He drove a black Audi Q8 when I last saw him. Loved his cars, though, so wouldn't surprise me if he's upgraded already.

I see the doors to the offices open. See people step out. In the distance, I see seagulls swooping overhead, over by the length of the docks. Quite a nice spot, the docks. Gorgeous on a sunny evening. Used to come for walks here when Charlie was little. One hand in mine, one in Gregg's. Walk him along the side of the docks and smile and laugh together. Those days were so good. They were so perfect.

But then I see the cracks. I see Charlie slipping out of my hand. Cutting his knee and crying.

I see Gregg rolling his eyes. Telling me I'm so irresponsible with Charlie. That I'm haphazard.

I see Charlie crying and—

No.

It's better to think of the good times.

It's better to think of the times when things were nice.

When things were perfect.

I watch the men and women leave the office, and I am alarmed not to see any sign of Gregg. It makes me wonder whether he's still here at all.

But then there's the other possibility, too. The chance he's just on a day off.

I lift my phone again. Hover over his name. Call him again.

Line dies, right in an instant.

I have an idea, then. TruCorps. It's just shy of five, but they have people working around the clock. I don't want to go storming inside, making a scene. But I can call them. I can get through to Gregg.

I Google their number, back in my car now. Hover over it. Question whether I'm actually really doing this. Then realise it's the right thing to do. Definitely, the right thing to do.

I hit their number, and then I wait.

The wait is torturous. Lasts forever. My heart beats faster, faster. I start to regret this. I'm in the wrong. I need to put the phone down and I need to get away from here and I need to—

"Good evening, TruCorps Tech, how may I help?"

I freeze. For a moment, I think it's him. I am convinced.

"Hello," I say. Then I clear my throat. Realising I'm going to have to lie a little here. "Is Gregg in? It's—it's his Mrs. Can't get hold of him on his mobile."

There's a pause. Static at the other end. Rustling.

"Hello?" I say.

"Gregg, you say?"

"Yeah. Gregg—Gregg Evatt."

Another pause.

"And it's his Mrs?"

I feel my stomach tightening. Something is wrong here. Something is wrong, and it's going to bite me on the arse if I'm not careful.

"It is, yeah," I say, trying to come across more confident. "Is there a problem?"

Another pause.

Then: "A couple, yeah."

My stomach sinks.

"First off, Gregg Evatt hasn't worked here for six months."

A punch to my gut.

Embarrassment. Crippling embarrassment. Like a kid caught in the sweet jar.

"I—I'm sorry. I've—I've rung his old work by mistake." It's the best excuse I can think of.

"That'd be a viable explanation," he says. "Nice save. Only unless you're a ghost or unless Gregg's moved on superfast, that's not possible."

I frown. "What?"

"Gregg Evatt's fiancee died. Six months ago. He's been off work ever since. Whoever you are, lady, don't call here again. And leave Gregg the fuck alone. He's been through enough."

The line goes dead.

I sit there. Heart pounding. Hand shaking.

Gregg doesn't work here anymore.

His new fiancée is dead.

And I'm back at square one.

CHAPTER THIRTY-FOUR

I t doesn't take me long to find the details of Gregg's fiancée's death.

I decided to go home last night after going to Gregg's old workplace. I didn't want Freddie getting suspicious. Today, I'm in a rough little estate just outside of town. I can hear dogs barking nearby. Graffiti covers the walls of the terraced houses. On the street corner, I see a couple of teenagers in black hoodies smoking something that smells a lot like weed.

As I sit here in my car, I still wonder whether I've got this right. Because this can't be right. Gregg was always a bit of a snob. No way he'd move to a place like this.

But then I remember the details. I remember exactly what I saw.

The obituary for his fiancée, Yara. Yara Nimikov. Easy to find. Obituary, Gregg and Preston, all in Google, all over the last few months.

And there she was.

Died of cancer just six months ago.

Place of residence not too hard to find with a few Google searches.

But as I sit here, pulled up to the pavement, I still can't quite believe it. Why did Gregg lie to me about where he was moving to? I mean, I get it. Really, I do. It's a shithole here. Nobody would exactly be *proud* living in a place like this. Especially moving from our little cottage in Broughton, which was so nice.

But then there's the other stuff, too. The woman at the cottage. The one I recognised. Why did Gregg give me her address? *Her* address, of all people?

Sure, the cottage she lived in was nice. The kind of place the pair of us might've looked at moving into many years ago. One we'd actually driven past and spoken about.

But the fact that the woman I recognised lived there made this more than just a coincidence.

There had to be more to this than there seemed on the surface.

I look at my phone. Hold it tight in my sweaty hand. I see a text from Freddie pop through.

You okay, hun? Chinese tonight? Love you x

And I feel so guilty. Because he's so sweet. Sure, he's been frustrated lately. He's been mad lately. But he loves me. He cares. And really, he's been far more patient than I've deserved.

And I need to be really, really careful not to drive him away.

I write him a quick text back before I do what I know will inevitably make me feel very fucking guilty.

All good. Can't wait. Love you too xx

I send it, swallow a lump in my throat, and I get out of the car.

I walk past a few of the terraced houses on this street. Honestly, being on the street makes me realise it's even more of a shithole than I first thought. There are yards covered in cigarette stubs. Broken gnomes. That sort of thing. Most of the windows are dirty. And most of the houses reek of weed.

And as I walk towards number 49, I can't help wondering

again just how Gregg ended up falling so far from grace in such a short space of time.

But then I guess it made sense, didn't it?

Grief.

Charlie.

Me.

And his fiancée, Yara.

I reach number 49, and I stop right outside.

Number 49 looks in better nick than the rest of the terraced houses, but not by much. The windows are clean, at least. There's a few plants in the yard, something Gregg used to enjoy—and something that I teased him for. My very own Alan Titchmarsh.

I tense my fists. Wonder whether I really want to do this. Because if Gregg wanted me to find him, he'd have got in touch. He'd have given me his real address.

I know there are things he would rather not talk about.

I know seeing him might awaken a lot of memories. A lot of dark memories suppressed from my past.

But I know this is what I have to do. There are things I need to ask Gregg. Things I need to know. Things I am beginning to doubt about myself.

Gregg will put me straight. He'll put me back on track.

I walk down the pathway towards the front door and knock three times on the window.

It seems silent here. Silent, but for the dogs barking. The sound of bicycle chains whizzing by.

But Gregg's place. It's silent.

I squint through the window.

Dark in there. Empty.

I go to knock again. As much as I want any excuse to get off this street, I'm here now, so I might as well try. Can't go giving up now.

I knock again, a couple more times when I hear a door to my right open.

I look around. See a man standing there. Bald bloke. Big belly. Wearing a sweaty vest, yellow at the pits. I can tell right away he's a creep, the way he's staring at my tits, practically drooling.

"You alright, love?"

I nod. "I'm just... Is Gregg about?"

The man shrugs. I realise then he's only in his boxer shorts, and he has a rapidly sprouting erection. "Don't see Posh Man much. None of us do. Never up for our barbecues. Never even fancies a beer with us. Dunno what his problem is."

I want to tell this lowlife scrote that I know exactly what my ex-husband's problem is. His problem is people like him. Losers. Creeps.

And then I realise it's strange how defensive I'm getting over Gregg, over my ex-husband.

But then we go back a long way, don't we?

We have a lot of history.

The man stays there. Stares quite openly at my breasts, now. "Y'sure you don't fancy a brew with me? While we wait for him to get back or whatever?"

I shake my head, feeling a little nauseous. "No. I'm fine. Thank you. I'll just come back another time."

I look back at the glass window in the door, hoping I'll see movement. Hoping I'll see *somebody*.

Nobody is there.

I sigh. Lower my head and turn around. It was always a long shot coming here anyway. Even if Gregg *was* in, why the hell would he want to see me?

Besides. Maybe Freddie is right. Things *have* been better recently. After the weirdness of a couple of weeks ago, things *have* settled since I've got back on my meds.

Maybe I should seize this opportunity for peace with both hands.

But then who knows how long it'll be before something sparks my fears, all over again?

I reach the end of the pathway when I hear a door creak open.

"Shit," the neighbour says. "Looks like you're in luck, love."

I turn around.

I see a man standing there.

Chubbier than I remember. Paler than I remember. Greyer than I remember and with a bushy beard.

But he looks at me, and I look at him, and right away, I know.

"Sarah?" he says.

I swallow a lump in my throat as I stare into his wide blue eyes, and I force myself to smile. "Hello, Gregg."

CHAPTER THIRTY-FIVE

I sit in Gregg's living room with a brew in hand, and I can't believe I am actually here.

It's not much nicer inside here than outside, which surprises me from a man as house proud as Gregg. The air is sickly sweet with air freshener, just about masking the strong hint of body odour coming off him. I can smell stale booze as well, spilled somewhere on the otherwise pristine brown carpet. There are plants all around the room, but they've gone brown and dehydrated. Dusty television in the corner.

And photographs everywhere of Gregg and this gorgeous brunette who I can only assume to be Yara.

I sip my brew. Glance up at Gregg, who stares at me. I still can't get over how much he's changed. He always used to be so well-trimmed. Took such pride in his appearance. But he's lost it. Greying. Overweight. Slight hint of weed about him, too.

"Always made a cracking brew," I say, attempting to break the ice—and pay him a compliment as he can quite clearly see I'm staring.

He hesitates a moment, then smiles. It's like I've caught him off guard. And as I sit here, phone on silent, I wonder how insane

I'm actually being. Because Gregg could be involved in the weird events that have been happening to me lately. I find it hard to believe, but I can't discount it.

But then, if he is, what's he doing inviting me into his home?

What's he doing offering me a brew?

What's he doing being so... well, calm?

"Nice place you've got," I say, looking around at the room.

"Don't patronise me," he says. "I was married to you for years. I know you think it's a shithole."

"Well," I say, lowering my brew, placing it on a mat on the wooden table before me. I see a cat underneath, hiding. Purring away. Staring up at me. "I didn't think this part of Preston was your cup of tea. But I guess things change."

"This was just a stopgap," Gregg says. "My ex. Who I'm assuming you know about. Especially since you've been ringing my old work asking about me. I'm guessing that was you, right?"

I lower my head, blushing a little. "I just... I needed to find you."

"Why are you here, Sarah?"

I look up at him. He's so direct. So to the point. He looks exhausted. Like a ghost of his former self. A ghost of the man I once fell in love with.

"I'm sorry," I say. "About your fiancée."

He shakes his head. "Me and Yara fell in love fast. The times we had... they were good. Precious. But it was all just such a shock, you know? The diagnosis came fast. And at that point, she only had six weeks to live."

"I'm so sorry."

He shakes his head. Sighs. "It was so hard to believe. Because she wasn't even that ill, you know? Like... how she got from the place she was to how she was at the end..."

He shakes his head. Closes his eyes.

"How's things with you?" he asks.

"I'm..."

"Guessing it's not all dandy, seeing as you're here now. Looking at me like you pity me."

I don't see any point in beating around the bush. Not anymore. "Things have been... quiet. Until recently."

Gregg nods for me to continue.

"Gregg," I say. "I don't... I don't know how else to say this. But weird things have been happening."

He raises an eyebrow.

"I moved recently. With my boyfriend. Freddie. I... I got this parcel. In the post. A note. *I KNOW EVERYTHING*. And something else, too."

"Something else?"

I'm not sure I want to say it. Not sure I want to admit it to myself.

Because it takes me back.

It takes me back, and admitting it makes it real. It crystallises it.

I can't hide from it if I admit it.

But I know it is time.

I take a deep breath.

Clench my nails into my palms.

"Some strands of hair. Blonde hair. The blondest hair."

He stares at me with those wide blue eyes.

"Blonde hair with a speck of... of blood on it."

I see him go another shade of pale.

"But—but weird things happened. The note. The hair. Both of them went—went missing."

"Went missing? What do you mean they went missing?"

"As in disappeared. One day, there. The next, gone. I had them in the kitchen. Passed out. Wake up, and there's no sign. And then—and then I'm back at Broughton one day. I'm standing there in the woods, and I find them again. Only I took them back home, and they vanished again and then—then the guy who gave me the parcel said he wasn't who I thought he was and—"

"Wait, wait. Slow down, Sarah. Slow down. Please. This isn't... this isn't really making any sense to me."

I puff out my lips. "You're not the first person to say that. Freddie thinks I'm insane. I mean, he's sweet. He's understanding. But he definitely thinks I've a screw loose."

Gregg nods. I hate to admit it, but I know he thinks the same. He has seen me at my worst.

"And you've been to the doctor?"

"Yes," I say. "And I know how this sounds. I... I know exactly how it sounds. But I... Gregg, I don't know why I'm here exactly. But some things just aren't adding up. I guess... I guess I want to just speak to someone who knows who I really am. *How* I really am. And maybe that will bring me some comfort. But I need to ask you something. The place you said you lived. The cottage over in Grimsargh. Why did you tell me you lived there?"

He narrows his eyes for a moment, then raises his eyebrows. Smiles. "Shit. I did tell you that, didn't I? I guess when I moved in with Yara, I was jealous. Happy you still had the cottage in Broughton, sure, but jealous. Because it felt like I was down-grading. Work wasn't stable, even then. So I... I wanted to prepare for the worst. Get somewhere I could at least call home, I guess. And it's far nicer than Yara's old place, anyway. But yeah. I gave you the other address because you always used to go on about how nice that place was whenever we were driving to Beacon Fell. Not my best move, maybe, but I figured you and I were done and dusted. So I didn't see the harm it'd do."

The memories are blurry. I don't really remember making any comments about that house. I'm not totally convinced. Totally satisfied.

"And you don't know who lives there?"

Gregg frowned. "Not a clue. Why?"

I open my mouth. I want to tell him. But then I close it. Shake my head. It isn't important. His story is legitimate enough.

And as weird a coincidence as it seems, I sense myself believing him. "It doesn't matter."

"Are you sure?"

"I..."

I think about Charlie.

I think about Broughton.

I think about the fete.

But more than anything, I think about that summer's day.

A teenager. On my own. Outcast. Lost.

And I think about how he saved me.

I want to ask how he's doing. I want to ask how he's coping. I want to ask so, so many things.

But in the end, I can only swallow a lump in my throat.

I don't want to bring Charlie up.

I want to keep that to myself.

For now.

"The hair. The note. Do you think maybe that could..." Gregg starts.

"Could what?"

"I just... I mean, the field. The school field. Do you think maybe..."

He stops, but I know what he's about to ask already.

He closes his mouth. Shakes his head. "It's been nice seeing you today."

I look into his eyes, and I want to tell him that yes, it's been nice. I don't find him attractive anymore. Not in that way. But my love for Gregg will never die. That love for a spouse never dies, especially your first love.

Especially a love as strong as ours.

"I haven't really seen anyone. Nobody from the old days, anyway. Except for Glynn, weirdly enough."

My mouth goes dry. "Glynn?"

"Yeah," Gregg says. "Glynn. And I know. Weird right? But they say time is a healer and all that."

My heart starts thumping. Gregg is in contact with Glynn? The guy I had an affair with?

The guy who got me pregnant?

Why didn't Glynn mention anything when I saw him?

"I—I saw Glynn too," I say. "A few weeks back."

"Really?" Gregg says frowning. "He never mentioned anything. And I grab a pint with him pretty much every weekend these days. Ever since Holly stormed out and took Alan with her, anyway. Crazy bitch, that one. Used to beat him up, you know?"

"Wait. Holly left?"

"Sarah? Are you okay?"

I sit there, heart racing, mouth dry. I can't wrap my head around this. Can't make sense of any of it.

I can only think of running into Glynn that day.

The same day I found the parcel in the woods.

How coincidental it seemed to bump into him in the first place.

But now this?

He told me Holly and Alan were doing well.

He didn't tell me anything about Gregg.

And he didn't tell Gregg anything about me, either.

I stand up. I feel sick. Uneasy. And I'm not even sure why. Only that I need to get out of here.

Something isn't right.

Something is rotten.

And Glynn is at the centre of it.

"Sarah?" Gregg says. "Are you..."

"I'm sorry," I say, shaking. "But I need to leave."

"Don't you want another brew or—"

"I'm sorry," I say. Reaching the front door. "But I really need to go. It's been nice seeing you again. Really. It has. And I'm—I'm sorry about everything. But I need to go."

I see a look in his eyes as I stand by the door.

I see that temper.

A rare temper, but there.

Especially when he was jealous.

I see it, and I can't make sense of anything right now.

I just feel my instinctive urge to get out of this house.

"Goodbye, Sarah," he says.

"Yeah," I say. "Sorry. Goodbye."

I turn the handle, and I rush out into the warmth of the summer sun.

I rush down the pathway. Past the creepy bald bloke next door.

I scramble for my car keys, worrying for a moment that I've left them inside Gregg's.

And then I find them with my shaking hands, and I unlock the door, climb inside and lock the door again right away.

I sit there for a second. Hands on the wheel. Heart racing. Hands shaking.

I don't understand what's happening.

I don't understand *why* I feel so uneasy.

Just that something is wrong.

Something is bitterly wrong.

Glynn lied to me.

And now something is happening with him and Gregg.

I hear my phone buzz, and I almost jump out of my skin.

I lift it. See a message from Freddie.

Nipping 2 Co Op. Want anything? x

I'm about to reply with my shivering fingers when I see something else.

A reminder that I still have an unread Snapchat message.

I don't know what possesses me to open it.

To tap on it.

I don't know what compels me to do it, right at this moment.

But when I do, I lose all sense of my surroundings.

Because of that image staring back at me.

It's from an account I don't recognise.

There's a message on there.

A photo of a message in a dark backdrop.

The only thing that isn't dark is a weird frayed cream poster, right at the edge of the image.

But it's not the poster I'm looking at.

It's the message.

I KNOW EVERYTHING.

And then right there, right beside it, there's those blonde strands of hair.

Smothered in blood.

CHAPTER THIRTY-SIX

I sit in my car and clench hold of the steering wheel. Tight.

My phone has rung a few times. It's boiling in here. The air con must've packed in again. Really need to get it seen to. Especially in the middle of summer.

I've driven far away from Gregg's place. Far away from my home at Cottam. I've driven right back to Broughton and parked in the church car park. I'm not sure what's brought me back here. Sometimes I do this when I'm lost, directionless. Mentally, rather than literally.

I let the place decide where I'm driving to rather than the other way round.

And naturally, I'm right back where I came from.

Right back where I belong.

I'm sweating. My heart races. My chest is tight. I hear my phone buzz and ping again. I know it's Freddie, and I know he's probably just worried about me.

But I can't face him. I can't face anything. Not right now.

Because nothing makes sense.

First, the news about Glynn going to visit Gregg regularly. What the fuck's all that about? I cheated on Gregg with Glynn.

Felt guilty as fuck about it, sure, but it is what it is. Glynn even got me pregnant, for fuck's sake.

And I'm supposed to believe they're now just best buddies? And for what? All because Glynn's wife left him?

It just feels... off. It doesn't feel right. Not at all.

And then I think of bumping into Glynn in Broughton a few weeks ago. He told me he was still with Holly, I'm sure of it. Told me Alan was fine.

He looked me in the eyes, and he didn't say a word about his new pally friendship with Gregg.

Why?

Why did he hide that from me?

Somewhere, somebody is lying.

And I don't even know where or why, but I know that somehow, Glynn is involved now.

I feel betrayed. I pitied him so much when he came round, night after night. Alan playing upstairs on Charlie's Xbox. Or was it a PlayStation? I can't remember. The details are irrelevant.

I think of the number of times he visited.

How much I hate to admit it.

How much I've tried to bury the truth, even from myself, because of the shame I feel.

The times we'd do it in parks. In woods. In his car or my car.

In the maize fields.

The maize fields...

I think of his hands all over me, and I think of Charlie and—

I hear a horn honk. I look around. I'm blocking someone from getting out of the church car park.

I hold up a hand, apologise. Then I drive out the way, find a quieter area where I'm less obstructive. I know I should call Freddie back. I know I should go home.

But I'm not sure I'll be able to look him in the eye and pretend everything is okay anymore.

Not after the Snapchat.

I feel a sickly sensation in my stomach. My chest tightens. The note. *I KNOW EVERYTHING.*

And the hair.

Those blonde strands of hair.

The blood on them.

I know what that means.

I know *exactly* what that means.

And I have been trying to run from it ever since I got that parcel from a man who claims never to have given me that parcel.

I pull my phone out of my pocket. It's three. Shit. I have eight missed calls from Freddie and a bunch of messages.

Where r u?

R u ok?

Sarah, I need 2 speak 2 u about something x

I see these messages, and I close them because I have no time for them. I have no time for *him*. Not now.

I open up Snapchat.

My Snapchat profile is anaemic, to say the least. It isn't an app I frequent. I only downloaded it because apparently everyone was downloading it a few years back. Fun way to take photos with Charlie, with all those filters they have.

I can see the message right there at the top of the screen.

The username, which I didn't register before.

0891deRrepooCiniM

Does it mean anything? I don't know. Doesn't spark any memories.

And yet, there's something about it.

An air of familiarity about it.

I just don't know it yet.

I tap on the message. But the photo doesn't show up again. I can just see a message window. Like a chat box.

A little blue man pops up at the bottom.

And then disappears. Right away.

I exit the app. My heart beats. Fast.

Someone sent me that photo, which has now vanished—vanishing messages being the novelty of Snapchat.

And that same person is there at the other end of the line.

Watching.

Waiting for my response.

My phone buzzes again.

I feel sick with anticipation.

Because it feels like they are taunting me.

Baiting me into replying.

When I lift the phone, I realise it is Freddie again.

Please love. Come home. Need to tell u about something

I want to ignore him again, but I can't.

So I text back.

Sorry. Been for a drive to countryside. Signal bad. Back soon. Love you. x

He texts back immediately, and I know something is wrong.

Love you. Sorry 2 worry u. See you soon. xxx

And then I hover over the Snapchat app.

Maybe I can engage whoever is speaking with me.

Maybe I can bait them into sending more. Something to incriminate them.

I can't run from the past anymore.

But maybe I can find something that puts whoever is stalking me in the red so I have something on them.

I open the app.

Hover over the message with my thumb for just a little too long.

That's when I notice something.

The message.

The message I received. The photo.

It reloads.

Snapchat lets you reload an image, just once.

My eyes widen.

My heart beats faster.

I'm not sure I want to see this.

But I know now I have an opportunity to capture this, once and for all.

And prove I am not crazy to Freddie.

To everyone.

I open the message.

See it there again.

The dark background.

The note.

I KNOW EVERYTHING

And the little strands of blonde hair splattered with blood.

I take a screenshot. "Gotcha, you bastard."

And then I close the app right away, stick my phone in silent, and shove it in the glove compartment, out of sight and in a compartment in my mind, too.

Then, I start up the car.

I am not looking forward to what I'm about to do.

But I realise now I have no choice.

I can deal with Glynn another time.

I am going to go home.

I am going to tell Freddie about the past.

And maybe then he will start taking all this just as seriously as me.

CHAPTER THIRTY-SEVEN

When I pull up at home, I'm slightly alarmed to find that Freddie's van isn't outside.

I get out of the car. Out into the heat of the August sun. I'm famished, and I'm dehydrated, so I'm surprised to see Freddie isn't back yet. I try calling him, but I go straight to voicemail. Try leaving him a couple of texts, but nothing.

I shrug. Figure he's probably just nipped out for something or other. It's not exactly out of the ordinary.

But it just feels somewhat... off.

Especially after my discovery about Gregg and Glynn. If I can even count that as a discovery at all.

And then the other thing.

The screenshot.

The screenshot of the photo I've got from Snapchat.

I tense up at the thought of it. At the thought of coming clean to Freddie about it. At telling him about the whole thing.

I step inside and, after trying Freddie again, I slump on the sofa. My mind is racing, but I can't think. Not for a moment.

I don't know where to go from here.

I don't know what to do.

I know I need to speak to Glynn at some stage. I need to get my head around why he lied to me the other day. And figure out if he has some involvement in this.

Because I'm starting to wonder.

Appearing at Broughton, conveniently, the same day I was there?

The very same day I found the parcel in the woods?

I tense up.

The silhouette standing outside the other week.

The duo Moira told me about, too.

Could they have been there all along?

Could they have sneaked inside?

Taken the parcel from me?

Working with Calvin—or Cameron or whoever the hell he was —all along?

It doesn't add up. It doesn't make sense.

There's only one reason *why* Glynn might be doing this to me, and I can't see how that is possible.

Because why now?

Why now, after all these years?

But nothing is making sense. Nothing at all. All I know is the parcel—the note, the strands of hair—they are real. They are real, and I have evidence they are real now.

I decide to grab my MacBook and log into Facebook and do some Glynn stalking. It's years since I've logged in. Deactivated a long, long time ago.

But I figure if I sign in now, all my old friends—or rather *Gregg's* old friends—will still be on there.

I enter my email. My old password, the same one I use for everything. *MiniCooperRed1980*. Capitals, numbers, always the best way, or so Gregg used to tell me, even though he insisted mine wasn't quite strong enough because it was too easy to guess, too...

A shiver creeps up my spine.

o891deRrepooCiniM

The username.

The Snapchat username I received the image from.

It's my password.

My password in reverse.

I start to shake. Another sign that this person, whoever the hell it is, knows things about me they shouldn't know.

They know my Snapchat account name. How? I don't give that out to anybody.

And they know my password, too.

Fuck.

All these years I've spent convincing myself I can get away with one random password, and finally, it's come back to bite me.

But as Facebook logs in and I am welcomed by people and acquaintances I once cared about, I am distracted. I can worry about the password later. I need to check on Glynn now.

I search his name in my friends list. No sign. Shit. Must've deactivated or deleted. Not surprising, really. We were friends when Gregg and I were together, but I deleted before the whole fallout of the affair. And I didn't really log in after that anyway, so he could've deleted me right away for all I know.

I type his name into the search bar.

Glynn Maynard

Nothing at all.

Shit.

I delete his name. Then I decide to take a look at his wife's profile. See if I can find anything out about her and him.

I type in her name. *Holly Maynard*. But I'm struggling to find her. Loads of Holly Maynards.

I'm about to give up when I see her.

There she is.

Holly Maynard.

Blonde and beautiful as ever.

I click on her profile and am surprised to see a photo of her and Glynn. Look like they're abroad somewhere. Palm trees in the background. Nice tans.

Alan standing in front of them.

He looks older. So much more mature. Always used to be such a cheeky chappy.

But there's this look to him.

A look I can't pinpoint. That I can't put my finger on.

This deadness to his eyes.

But there's something else that catches my attention. That I hone in on above anything else.

Holly's photo.

It was uploaded a week ago.

She and Glynn are still together.

I sit there. Laptop on my knee. Stare at the screen. I don't understand. Gregg told me he met Glynn. That Glynn and Holly split up.

Then why is Holly still posting photos of her and Glynn?

Why is—

The front door opens and makes me jump.

I'm immediately greeted with the smell of Chinese food.

Freddie stands there, wiping his shoes. "Sarah," he says. "Sorry. Nipped out to grab Chinese for us. King Prawn Fried Rice and curry sauce. That good?"

I smile. Nod. "That's... That's good. Listen. Freddie. I have to—"

"Before you start," he says. "There's something I have to tell you."

I freeze. Dread creeps up my spine. Something is wrong. He knows something. Or something has happened.

I remember the texts.

The urgency with which he wanted me home.

And I wonder just what is going on.

"What?" I say, trying to be as calm as I can.

He stands there. Stares at me for a moment.

Then a big smile bursts across his face. "Managed to book us a last-minute flight to the Costa del Sol. Next weekend. One week. No work. None of this crap. Just a chill on the beach with plenty of cocktails. Put all this shit of the last few weeks behind us. Just for a little while. Our time. What do you reckon?"

I want to smile.

I want to thank him.

I want to be so grateful.

But instead, I burst into tears.

"Sarah?"

He puts the Chinese down. Walks over to me. Wraps those big arms around me.

"What's wrong? I thought—I thought you'd be happy."

I want to lie to him. I want to convince him all is good. That everything is okay.

But I can't keep the pretence going any longer.

"I am happy. Really. But I... I need to show you something, Freddie."

I reach for my phone. Pull it out of my pocket. Open my photos. Go to tap on the screenshot.

And then I freeze.

"It... it was here."

"What was there, Sarah? What is it?"

I stare at my photo library.

There is no trace of the photo.

I close the photos. Go into my recently deleted.

It's not there either.

"It—I got a screenshot of it. It was here."

"Sarah, you're scaring me a little."

"They sent me a Snap," I say.

"A what?"

"The person. The person who—who is following me. Who is tormenting me. They sent me a snap, and I screenshotted it, and it's... it's gone."

I look up at Freddie, and I can see in his eyes already that he doubts me.

"They've got an account," I say. "I can show you. Their username. It's like my password. It's... I'll show you."

I open Snapchat, barely able to keep my hands still.

I go to click on the message again, even though I know it'll be gone and even though I know I won't be able to see it again.

But again, I freeze.

There is no message there.

The profile is gone.

There is no trace of *o891deRrepooCiniM* on my Snapchat.

Or of the note and the strands of hair in my photos.

It's gone.

CHAPTER THIRTY-EIGHT

"It... it was here, Freddie."

I stand and stare at my phone and try to wrap my head around it.

The photo.

The screenshot of the note.

I KNOW EVERYTHING

And the other thing.

The strands of blonde hair with blood specks on it.

I took a screenshot of it from Snapchat.

And now it is gone.

Not even in my Recently Deleted.

Totally gone.

"Sarah," Freddie says. I can sense he's trying to calm me. Trying to reassure me. But it's not working.

"I had a photo," I say. "A—a screenshot."

"I think you should sit down."

"I don't *want* to sit down."

"Lower your voice. Please."

I know he's right. I know it makes sense. I know I can't lose my shit. Not now.

But everything from today is just driving me crazy.

The Gregg thing.

The Glynn thing.

The Snapchat account with my password as the name.

And now this...

The account. Vanishing.

No trace it ever even existed at all.

"Do you believe me?" I ask.

I see it in his eyes again. Sadness. But also disappointment, too.

He's booked a holiday for us. Done something for the pair of us to get us away. To take our minds off all the shit we've both been through lately.

And after things have gone so much calmer lately, so much more peaceful, this goes and happens.

"Do you believe me, Freddie?"

He opens his mouth. And I can tell he's about to tell me what he wants me to hear. He's about to comfort me. He's about to reassure me.

Then he closes his mouth and shakes his head.

"No, Sarah. No, I don't."

It hits me like a punch to the gut. Hearing it as clear as day.

My boyfriend doesn't believe me.

And he isn't even pretending to believe me anymore.

"It's like I said. I believe *you* truly believe what you're saying. I don't think you're lying to me or anything. Not consciously. But I... I've got to look at the evidence, Sarah. And you haven't even told me what was in this parcel yet. You haven't let me into the doctor's with you. You haven't told me anything other than you had a breakdown after Charlie disappeared, and it sent you a bit... downhill. And I feel like that's happening again. And I... I'm starting to feel like it's time we got someone else involved."

I narrow my eyes. I don't know what he's saying. What he's implying.

"What're you talking about?"

He lifts his phone. "I'm—I'm going to ring somebody. The meds, I thought they were helping at first; I really did. But now I'm starting to wonder if we need... more help than that."

My heart races.

My stomach tightens.

I know what he is saying. What he is implying now.

"You're—you're going to have me sectioned, aren't you?"

"I don't want to do this, Sarah."

"Fuck. You—you think I'm crazy. You think I'm insane—"

"Look at the fucking evidence in front of me, Sarah! Look at things from my perspective for one fucking moment. You're saying things that don't make sense. You're claiming things are there when they aren't. And you won't be specific about anything. Anything at all. I love you. And I'm not leaving you. I want to help you. But... but you're not cooperating with me. You're not opening up to me."

"I want to. I really want to."

"Then tell me where you were today."

I open my mouth. I can't tell whether this is a test or not. Whether he already knows.

"Tell me, Sarah. Please."

I want to lie. I want to cover up the truth.

But I don't see how I can anymore.

I don't see where it will get me.

"I was at Gregg's," I say.

Silence. A pause. I can barely bring myself to look into his eyes.

"Gregg's?"

"Gregg's. My—my ex-husband."

"Your ex..."

He looks away. I can see his eyes are bloodshot. Tearful. I can see how upset he is. How little he understands.

"There's nothing going on," I say before he can suggest it. He does get a bit jealous like that. "I went to see him because I wanted him to confirm a few things about my past."

He looks right at me. "And that's why you visited him the other week, too?"

I frown. "I didn't..."

"Don't bullshit me, Sarah. I know you've been sneaking off a lot lately. That where you went instead of the doctors the other week, too?"

"I... No. That wasn't to see Gregg."

"Then where was it?"

Fuck. Where did I say I'd gone?

Because I can't tell him the truth on this.

Not because there's anything sordid going on. There isn't.

Not because I'm technically doing anything wrong.

Just... because.

"I—I met Cindy."

"No," he says. "No, you didn't."

"I—I think I—"

"Why don't we give Cindy a call then?"

I frown. My throat tenses up. "I don't—I don't want to involve her in this."

"The famous, mystery Cindy. Why don't you pick up your phone and give her a call right now?"

"Freddie. Please don't make me do this. Please."

"Okay. I don't want to play mean here. But I'm going to give you a choice. Pick up the phone. Ring Cindy. Or I ring the police, and I'll see about getting you get sectioned for your own good."

"You—you wouldn't."

"Cindy, Sarah," he says. "Do it."

I lift my phone and can't believe this is happening.

I open my contacts.

I scroll through.

Right down to Cindy.

And I don't know what to say.

What to do.

I look back up at him. "I—"

"Now. Now."

I think about hitting a random contact.

I think about telling him some lie.

I think about hiding, and I think about pretending.

But at this moment, this dark moment where I feel so lost and cornered, there is only one thing I can do.

I lower my phone.

I put it in my pocket.

Freddie watches me. Narrows his eyes.

"So you won't ring her? Not even for me?"

I swallow a lump in my throat and prepare for my whole world to fall apart.

"I won't ring her because I can't," I say.

Freddie frowns. "What—what are you talking about?"

"I can't ring her," I say, wanting to fall into a hole, wanting to die, wanting all this to end. "I can't ring her because... because she doesn't exist."

Freddie is silent.

But I can still hear my own words echoing around the room, around my mind.

"What?" he says.

"She doesn't exist," I say. "I don't have a best friend called Cindy. I didn't go to meet her. I never have. Cindy—Cindy doesn't exist."

CHAPTER THIRTY-NINE

Okay. So maybe I've not been *entirely* honest about some things.

But it's like I said earlier.

If you thought I was being entirely honest about everything, you *really* haven't been paying attention, have you?

It's not for any bad reasons, though. I don't have any nefarious intentions. It's just the way we all are, right?

Don't we all keep secrets from ourselves?

Don't we all tell ourselves lies because the truth is a whole lot harder to swallow the vast majority of the time?

Don't we live fantasies?

Don't we gloss over the darkness of the past and emphasise the light—and vice versa, where necessary?

Aren't deep down, we all just messed up fuckers?

Lying is human nature.

And I'm the most honest fucking person here because I actually dare to admit that, so don't you dare judge me for it.

* * *

I STAND in my living room opposite Freddie. I still can't believe the words just exited my mouth.

And the way Freddie is looking at me, neither can he.

"What—what do you mean Cindy doesn't exist?"

I hear Freddie say those words, and I can't believe I've actually said it. I can't believe I've actually admitted it to him.

The number of times I've said I'm off for coffee with her.

The number of times I've told him she won't be coming around for whatever fucking reason or other.

The number of times I have lied to him.

I've hidden the truth from him because I wanted to protect him.

And pretending I have a best friend. Pretending there is actually somebody out there who cares. Sometimes that makes me easier to digest for other people. Makes me seem more... well. Normal. Ordinary.

And sometimes I tell myself I have someone, too. Just so I feel a little more normal in this world.

A little less... lonely.

Is there any harm in that, really?

"Sarah?" Freddie says. And I can hear the urgency in his voice now. The intensity. "Speak to me. What do you mean Cindy isn't real? What... what are you talking about?"

I look at him, and I don't know what to say. So I simply shake my head, and I shrug. "I don't have a friend called Cindy. What else can I say?"

"But—but you meet her. For coffee and lunch and—"

"You've never met her, have you?"

He opens his mouth. "But... but you even went for a weekend away with her. A couple of months back. What... Where were you, Sarah? What—what's happening?"

I hear his questions and see the confusion, and I feel so desperately sorry for him. But really, I was fooling myself, wasn't I?

Did I really expect to spend my whole life with this man and for him never to find out the truth about me?

Did I really plan on keeping this from him forever?

And just how deluded does that make me?

"I lied to you," I say. "I lied to myself. And I'm sorry. Really—"

"You're insane."

I hear his words, and they cut me deep. "Yeah," I say. "Yeah, I probably am."

"You need help, Sarah. All this time and you've been lying to me."

"It's not like it sounds."

"So what is it?"

"What?"

"Is it another bloke or something?"

"Freddie, no. That's not how it is—"

"It's him, isn't it?"

"Who?"

"Gregg. All along, it's him."

"Freddie," I say. "I am not having an affair. I know how this sounds. And you are right. I... I do need help. But I can tell you something else, too. I am not crazy when it comes to the things that have been happening to me. I know what is happening. And I believe it. Really. I do. But... but you're right. It's time I started being honest with you about things. Fully honest with you about things."

But he just stands there. He just stares at me. Shakes his head.

"I'm not sure I can believe another word that comes out of your mouth."

I look him in the eye, and I know I have no choice now.

I know I have to go back there.

Way, way back.

As much as I don't want to.

As much as it horrifies me to revisit it.

I have to open the door.

I take a deep breath, and I get ready to let it all out.

"When I was a child, I was raised in a sect. A cult. Call it whatever you want. But that's how it was for me. We called it the Family.

"It was nice there. Boys did their thing. Girls did their thing. We were separate, but it was... well, it was nice. We got a proper education. We went away on holidays. Everything *seemed* normal and fine.

"I didn't know any different. You've seen Midsommar, right? Well, picture Midsommar, only without the sporadic murders.

"My parents, they did their best. But they were lost in this cult. They were caught up in it. And I was always an inquisitive kid, so I never really totally fit in. I always wanted to break out. But my parents were completely caught up. Some... some horrible things happened. Disagreements happened. And... and well. In the end, I got out. I escaped. I don't know what happened to my parents. I don't know what happened to any of them. And that's... that's where I went the other day. To the place we used to live. There's nobody there anymore. No sign of life there. I got away, and I escaped them, and I made a life for myself. But it wasn't easy. I... I maybe haven't been totally truthful about one thing. And that's... I was psychologically scarred by what happened to me in that cult. So my mental fragility... that predates Charlie's disappearance.

"But... almost a month ago, I received a parcel with something that only somebody involved in that same cult could know. And the things that have been happening to me since... It's exactly the same. Someone is following me. Someone is taunting me. And something deep inside me makes me wonder if it was them who did something to Charlie all along. To get back at me."

Freddie just stands there. I want him to say something. I want him to tell me he understands.

But he just stands there.

And then he opens his mouth.

"Your... your parents—"

"I haven't seen my parents in years."

He is quiet. Silent. I can see him trying to understand it. Trying to process it.

"And your sister? Elana?"

I open my mouth. Hesitate, just for a moment.

"Her neither."

He is quiet again. Doesn't say a thing. Time drags on; the moments stretch out forever.

And then, finally, he speaks.

"I'm sorry, Sarah. You've told... You've told me you struggle. With your memory. With what's true and what isn't true. And all this with Cindy..."

He hits the Dial button on the phone, and I know it is done.

"I'm so sorry, Sarah," he says. "But this is for you. It might not seem like it right now... but it's for you."

I know I should stay here with him. I know he is afraid. Confused.

But I am telling the truth.

I am telling the complete truth.

I hear the phone dial.

I see the pain in his eyes.

And I feel a weight off my shoulders. Telling Freddie this. As much as I've tried to run from it, as much as I've tried to hide it, I feel better now it is out in the open.

I have told my truth.

I have had my say.

But as he stands there, as the phone rings, I know there are things I need to do.

I know I need to understand.

I know that Gregg and Glynn must be involved somehow.

One of them is lying.

Maybe both of them are lying.

And I need to get to the bottom of it.

I need to understand.

I hear someone's voice on the other end of the phone.

And then Freddie. "Yes. It's—it's my girlfriend. We need to get her help. I think she's having some kind of breakdown..."

I don't hear the rest.

Because I look over at the door.

And then I look back at Freddie.

I see him realise what I'm planning, right in that instant.

"Sarah—"

I dash past him.

He grabs my arm, but I slip free.

I run out of the front door.

"Sarah!"

I slam it shut.

Run to my car.

Scramble for my keys.

"You okay, Sarah, love?"

A voice.

Moira.

Standing outside her house, watering a plant.

"Can't stop, Moira."

I unlock my car.

Clamber inside.

Freddie steps out the front door, just as I put my key in the ignition, start up the engine.

I look back at him as he stands there, phone in hand.

And I know that if this is my last act before I am sectioned and locked away—for my own good—then I have to make it count.

"I'm sorry," I mouth.

And then I drive.

I know exactly where I need to go.

CHAPTER FORTY

I sit in my car and stare at the nice little semi-detached house beside me, and I know it's time.

Freddie has tried calling me several times, so I've switched my phone on silent. I thought about messaging him to tell him I'll be okay, but I realise I'm long beyond convincing him of that. No matter what happens, I know how tonight ends. I know how it plays out. I know he thinks I am crazy.

And maybe I am crazy. Maybe there are things I'm paying far too much attention to and other things I am not paying enough attention to.

Maybe I am imagining things.

But I know one thing for sure.

Glynn's profile. He's still with his wife. Even though Gregg told me he and Glynn were in contact now. That they were friends now.

I found it hard to believe at the time. Found a lot of what Gregg said hard to believe.

But now I am at Glynn's. Because I need to see the truth for myself.

I get out of the car. It's a nice street. Quiet. Suburban. It's still light, but the tree-lined pavements make it feel dark, intense.

I see Glynn's house opposite, and I wonder whether I'm doing the right thing. I could contact him on Facebook. There are a whole host of other options and routes I could take right now.

But I know, deep down, I need to see for myself.

I need to look Glynn in the eye and ask him the important questions.

Because I think he is involved.

I don't know how, and I don't know why, but I think he is terrorising me.

I walk down the little pathway. Past the garden, the grass a little long. I walk up to the doorway, fully aware that if Glynn does really know the things he knows, that all bets are off the table at this point.

I pull the doorbell, an old-fashioned one that rings through the hallway, and I wait for an answer.

My heart beats. I feel like I haven't slept in days. Even when I have slept, I have been so lost in taunting dreams that I've barely rested.

All I can think of is Glynn and Gregg.

The inconsistencies in their stories.

Who is lying?

Who is telling the truth?

Is either of them telling the truth?

Or am I really just losing my grip on sanity after all?

I try the doorbell again. And again, nothing. And for some reason, I have a bad feeling. A really bad feeling.

It's dark inside.

There are no lights on.

The curtains are closed.

I look over my shoulder. Nobody around. An old woman curtain-twitching across the street, but nothing to worry about too much.

I turn back around and go to pull the doorbell one last time.

I wait.

Nothing.

I sigh. Glynn's car is in the drive. So maybe he's just ignoring me. Maybe he just doesn't want to see me.

But then I guess if he is involved somehow, that would make sense. He would want to avoid me. He wouldn't want any kind of contact with me.

I go to walk away when I notice a little path around the side of the house.

And at that moment, I want to go around there. I want to see. Because I am worried about Glynn. Worried about why he isn't answering the door.

But more because I want answers. I want the truth. Before Freddie's army of sectioneers are launched upon me and take me away.

I look around. No one in sight. And even if there is, what are they going to think? I'm just a concerned friend, that's all. Nothing more.

"Fuck it."

I wander around the back of the house. Have a glance through the side window. I can see a lot of boxes. Suitcases filled with clothes.

And I have a bad feeling, again. Because what Gregg said about Holly and Glynn splitting up. Maybe it *is* true.

Maybe it is Gregg I should be going to see after all.

I walk further around the back. Climb over the gate and into the garden. I see a football net, the goalposts rusting. A deflated ball by the side. The garden looks unkept. The grass long. A dog turd with flies buzzing around it. And not the only one.

I try not to breathe too deeply and walk around the back of the house to the conservatory. I look inside, squint through the window. I can't see anyone. But I can see one thing. The house looks bare. Like someone is moving out. Like they are in the process of moving out.

And again, it makes me feel uneasy.

Maybe I've got this completely wrong.

Maybe Gregg *was* telling the truth. A weird truth, sure.

But then the woman at the cottage...

I don't want to think about her.

I don't want to think about what running into her means.

Someone from the cult.

Living a normal life in a house Gregg claimed he lived at.

It couldn't just be coincidence.

My heart beats a little faster. I'm getting uneasy. I'm starting to worry I might find something. Something I don't want to see.

And that's when I hear the engine of a car out front.

I freeze. It sounds close. Really close.

And even though I know it's probably elsewhere, deep down in my bones, I sense it is someone from this house.

I hear doors close.

I hear mumbled voices.

I hear Glynn.

I hear a little boy, too. A little boy I know to be Alan.

And then a woman laughs, too.

And then a bark.

And the next thing I know, I hear Glynn say the words that make me freeze.

"...give it another go. But you'll have to excuse the house. It's not exactly in the best nick."

I freeze. So maybe Gregg is telling the truth. Maybe Glynn and Holly split up, and now they're rekindling things.

But if that's the case, why didn't Gregg say anything?

Maybe he doesn't know.

Maybe he hasn't heard yet.

Something just doesn't feel right.

I walk around the side of the house, heart racing, hands shaking, desperate to get out, desperate to get away. Desperate not to be seen. And I know there's only one place I can go, now. Gregg's.

I have to find Gregg.

I have to ask him some questions.

And then I have to face whatever fate lies before me.

I stand at the edge of the pathway. Stare at my car. The obstacles before it.

I wait for the front door to close.

For the voices to stop.

And then I wait until I'm absolutely sure the front door closes before making a dash for it.

I run down the drive.

Heart racing.

Chest tight.

Desperate to get away.

Desperate to—

"Sarah?"

I freeze.

Every muscle in my body goes weak.

I look around, and I see Glynn standing there.

Eyes wide.

Alan right beside him.

"What—what are you doing here?" he asks.

CHAPTER FORTY-ONE

"Sarah?" Glynn says. "Is—is everything okay?"

I see the panic in his eyes. I see the fear on Alan's face, who Glynn pushes behind him. I hear a dog barking somewhere behind them both. I hear Holly trying to calm the dog, Monty.

I see and hear all these things, and for a moment, I am back there.

Back at the school field that summer's day three years ago.

Holding Charlie's hand.

Seeing Glynn.

Glynn coming over to me as I let go of Charlie's hand, and he lets Alan run off into the distance, too, to watch the band.

Walking the long route to the maize fields.

Fucking him to the sound of the music and staring up at the blue skies.

Getting on my knees as he fucks me from behind—and not for the first time, even though he doesn't know he's got me pregnant, even though we swear this will be the last time, just like we always swear it...

Go on, go on, go on—

And then suddenly, something shifts inside me because I feel the tightness around my wrists and the water on my hands and see the brown mole staring down at me from his neck, and it brings it all back, brings it all back as much as I want to fight it, want to resist it, want to—

And then we are both stepping out of the maize fields. We are both walking back through the crowd. Excited but feeling shame. Alan is there. He looks at me, wide eyes. Head down.

Only there's no sign of Charlie.

"Have you seen Charlie?" I ask him.

He looks at me like I'm weird. His friends laugh at me. Mutter things under my breath.

And I see Glynn there, now, too. The redness of his cheeks.

"Have any of you seen Charlie?"

I don't want to remember what Glynn says to that.

I don't want to think about it.

Because that doesn't line up with the story I have told myself.

"Sarah?" Glynn says. And I am back in the moment now. Back in reality.

Although again, I am starting to question things.

The truth is breaking through.

A truth I have run from.

A truth I have denied.

"Glynn," I say. "It's..."

"What's she doing here?" Alan mutters.

And I feel it sting right away. The way he looks at me. Like I am crazy.

"Alan, go inside," Glynn says.

"But—"

"Go inside, Alan. I'll deal with this."

He looks at me, does Alan. Looks at me like I'm weird. Like I'm crazy.

Then he steps inside the house.

Glynn walks towards me. Rubs the back of his neck. "Sarah.

You shouldn't be here. My marriage isn't in the best state, and you being here isn't exactly going to help things—"

"Gregg," I say.

Glynn looks at me with wide eyes. And then he nods. "Your ex-husband. Yeah. What about him?"

"You're—you're friends with him now?"

He opens his mouth. And then he closes it. Sighs.

"Glynn, I'm barely holding on to reality here. Just—just give me a straight fucking answer, please."

"I didn't mention Gregg to you when I saw you because I didn't think it was relevant."

"Didn't think it was relevant? You fucking asked about our marriage."

"And I'm sorry. Gregg and I... I know it's unlikely, but we just drink together sometimes. I know. It's weird. I never expected it, but he needed someone to talk to, too, and I guess it just happened. But truth be told... well, the whole thing spooked me out a bit."

"Spooked you out?"

He rubs his neck again. "It freaked me out. Seeing you again. At Broughton, too. Especially after everything that happened between us."

I shake my head. Sigh. "Glynn, that's the past. What happened between us. The affair. The baby. That's the past."

"And you're too fucking right about that. And now I have a life. I have a marriage to rebuild. What happened with you... it should never have happened. But it did. You should never have even been there, Sarah. At the school. You should never have—"

"Don't go there."

He opens his mouth. And I know he's about to say it. Say the words that fill me with horror. With pain. The words I fear will break me.

"Do not go there," I say.

He closes his mouth, then. And he looks me right in the eye.

"I've met Gregg because me and him get on. Despite what happened in the past. He's been through a rough time. I've had a rough time myself. There's nothing more to it than that."

"Then what about the messages?" I say.

Glynn frowns. "The messages? What messages?"

"The Snapchat messages," I say. "The—the stuff about knowing something about my past. The note. The parcel. The—the hair." I'm beyond trying to hide it anymore. "Was that you? You were near the school field that day. The day I found the parcel there in the woods. Was it you? Was it Gregg? Because—because nothing else makes sense. Nothing at all makes sense."

Glynn walks over to me. He's close, now. And I can see Alan and Holly in the background, staring through the window.

He puts a hand on my shoulder. Gentle.

And with all the patience and calmness in the world, he looks me in the eye.

"Sarah. I'm saying this with absolute sincerity. You need to get yourself better again. Because you've been here before. You've been here before, and you've got yourself out of it. So you need to do it again. That's as compassionately as I can put it right now."

I know what he's talking about. I know what he's referring to. I know what he's trying to say.

But I can't bring myself to accept it.

I can't bring myself to admit it.

I can't bring myself to face the truth.

"Get help, Sarah," Glynn says. "Before you go down that hole you went down last time, all over again."

He turns around. Walks up to his front door.

"But how am I supposed to let it drop when I can't ever forgive myself for what happened that day?" I say. "How—how can I ever walk away when Charlie went missing that day because of me?"

He stops.

Looks around at me.

"You really want me to say it, don't you?"

Holly comes to the door. Appears over Glynn's shoulder. "What the fuck is that crazy bitch doing here?"

I ignore her. I have no time for petty arguments right now.

"You really want me to say it," Glynn said. "Don't you?"

I stand there, and I want to argue.

I want to fight.

I want to resist the truth.

I want to run from it, and I want to hide it and—

"Well, I'll say it," Glynn says. "For your own sake, more than anything."

"Glynn—"

"Charlie didn't go missing that day," he says.

"No."

No no no no no no no no—

"Charlie didn't go missing any day at all."

Please no please no no not again not again no—

"We went into the maize fields, we slept together, and then you cracked."

"Glynn—"

"But Charlie didn't go missing because Charlie didn't exist, Sarah. He didn't exist. And he never has fucking existed. At all."

CHAPTER FORTY-TWO

I think of my life in two distinct segments.
The days before Charlie went missing.
And the days after Charlie went missing.

* * *

I'M THERE AGAIN. On the school field. Charlie's hand in mine. I can feel the heat of his sweaty palms in mine. I can hear the other children laughing.

I remember being worried about him. Being concerned about him.

I remember the way he looked at me like there was a problem. Like there was something wrong. Like there was something unspoken.

And then, before I know it, I am with Glynn in the maize fields.

And then racing out and trying to find my son.

Only...

There's something different now.

I'm having other memories, too.

Memories of going home to Gregg.

Of Gregg holding me. His arms wrapped tightly around me.

"It's okay, Sarah. It's okay. I've got you. I've got you."

And then I have memories of some kind of psychiatric hospital.

A medicinal stench in the air.

I have memories of the same food, day after day. Mashed potato. Drugged up to my eyeballs.

I have memories of getting out of that place. Being so excited to see Gregg again.

Only Gregg visited me one day. Told me he'd met someone else. Not because of what had happened to me. And not even because of Glynn and the dishonesty.

But because he'd met someone else. As hard as it was to believe that it was as simple as he made it out to be.

He was moving on.

And it was time for me to move on, too.

I remember being alone at first. I remember feeling like my life was over. No friends. No son.

And that was the hardest thing to swallow. Even after everything, I couldn't accept that I didn't have a son. That Charlie wasn't real.

Because he *was* real.

Even if they told me in that patronising manner that he was "only real to me," I knew, and I still know deep down that there is another truth.

There is a longing.

Grief.

Grief for a boy everybody else is convinced didn't even exist.

I am standing outside Glynn's house. He has gone inside now. I see Holly and Alan keep on peeking through the window, muttering things under their breath.

And I remember what it was like. The glances I got that day at the school. The side glances. The little smirks on their faces.

"She's crazy," people would say.

And I remember feeling ashamed. Totally ashamed.

Because I knew deep down that I was hiding a lot of trauma. That's what they called it. Dissociative amnesia. An inability to recall important personal information that would not typically be lost with ordinary forgetting. Trauma fucking with my memory, basically.

But we worked through it.

I worked through it, and I got better.

And I got out of that place—the place where they gave me the drugs and the meds—and I found Freddie.

I stand there, and I see people staring at me from their gardens, from their houses. I see those looks on their faces.

And still, I can't understand this flood of memories—or are they even memories at all?—surging into my head right now.

I don't know what is real and what isn't real anymore.

I can't distinguish between what I should and shouldn't believe anymore.

I only know what they told me three years ago.

The same thing that Glynn is telling me now, as much as I don't want to accept it, as much as I want to believe this cannot be true.

"Charlie isn't real. He's never been real."

I turn around, and I rush to my car. Start up the engine. Put my foot on the gas, and I drive. Because I need to find Gregg. I need to ask him. I need to look him in the eye, and I need to ask him about my son.

About *our* son.

I feel my phone buzz. Freddie. He's rung eighteen times since I left, so many times that he's bypassed silent mode at this stage. There's an array of texts from him. I feel sad for him. He has every reason to be concerned. I'm concerned myself. Really fucking concerned.

I've tried to run from the version of the truth people once told me.

I've tried to convince myself my story is true.

To convince those around me my story is true.

And it is. I want you to believe me on this. Please, please believe me on this, if it's the only thing you do believe me on.

Not Glynn.

Not everybody else.

Me.

I hear a horn honk and jam my foot on the brakes.

A car hurtles past. The guy driving gives me the finger, curses under his breath. I know I shouldn't be driving. I'm in no fit state right now.

But I need to get to Gregg's.

I need to ask him for the truth.

The full truth.

I drive again. Rain pellets against the windscreen. My phone rings again. My head is busy with fragments of thoughts and memories and flashbacks and pain and—

Deep breaths.

Focus on the road.

Just get to Gregg and get your answers.

Get to Gregg, get your answers, then face whatever fate awaits you.

I drive. I hear more cars honk at me, so I know I am unsteady. I whizz through a light on red. I almost send a man hurtling off his bicycle.

But I need Gregg to tell me Glynn is wrong.

Glynn is lying.

But why would he lie?

I turn down Gregg's road. Pull up on the kerb and bang into the back of a Toyota Yaris as I stop.

I clamber out of the car, run past the Yaris, the alarm blaring.

I see people hurrying out of a house to my left. Shouting something at me. Ordering me to come back.

But I can't go back.

Not now.

It's too late for that.

I run down the pavement towards Gregg's house as the skies turn black, as more torrential rain hammers down from above.

I reach his front door, and I bang my hands against it. Again and again and again.

"Gregg!" I shout.

No answer.

I bang on the door again. Try the handle. "Gregg! Please! It's Sarah. Open up. I need to talk to you about Charlie. Please! I need to talk to you about Charlie!"

I'm not sure how long I am standing there, banging against the door.

I am not sure when it is I fall to my knees and feel the rain drench me.

I am not sure how long I spend on Gregg's pavement, huddled in a ball, crying, soaking, shivering.

I only know that eventually, I see flashing lights.

Eventually, I hear someone say something to me that cuts through the rest of the noise and the panic.

I feel a hand on my shoulder.

"Come on, miss. It'll be alright with us."

And then I am in the back of a car wrapped in a warm blanket and driving away, and I know that I have failed.

But I am safe now.

PART THREE

CHAPTER FORTY-THREE

I sit in the communal lounge and stare at the television.

But really, my eyes are only on the time.

It's half nine. Barely anyone else is up. Fat Jenna—and that's what she calls herself, so don't go accusing me of being "fat-phobic"—who is friendly enough but occasionally has tantrums that keep the whole lot of us up all night. Mary who sits there with a smile on her face. Honestly, all these people are okay in the low-security ward at the Crystal Lodge psychiatric hospital, just outside of Preston. Sometimes, the media creates an image of insanity when it comes to places like this. Archaic views of mental health and the old "lunatic asylum" create prejudice when it comes to people in rehabilitation, suffering, and recovering from mental health issues.

Truth be told, the bulk of these people are just ordinary people who've had a raw deal with their mental health. They're good people. They aren't threatening. They just want to get back to normal, just like everybody else.

But as much as I am grateful for my time here—for the acquaintances I have made in my three-month stay—I am so, so ready to get out of here.

Which is why I am staring at the clock.

I have my final meeting today with both the doctor and someone to speak to me about my rehabilitation and reintroduction into society. The rehab shit should be a breeze. After all, Freddie has stayed completely true to his word; bless him. In the three months since I was sectioned under the mental health act, he has visited me at every single opportunity. He has never missed a meeting. And he has never pushed me for any kind of information about my past, either.

And that's the part I appreciate the most. I am sure he has a lot of questions. Especially now he knows the truth about me.

We've spoken about a lot of things. He's allowed me to be open with him without forcing me. Given me the opportunity to come totally clean, in my own time. The truth about my conversation with Doctor Murray back when I refused to let him in her office with me, mostly because I was afraid of my past mental health history coming up in front of him.

And even where I went the last time I visited the surgery, where I ran off before I even went to my appointment without telling him where I was going.

I got on a train. A train somewhere. A train to a place that reminded me of my past. But I soon realised I didn't want to go back there. I didn't want to awaken any more demons from my past.

And that's all I told him.

He let me leave it at that. Bless him.

I am sure he has thoughts about leaving me, wondered whether I am worth sticking by, all this time, especially after the things he now knows.

But he has stood right by me.

And as the autumn leaves cover the ground with their crunchiness, I am going home to him.

Today.

I hear a voice behind me. "Sarah?"

When I look around, I see Dr Maubid.

We all laugh at his name, and he is in on the joke, too. But he's a nice guy. Short. Looks really childlike, tiny fella. Like someone playing at being a doctor rather than an actual doctor.

But he's a good bloke. He's understanding. Patient. He's helped me a lot.

"Would you like to join me?"

I stand up, trying to keep my calm, my composure. Not wanting to appear too eager. After all, if I am to be released today, I need to appear as normal as I possibly can.

It won't be a proper release. After all, I'm still in deep shit for my reckless driving on the day my world fell apart. I have a date in court due, although the judge is expected to find me not guilty on the grounds of diminished responsibility due to my mental health issues.

But still. I'll probably lose my licence. And a whole host of my freedom along with that.

And besides. I need to be careful. Because I've been here before. I've been this *healed* before. And I snapped. Again.

"Would you like to follow me?" he asks.

I follow him into his office.

"Good luck, Saz."

I nod at Jenna. Smile. "Thanks."

"I'll miss you as much as it pains me to admit it."

"Yeah," I say. "Me too." And I'm serious. I will weirdly miss the people here.

But it's like missing acquaintances at school after spending all day with them. Home is still preferable. Always.

I follow Dr Maubid into his office. I notice photos of his family on his ultra-tidy desk.

"Take a seat."

"Thanks."

I sit in his comfy leather chair for what I hope will be the final time. But again, I feel like I will miss these weekly visits, strangely.

"So, big day today," he says.

"Yeah. Let's hope!"

"How are you feeling about it?"

"I can't wait. No offence. But I'll kind of miss your company."

He laughs. "And you too, Sarah. Any nerves?"

"A few. Naturally. I mean. I feel like I'm going to have to get to know my boyfriend again. Properly, you know. Because as good as he's been... there's always going to be conversations to have."

He sits there. Nods. "Well, if it's any consolation, I am exceptionally impressed with the progress you have made. From the condition you were in when you first came in here, to now... I have to say... I am mightily pleased with how well you are doing."

There is a silence between us. A silence where he flips a few papers over, glances at them. And I sense something is coming. A final test.

"Sarah, before we do let you go into the next stage of the rehabilitation process, which is a return home with a close focus on your aftercare—which I really want to sanction today and see no issues with—I'd just like to run through the circumstances that led to your breakdown one final time. Would you be comfortable with that?"

A knot in my stomach.

My mouth goes dry in an instant, so I gulp spontaneously.

Then I smile.

Because I know I have to keep my cool.

I know I have to convince the doctor I am fit and I am healthy, and I am ready for release.

"Of course," I say.

"Okay," he says, smiling. "I know this isn't... easy. I know we've been to some deep places. Some dark places. So we'll take it all gently. We'll take it all one step at a time. There's no rush. So we—"

"Three years ago, I had a breakdown," I say, speeding ahead of him, eager to prove my sanity. And to prove I accept the truth, now, bitter as it is to swallow. "It was prompted by a trigger. PTSD. The maize fields. Something that... something that happened in my childhood."

Dr Maubid stares right at me. "Sarah, we don't have to go this fast—"

"I was having an affair with a man called Glynn. We started as just friends, and then things got... out of hand. He'd come round sometimes. Bring his son, Alan. We made love a lot. But I... I think Alan saw us once. I got pregnant. And that day, the day of the fete three years ago, I... I went into the maize fields with Glynn, and something about it... something about it brought back a memory. A memory from years ago. And it unsettled me. It destabilised me. I had a breakdown, and I found myself... I found myself convinced I had a son. False Memory Syndrome, apparently. Convinced I had a son called Charlie. That he was missing. Only... only that's not true."

It hurts me to say it. Pains me to admit it. The truth is, I'm grieving. Grieving for a son I never had. Because even though I know I never had this son now... he was still real to me.

And that's an impossible situation to explain to anyone who hasn't suffered the way I have suffered.

The loss of a son who never existed to anyone else.

But who felt so real to me.

"I went into the psychiatric hospital. I got better. I came out, and I... My husband and I were over, but I had three good years. I rebuilt my life. But deep down in my mind, I still lived with the belief I had a son. That I'd lost a son. I told Freddie this, my new partner. And I made him believe the lie. It made living... easier, somehow. It made me feel more normal. And I told myself I had it under control. I told myself I wouldn't let it spiral like it did the first time. Only something... something triggered another breakdown. Maybe the stress of the move. Maybe the pretence of all the lies. I'm not sure."

Dr Maubid nods. Because I am saying everything he wants me to say. Everything he wants me to believe.

Even though deep inside, I still have doubts about it all.

But first, let me tell you a bit about False Memory Syndrome, the beautiful fuckery of a mental health condition I have along with its abusive partner, dissociative amnesia.

Quite the double act.

A recipe for traumatic disaster.

False Memory Syndrome is a condition where a person's identity and relationships are affected by false memories.

I remember hearing how it worked and being somewhat fascinated. Apparently, glutamate and GABA, two amino acids, steer emotions and decide whether nerve cells are excited or chilled.

In normal conditions, the system is balanced. But when people get anxious and over the top, glutamate surges.

Oh, and glutamate just so happens to be the main chemical that makes it easy to remember memories stored in the brain.

So that's how the whole false memory thing is supposed to work. What happened that day in the maize fields, it apparently rooted in my mind as a trauma memory.

And when I was there with Glynn, fucking in the fields, it brought it out again.

The glutamate was stimulated.

My system went into overdrive.

Only that FMS was so strong that it triggered my dissociative amnesia.

It convinced me I had a son.

Even though I'd been fucking Glynn and there had been no mention of a son in our entire affair, I became convinced.

In the end, it was Gregg who reassured me it wasn't true. Who got me sectioned for the best. And then ended up leaving me while I was in there, something I couldn't really blame him for, right?

"I became... I became plagued by false memories again. And I started suffering from dissociative amnesia. I blocked out the trauma of my previous breakdown. My mind became obsessed with the idea of Charlie again. With finding him. With the idea that he was lost, and he was out there. I suffered from—from paranoia-induced hallucinations and became convinced somebody was following me. That I'd done something bad a long time ago and that somebody knew about it.

"But now... but now I know none of that was real. None of that was true. Charlie... Charlie never existed. I've grieved for a son I never had so many times. But he—he never existed."

It is so hard to admit this. So hard to accept it. I'm still not entirely sure I believe it.

There are vivid memories I have.

Memories of holding Charlie's hand in the school field.

Memories of Glynn bringing Alan around to play with Charlie, only apparently there was only one occasion where Alan came round, and we sent him upstairs to play on Gregg's Xbox while he was away.

Memories of holding a crying baby Charlie in my arms in the summer heat.

And all the stuff with the note. *I KNOW EVERYTHING*. The strands of blonde hair.

Every memory I have of my son and of losing my son.

There was no evidence any of that even happened.

None at all.

So as real as it felt, we were chalking it down to my fragile mental state.

My trauma.

My False Memory Syndrome and my dissociative amnesia.

I suffered a trauma years ago. A trauma I cannot remember. A trauma I do not *want* to remember.

It resurfaced again three years ago, and it resulted in me being sectioned.

I never truly recovered and became increasingly paranoid and convinced of Charlie's existence and that someone was out to get me.

But it's not true.

None of it is true.

"My husband—my ex-husband—he tried to protect me. But he couldn't handle it. Not anymore. But Freddie. My boyfriend. He—he is much better. He is more understanding. I have a lot of... a lot of things to explain to him. I've told him what happened now. I've told him my story. And hard as it is for him to understand, he gets it. He really gets it. There's a long road ahead. But I... I can see the truth now. I can see it, and it's so clear. And that's all thanks to your help."

Dr Maubid smiles. "Flattered as I am, it's thanks to your hard work, Sarah."

I nod. I appreciate it. It means I am saying all the right things, even though deep down inside, that voice of doubt still speaks up.

"There is one more thing I would like to speak about," he says.

My stomach turns because I think I know what is coming.

"There is one section of your past you seem particularly reluctant to talk about. The years before Gregg. Your teenage years. The years we have identified as... as being the years your trauma was prompted."

My body seizes up, goes totally rigid.

"You alluded to something... something to do with a cult. With summer weather. Maize fields. Is there anything you'd like to say about that?"

I feel my face getting hot. Surely this isn't right? Aren't you supposed to be fucking careful around trauma memories rather than being so, well, haphazard?

"Sarah?" Dr Maubid says.

I swallow a lump in my dry throat. Take a deep breath. Shake my head. "That's the past. It's gone now. It's over now. All of it."

He looks at me for a few seconds. Like he's trying to figure out whether he really believes me.

Then, he smiles.

"In that case, I'm happy to let you leave today if everybody else is. Which considering your cooperation and your improvement, I see no reason to doubt that."

My eyes light up. A smile stretches across my face. "Thank you. Thank you so, so much."

"Thank yourself, Sarah. You've made an excellent recovery. Coming to terms with some of the things you've had to come to terms with cannot be easy for anyone. Not by any stretch."

I sit there, and I smile.

Because I know my story now.

Charlie never existed.

The note and the strands of hair and all the terrorising and stalking that happened to me three months ago were all just a product of my fragile mind.

I am a mess of false memories, of dissociative amnesia, of post-traumatic stress disorder.

But I know what is and isn't real anymore.

At least, that's the story I tell those around me.

Because deep down, even though I sit there and smile and take my meds and do as I am told, I don't believe them.

Not on a deep level.

On an instinctive level.

Because in my mind, I had a son called Charlie.

In my mind, I suffered a loss. A great loss.

And in my mind, somebody really *was* terrorising me about a past I cannot talk of.

A past where I can barely even bring myself to look at myself.

Call it trauma burial.

Call it dissociative amnesia.

Call it whatever the fuck you want.

This is my secret.

And it's one thing I am not sharing with a soul.

I just have to pretend to be healthy.

I just have to pretend to be well.

That's my only way forward, now.

"So," Dr Maubid says. "Ready to chat with the relevant authorities before getting out of here?"

I take a deep breath.

I am Sarah Evatt.

I have no son, and I have never had a son.

I had a breakdown, and I became convinced I was being stalked and followed.

But now I am better again.

I am ready to live a normal life again.

I swallow a lump in my throat, take another deep breath, and I smile.

I see the maize fields in the periphery of my mind.

And I push them away.

"I'm ready," I say.

CHAPTER FORTY-FOUR

I am in the waiting room, and time is going incredibly, painfully slowly.

I have a rucksack on my knee with my things. Nothing sharp, of course. And I've practically spent the last three months wearing trackies, which barely fit me at first. But I've grown into them. Eaten pretty well in here, in all truth. The food really isn't as bad as it's made out to be. Pretty damned healthy, in fact. Probably better than most people cook for themselves. Obviously, that's the way it goes nowadays. All these places need to have tip-top health policies. Anything less than stellar, and it reflects badly on the whole institution.

I feel healthier. I've put on weight, so I'm not rake thin anymore. I even have a healthy glow to my face.

But honestly, I can't wait to just get out of here and get back to my normal life. To takeaways with Freddie on a Friday night, sometimes midweek, too. To lounging on the sofa in his arms, watching whatever crap's on telly.

I just long for those days again. The good days. The days before all this crap entered our lives.

I sit in the waiting room, and I keep checking the clock.

There's a woman at reception, rather chubby, with long pink nails. They remind me of my doctor from three months ago. Doctor Murray, or whatever she was called. The conversation I had with her. The increasing of the dosage of my medication to help with my symptoms. Symptoms I was convinced were some kind of conspiracy.

I remember flushing them down the toilet every single day.

Because I didn't need them.

As far as I was concerned, I wasn't suffering any illness at all.

But I see now how wrong I was back then.

I see now that it's important I take my medication. Because some days, I wake up, and I'm still convinced all those things actually happened to me.

That Charlie actually *was* my child.

That my grief was real.

And that I really was stalked three months ago by somebody who knew more about my past than I was comfortable with.

Maybe you were.

I shake my head.

Just thoughts.

Observe the thoughts, let them go.

Do not go down the trail.

Do not follow the automaticity of thought.

I hear the woman at the reception desk tapping away at the keyboard. See a few folks walk in from their trips out of low secure, which are allowed for a few hours each day. Something I've taken advantage of, meeting Freddie for a brew a few times.

The wait goes on. That long wait for Freddie's arrival.

And as I sit here, I wonder if maybe he won't show. If maybe he will bail. Just like Gregg did all those years ago.

It's something I pushed from my mind. Something I chose to forget. Dissociative amnesia, they call it. Totally psychological. And coupled with my supposed tendency for false memories, a nightmare when it gets out of hand.

But now I remember three years ago so, so clearly.

Being locked away in a psychiatric hospital. And one not as nice as this, either.

Waiting there for Gregg to come to pick me up, even though he hadn't visited for three weeks.

Getting a call from him to say he couldn't make it.

And leaving on my own.

Completely on my own.

I feel betrayed by Gregg. Freshly betrayed. He was always nice to me. Always good to me. But at the end, he was a shit towards me. He ran away from me. Ran away from any sense of responsibility towards me. Broke up with me in my lowest moment.

I should never have been so forgiving towards him.

But my mind chose not to remember that part of my life.

Because it was intertwined with far too much trauma.

A door opens.

I turn around. Expect to see Freddie.

But it's not Freddie. It's another one of the receptionists. A short, skinny bloke. Camp looking. Definitely wearing some makeup.

He looks at me and smiles, and I can only smile back.

I look at the clock. Ten past four now. Where is he? He was supposed to be here ten minutes ago. I want to call him, but I don't have a phone. I see the two receptionists peeking over the desk at me, muttering under their breath. I feel their sympathetic gazes burning into me.

I know they must see this so often. Someone left behind. Or someone waiting for someone to pick them up, someone who never ends up showing.

I wonder just how many people who walk through these doors end up walking straight back into them again. Like prisoners. Unable to hack the outside world, so end up reoffending just to get back inside.

It's a comfort. A weirdly small comfort.

If all goes to shit on the outside, I can just play crazy and get myself locked back in here again.

The clock hits half past. He's half an hour late. The receptionists are getting antsy. I wonder how long I wait here before stepping outside, before giving up. They won't let me go without him because that's what's been agreed. You have to state who is picking you up. If nobody, they get somebody to escort you out. The last act of care before throwing you back into the outside world.

I stand up. Pace back and forward. I'm starting to get nervous now. And whenever I get nervous, I panic because I begin to question everything.

Am I going to slip down the same dark path as I did the last time I got sectioned?

Is it all going to happen, all over again?

The forgetting?

The paranoia?

The dread?

Am I going to have to start my life all over again?

I see one of the receptionists—the camp one—climb off his stool, and I know he's going to walk over to me to tell me to sit down when I hear the door creak open.

I turn around.

And then I see him.

Tall.

Muscular.

Handsome.

Just as I remember him.

Smile beaming across his face.

"Freddie," I say.

He walks towards me.

Grabs me in his arms.

Holds me. Tight.

"I've missed you," he says.

"You soft git," I say, tears rolling down my cheeks. I can see he is crying, too. Eyes bloodshot. "I saw you on bloody Wednesday."

"I know," he says. "I—I got caught in traffic. I was getting us Chinese."

I laugh. And I cry. I can't contain myself anymore.

The pair of us stand there, together in this waiting room.

Freddie takes my hand.

"Come on, love. Let's take you home."

I look at the receptionists, both of them smiling.

I look back at the door towards the place I've just spent the last three months of my life.

The place I am actually weirdly grateful for.

And I take a deep breath and turn around.

I take a step, out of the front door, out into the crisp, crunchy autumn leaves, and into whatever my new life holds for me.

CHAPTER FORTY-FIVE

ONE MONTH LATER

I have been home one month, and life could not be better.

It's the start of December. Christmas is just around the corner, but we put the trees and the lights up early because fuck it. We don't give a shit what anyone thinks. What anyone might say. I love Christmas, and I always have. And the second Freddie heard that, he rigged up the cheesiest, most novelty lights setup possible. Big inflatable Santa on the roof, something that Moira didn't seem too impressed about, seeing as she's directly attached to our place. But she can't talk about fire hazards with all her smoking, the crazy old fool.

A big light display outside, with lasers and everything. Even a fake snow machine, something the kids on the street love.

It's cheesy as fuck, but I love it.

Really, life is good right now.

I'm sitting outside in the backyard around a patio heater. It's one Freddie got from work. Made out of an old washing machine drum. The flames crackle away, giving off an immense amount of heat. We're at that weird point of the year where the orange of autumn has fully made way for the cobalt grey of winter. It's a sort of limbo state. That no-place between dying and death.

And yet, there's a beauty to it. A real beauty.

Freddie holds a stick with a marshmallow on the end over the open flame. He looks up at me and grins. "Go on. Your turn."

I shake my head, laugh a little as he holds that marshmallow to my mouth. "Won't it be hot?"

"Oh, yeah. Excruciatingly hot. Like burning alive."

"Nice. Very poetic."

"Go on. Just take a bite. It won't do you any harm."

I go to take a bite out of the marshmallow, and Freddie jolts back the stick, making a funny noise as he does.

"Damn it, Freddie," I say, laughing. "You scared the shit out of me."

He leans back, laughing. I can see he's pale. I can see he's lost a lot of weight. And I can see he has suffered along with me.

But he's been amazing since I got back. While I was inside, he was amazing too. But since I got back... he's made life fun. He's made me feel loved. He's taken a full month off work just to make sure I'm comfortable.

He's insisted he'll give me my space. He's trusted me not to turn into some suicidal wreck at the first sign of loneliness. Really, he's been perfect.

He goes back to work tomorrow. Which, admittedly, makes me a little nervous.

But honestly, I'm feeling better than I've felt in a long time.

I managed to keep my driving licence. The dangerous driving case was dismissed. I'm so grateful for that element of freedom, but I know I'll be in big trouble if anything like that ever happens again. The judge was particularly lenient. So glad I caught him on a good day.

I'm taking my meds, for one. Regularly. New meds. New doses of old meds.

I'm being supported by the doctors and the psychiatric

hospital I stayed in. Good aftercare, where I have regular phone calls, visits, all that stuff. I even see Doctor Maubid again from time to time. It feels like they really care about me this time. Like they are really looking out for me and don't want to see me fall back down a dark road again. Especially not after last time.

I'm doing therapy, too. Regular therapy. And while there are things in my memory I don't want to touch on... honestly, I'm not even sure what is real and what isn't real from my past. Not anymore.

There is trauma there, sure. Trauma from somewhere.

And there is grief there, too. Grief for a child who didn't exist.

But for all of this, I'm doing all the right things.

I'm taking my life one step at a time.

And I am enjoying every minute.

"Want to be careful burning stuff like that." A voice from over the wall. Moira. "Wouldn't want the whole building to go up in flames. Especially not with all those lights."

I smile at Moira. Nod. She hasn't liked me since my break-down, really. Seemed nice at first. I actually pitied her.

But she's of that generation who judges mental illness just like she judges pre-marital sex.

She's naive. I can't really blame the environment she grew up in. We all have our stories. We all have our flaws.

We all have our secrets.

I've told Freddie everything I know now to be true. About Charlie. About losing contact with my mum and dad. About my lack of contact with my sister. I've told him everything.

Or at least, everything that is relevant, anyway.

And truth be told... I'm really starting to believe the official story of what happened to me now. Or rather, what *didn't* happen to me.

I'm starting to believe that I really did just have a mental breakdown. Because all the evidence suggests I did. Especially when it has happened before.

And that is just another step on my road to recovery.

"Give me a sec," I say. "Just grabbing a cardie."

"Can you grab my hoodie while you're in there? Freezing my balls off."

"Your hoodie isn't going to do much for your balls; I'm afraid to say."

"Hey. It's a large hoodie. And I have such microscopic balls, of course."

I laugh. Both of us laugh. It's been like this for a month. Perfect. Almost teenage.

And sure. The sex isn't *quite* there yet.

But we're taking our time. Freddie is being super patient. I'm so, so grateful for him.

I step into the kitchen to get my cardigan and Freddie's hoodie, and I notice my phone flash on the side. I walk over to it. Pick it up.

And that's when I see something that makes me stop, right in my tracks.

There is a Facebook message there.

It's from a profile I don't recognise.

A little grey figure and no name.

Just "Facebook User."

I read the words, and right then, my whole world stands still.

Woodplumpton Village Church. Tomorrow. 3pm. Be there. We need to talk.

CHAPTER FORTY-SIX

Woodplumpton Village Church. Tomorrow. 3pm. Be there. We need to talk.

I read the words repeatedly, and I have to pinch myself a few times to check I am not imagining things.

The rest of the room has dissolved around me. And suddenly, I am back in a hole, back in that void I was in four months ago. I can feel that same darkness inside. That sense of dread. The memories all coming back, rearing their head once more.

The stalking.

The message and the parcel I received.

All of the shit that happened.

Everything that followed.

I'd cast it aside. Put it down to my fragile mental state.

But now I am here, staring at the message, and I can see it is true.

I hear Freddie outside, shuffling around. I know what I need to do. I need to go out there. I need to show him this. And then maybe he'll believe I was telling the truth all along. Maybe he'll see I'm not crazy. Maybe it'll make him reassess everything.

But then even I'm fucking confused. Even I'm not sure what I'm seeing is real right now.

But this message. It's still right here. Still right in front of me.

I close the phone. Lock it. And I walk outside. Shaking a little.

Freddie is still sitting around the fire. Rubbing his legs in the cool winter air. "You okay, Sarah?"

"Freddie," I say. Reaching for my phone. Shaking. I can still hardly believe this is actually happening to me. "I... I need to show you something."

He frowns. That momentary flicker of concern across his face. A reminder of how he used to look at me three months ago when everything was falling apart. "Are you okay?"

I reach for my phone and go to open up the message when I realise it is gone.

Gone.

Completely gone.

Not a trace of it.

I stand there and stare at the screen, and I wonder. Either it was a disappearing message, which is a distinct possibility on Facebook nowadays.

Or I imagined the whole thing.

I swallow a lump in my throat. I want to tell Freddie what I saw. But at the same time, I know it'll only worry him. It'll only make him fear I'm deteriorating. And I can't have him thinking that.

I lower my phone. Put it in my pocket. "Nothing," I say.

He frowns even more. "You sure? You looked a little alarmed for a moment there."

I take a deep breath.

"I... I thought I saw something. On my phone. A message. But —but I didn't. There's nothing there. No evidence of it existing. So it mustn't exist. Right?"

He stares at me. And I can tell he is a little concerned, now.

"What did the message say?"

I open my mouth to tell him, and for some reason, I want to keep the details to myself.

"It was just to do with—with Charlie. But I... The doctors told me I will have relapses occasionally. It's natural. But I know what's real and what isn't anymore. It's nothing. Really. I'll log it and tell the doctor about it."

He stands up. Walks over to me. Smiles. And then he leans in and kisses me, wrapping his big arms around me.

"I'm so proud of you," he says. "You've come so far. I love you."

He steps away from me, then.

"Actually, I was going to ask you something. I realise it's early days. I don't want to stress you out. But I, um..."

I narrow my eyes. "What?"

"I was wondering if... if maybe... well. I guess this is the part where I'm supposed to get on one knee, isn't it?"

"Are you... wait. Is this your elaborate way of asking me to marry you right now?"

He laughs. His cheeks are flushed. "I—I guess it is."

I laugh. Shake my head. And then he gets down on one knee and holds out a marshmallow. "You'll have to bear with me for the ring. A marshmallow will do for now, for my queen?"

I laugh. And as much as I feel uneasy about the message, as much as I feel like the tentacles of the past are wrapping around me, I laugh, and I reach down and wrap my arms around Freddie.

"Yes," I say. "I'll do it. I'll marry you."

I am happy.

So happy.

But I can't deny the slight hint of discontent as I feel the weight of my phone press against my thigh...

CHAPTER FORTY-SEVEN

I lie awake in bed, and I can't stop thinking about the message.

We've had a beautiful evening, Freddie and I. I can hear him snoring away now. Not surprised after all the sex we had. It was very romantic. Very slow. Very emotional, very intense. And that in itself was tiring.

But it's been such a nice day. Such a nice evening. Our first evening as an engaged couple.

It should be happy. It should be a time of complete and utter elation.

But that message.

Woodplumpton Church. 3pm tomorrow. Be there.

I can't stop thinking about it. I am torn. One part of my mind tells me it's all in my head. The message disappeared, after all. There's no trace of it. No way of proving it happened to anyone else and no way of even proving it to myself.

And that was always touted as a key part of my recovery. Always ask the questions; can you verify it yourself? Can someone else verify it?

The answer is obviously no to both these questions.

And yet still, there is something about that message that draws me in.

Especially with disappearing, self-destructing messages being a thing, these days.

Freddie is back at work tomorrow. I will have a free day to myself. And if I go to Woodplumpton, maybe I can record whatever happens to show Freddie if I have to.

But no. I am insane for even thinking about going to Woodplumpton.

This is just in my head.

It isn't real.

It's just like the parcel and the *I KNOW EVERYTHING* letter.

But then I think of the maize fields.

I think of the rat.

The rat.

The dying rat that appeared in our kitchen that day.

The way Freddie described it.

Just like the rat from my childhood.

Just like the—

I hear crying.

I feel the burning heat of the sun.

I look down at him, and I feel tears rolling down my face.

A cracking sound.

Blood.

Wet palms.

Crying.

And...

I jolt upright. My heart races. I am covered in sweat.

Because I feel like I've just had a memory.

And whatever it was, as fragmented as it was... it felt real.

I lie back down. Freddie still snoring away. I look out of the gap between the curtains, out at the light. And as much as I want to let this go, it's not in my nature.

I know already exactly what I am going to do tomorrow.

Regardless of the consequences.

I take a deep breath, swallow a lump in my throat, and close my eyes.

I won't sleep tonight.

That is absolutely guaranteed.

But tomorrow, at 3 p.m., I am going to go to Woodplumpton Church.

And I am going to find out the truth about the legitimacy of that message.

Once and for all.

CHAPTER FORTY-EIGHT

I sit in my car outside Woodplumpton Church graveyard, and I am not sure I want to do this at all.

It's freezing cold. Cloudy. Woodplumpton is a sleepy little village, so there's barely a soul around. I've always liked it here. Such a nice little graveyard. Always said I'd want to be buried here, as morbid as that sounds. Just something comforting about it. Something cosy about it. Fields all around, with cows and sheep. A cute little church. A warm feeling about it all.

There is nobody in sight.

I look at my phone. Three o'clock. Bang on. And it seems like nobody is here, which makes me question whether I really did receive that message at all. Chances are, it was all just a hallucination. All in my head.

But still, that urgency to discover, to know, it plagues me...

Freddie messages me.

How's the village? x

I've told him the truth. Well. A version of the truth. I've told him I'm going for a walk around Woodplumpton. Clearing my head while he's back at work.

But I haven't told him about the message.

I don't want to worry him. I don't want him to think I'm going downhill again. Losing my mind. I've just come here because there are things I want to settle. Things I want to come to terms with at my own pace.

This is a part of my healing. A part of my recovery. Coming to terms with the fact that this is some kind of hallucination.

Or maybe something else...

I shake my head. I know that's probably not true.

But a part of me can't help feeling disappointed, somehow.

A part of me wants to believe what happened four months ago wasn't all the product of a breakdown.

And what happened three *years* ago wasn't just the product of a breakdown, either.

I look at the little GoPro camera attached just under my shirt. I don't know how it works really, and I've already had a nightmare setting it up. Tiny little thing with a big Share button that I keep accidentally hitting and uploading stuff to YouTube and social media. And that got me in a whole mess of having to change my passwords for every bloody thing.

But that doesn't matter. What matters is I have a camera on me now. And its sole purpose is so I can prove to others—and to myself—that I am not lying.

Apparently, there's a good six hours recording time on there because it's one of the more expensive models, something I didn't even realise at the time. I was desperate at the end of the day, and it was the only one in stock.

I figure I can just keep it running throughout this conversation.

I get out of the car. Figure there's no harm in stretching my legs. I walk through the graveyard, past all the headstones. It's so windy, so cold. My hair flies all over the place.

I look at the years. Look at the names. This place fills up every time you look at it. Soon, it'll be totally full. I wonder if they'll expand. Or if they'll just start ripping the old headstones out and replacing them with new ones.

Quite sad, in a way. Seeing the newer headstones with all the flowers. The older ones, abandoned.

A reminder that nothing is permanent. Not really.

I reach the witch's grave, and I stand by it for a bit. Apparently, a woman was executed for being a witch many years ago. They drowned her. Dunked her head in and out of the water, even though she was innocent.

And sure. She would have her secrets. But she was still innocent of what they accused her of. She was still just a human. Just suffering.

I look at this headstone, and I think of the maize fields, and I wonder what people would say of me.

Of the things I've done.

I wonder if people would think of me as a witch.

If people would...

No.

That's the past.

No. Not the past.

It's not real.

This is all that's real.

This is all that matters.

I put my hand on the cold stone and imagine that poor, innocent woman's horror as she drowns. I imagine her keeping her mouth tightly shut. I imagine her kicking. Screaming. I imagine her reaching out, softly placing her hand on the back of those holding her down and—

Maize fields.

Stream.

Damp hands.

I step back. My heart picks up again. These visions. The same as last night. They keep on emerging in my mind. Sparking up, surfacing.

And the weird part is, I don't even know if they are real anymore.

I look at my watch. Quarter past three. At least that's something. The message. It was all in my head. There is no meeting. There's nothing here.

And that means everything else I'm seeing, envisaging, imagining... yes. That's all in my head too. It's not real.

I turn around to walk away from the graveyard, and I feel somewhat disappointed not to be proven right. But I have to be humble. I have to accept the evidence before me.

That's when I see him standing right opposite me.

"Hello, Sarah," he says. "Thanks for coming. We really need to talk."

CHAPTER FORTY-NINE

"Hello, Sarah. It's about time we had a proper conversation, huh?"

I stare at the man standing opposite me, and I have to blink a few times to check I'm not imagining things. To check I'm not hallucinating.

All I can do is stand.

All I can do is stare.

Because standing opposite me is a man I recognise.

Slicked back dark hair.

Short. With a paunch of a stomach.

Not smiling with those yellow teeth as usual. Looking far more concerned and serious than the first time I saw him.

And even from here, I can smell that onion breath.

"Calvin," I say. "Or is it Cameron?"

He walks towards me, and I want to bolt. I want to run. Because this is real. The man who started this whole saga four months ago when he handed me the parcel. It's him, and it's real.

"It's—it's Cameron," he says, not sounding as over-the-top northern as he did when I first met him. "Sorry. I know you're probably a bit spooked out right now. And I fully understand if you want to bolt. But—but I can't have this shit go on any longer."

I do want to turn. I do want to run. I want to disappear back to the happy life I've been living for the last month, ever since I got back from the psychiatric hospital, ever since I recovered.

But I can't turn away from this.

"How did you find me?"

"You're on Facebook, love. It ain't too hard to find someone on there."

"The Snapchat messages. Everything else. Was that you too?"

Cameron looks me right in the eyes, and he shakes his head very defiantly. "It wasn't me. I swear."

And I know I should doubt him. I know I should question his every word.

But I believe him.

Weirdly, I believe him.

"You came to visit me. You... you didn't repair my boiler. Right?"

Cameron looks at the ground of the graveyard path and nods. "I'm sorry. You're right. I came to see you. I small-talked with you at the door. Handed you a parcel. Then I walked away."

I feel it hit me like a punch to the gut.

"So I'm... I'm not crazy. I didn't imagine it all."

"Sarah, I'm so sorry, love. I know this ain't gonna be easy to believe, but I ain't a bad man."

"You made—you made people think I was crazy—"

"And I've lived with the bloody guilt of that every bloody day. I toyed with telling you. The day you saw me on the street, I was gonna tell you. And there was another night, too. I came by your house, and I was gonna knock on your door and tell you everything. But I didn't. I didn't, and I'm sorry."

I feel it all slipping into place.

The night when I saw someone across the road staring up into my bedroom window.

That was Cameron.

"But then what about... the school field?"

Cameron frowns. "I'm sorry. But I don't know what you're on about. But... Well, I should probably be honest about summat else, too. We did meet. A long, long time ago. Lytham Festival. You were there with your fella. I was there with my grandkids. Remember?"

And then it hits me.

Lytham Festival with Gregg.

The heat of the summer.

The live band playing.

And Cameron and his onion breath commenting on what a nice day it was.

My memories jumbled together. It *did* happen. I did remember him from a festival.

Just not as I thought I did.

"I remember," I say.

Cameron nods. "Look. I ain't proud of what I did. And when I heard you got sectioned... shit, I've been living with the guilt ever since. I wanted to reach out to you. Wanted to tell you. But there was never a right time. Not until... not until he came to me again."

I frown. A shiver creeps down my spine as the breeze blows against me. "Who came to you?"

He looks over his shoulder like he's worried. "Four months ago, I was at a low ebb. I was low on cash and deep in debt. And some bloke I've never met comes to me and asks me to hand you summat. A parcel."

I cannot believe what I am hearing.

I cannot believe this is even real.

But it makes sense.

It makes total sense.

"He told me the job was simple. Hand you the parcel. Tell you some bullshit about a fake address. And then disappear. Do all that, and he gives me ten grand."

I swallow a lump in my throat. So this was targeted. It was all real. It actually happened.

"Now, trust me. I felt uneasy about it, like. I even came back to warn you a few times but got cold feet. That's what happened when—when you caught me that day in the street. But anyway. I did it, and I ain't proud of it. And listen, ten grand's a lot of money, and when you're struggling, it's even more. But I did it. Didn't think much of it. Not until he came to see me again a week back and asked if I'd do summat awful. Really awful."

I hold my breath. "What did he ask you to do?"

"To—to break in. To break into your house all masked up and drive you away somewhere. Shake you up. Not harm you or hurt you, just—just fuck with you, you know?"

My mouth goes dry. I can't believe what I'm hearing.

"I couldn't do it. Not anymore. Told the bloke flat out I wasn't gonna be his lackey anymore. But—but then yesterday, he paid me a visit. He gave me five more grand and told me to get the job done and not to tell the police about owt. And that if I didn't do it or if I told the police, I'd be in trouble. My grandkids would be in trouble. Just turned up, he did. Handed 'em an ice cream. I knew then how much shit I was in. And he—he wanted me to tell you summat, too."

I swallow a lump in my throat. "What was it?"

"'I... I know what you did to Charlie.'"

My skin turns cold.

Everything goes numb.

"I don't know what it means," he says. "I don't know what any of it means. But someone's after you, love. And honestly, I took the money, and I'm gonna use it to get me and my family far away from here. As far away from him as possible. 'Cause I'm scared of him. I'm scared what might happen if I go to the police 'cause he says he has people everywhere. And I'm scared you're gonna get trapped in it all yourself. I just couldn't have you thinking you're crazy. 'Cause you ain't. Really, you ain't. It's real. It's all fucking real. And you need to be careful of this guy. You need to get yerself as far away from him as you can."

"Who—who is he?"

"That's the thing," Cameron says. "I didn't get a name. Not at first. Kept a very low profile, y'know. But I saw him. The night I came round to yours when the streetlamp went out. When you saw me. I—I saw him, and that's when it hit me."

"Who is he?" I ask.

"I dunno who he is," Cameron says. "And I don't know what he's called. But I do know one thing. That old woman who lives next door to you. You can't trust her. 'Cause I'm pretty sure it's her son."

CHAPTER FIFTY

I drive back home, and I still can't wrap my head around everything Cameron just told me.

Somebody paid Cameron to deliver me that parcel in the summer. The parcel, which was real.

Somebody paid Cameron to kidnap me.

To tell me they knew something about... about *Charlie*.

That they knew what I'd done to him.

And ever since then, Cameron has been battling with his own demons over whether to reach out to me or not, jeopardising his own safety in the process.

I can barely think. My mind is mush. I feel like I'm living in a dream. Or a nightmare.

Because there is no doubt in my mind that what just happened is real.

And I have the evidence to prove it.

I've recorded my conversation with Cameron via GoPro. I haven't even had time to stop the recording. Or to watch it back. Or anything like that.

I've just sat here and tried to wrap my head around it.

Tried to understand.

There are so many things that don't make sense to me.

But I cannot deny what Cameron told me.

I cannot deny that it adds up.

Someone is stalking me.

Someone really is terrorising me.

And according to Cameron, that someone is Moira's son.

But Moira said she didn't have a son. So it must be Kent. Her nephew.

Unless she was lying about not having a son.

Either way, I cannot trust her.

I remember the night I went to the window. I remember looking outside, seeing that figure staring back at me in the darkness.

And I remember Moira speaking to someone getting into a red car in hushed tones. Looking up at me, right at me, then away.

And as I sit there, driving, barely able to focus, all of it slides into place.

The parcel.

I lost it around at Moira's.

Her son must've taken it, somehow.

Shit. Her son must've sneaked around that day I collapsed in the kitchen.

And come to think of it, when I went around to Moira's in search of that parcel, I distinctly remember hearing movement upstairs.

And the time I rushed back around later that day, I swore I heard her speaking to someone.

I turn into my road. I can't make sense of it. Any sense of it at all.

I just know that I have all the evidence I need now.

I need to get home.

And regardless of what Freddie thinks of me now, I have to show him.

I have to show him, so he knows I'm not crazy.

So he knows I'm not insane.

I drive past Moira's house, attached to my own, and I can barely look at it. I need to go inside. I need to find Freddie. I need to tell him everything, and then we need to go to the police.

But then the message.

The message Cameron was paid to deliver me, through terror.

I know what you did to Charlie.

I shiver when I think about it.

I don't want to think about it.

Because it's like everyone says.

Charlie never existed.

Charlie has never even *been* a thing.

It's all just trauma.

It's all just false memory.

It's all just...

I pull up outside, and I notice Freddie isn't home yet. I just need to get inside and lock the doors and hide upstairs.

Or... no. I need to just keep my cool. Moira's nephew, Kent. Or her son. Whoever he is, and whatever he knows about me, he could've done a number of things before now. Just because I suddenly know the truth doesn't mean he's any more likely to act, especially when he doesn't know what I know.

Right?

And then there's Moira.

What does she know?

She always seems a bit odd.

But *this* odd?

I look around at my house and decide the only course of action right now is to get inside, act as normal as possible, and wait for Freddie to come home.

I'll show him the footage.

Then we'll go to the police.

I climb out of my car. Keep my head down. I start rushing my way up the pathway, unable to keep my eyes off Moira's front lawn. The garden gnomes tumbled onto their sides. And that CCTV camera staring down at me.

And I wonder, then.

Has this CCTV camera been working all along?

Did she lie about that, and all this time, she's been stalking me, waiting for the perfect opportunities to make her moves?

I fumble around with my keys. Drop them to the ground. Pick them up.

And then I hear movement down the pathway to my left.

Whistling.

Moira.

I stick the key in the lock with my shaking hand.

I turn it.

Fast.

And then, just as I see her appear, I step inside, close the door shut and turn the lock.

I fall back against the door. Close my eyes. My heart races. I am covered in sweat. And as I slouch here, I just want Freddie to come home. I just want him to get back and to tell him everything, the whole lot.

And then we can go to the police and finish this, once and for all.

I feel bad for Cameron. He is scared. He is afraid. And his family is in danger.

But he did something bad. Really bad. And it has put me through hell.

So if he thinks I'm not going to use his words against him, he is mistaken.

I will try not to. But I cannot make any promises.

I suddenly hear a floorboard creak upstairs.

I open my eyes.

My heart skips a beat.

I heard something.

Like footsteps.

Like somebody is up there.

After sitting there for what feels like an eternity, I finally manage to stand.

I walk across the room. Grab a heavy metal clock we've got on the mantlepiece, and I stand at the bottom of the staircase.

I know what I heard. And it could be nothing. After all, I always hear creaking around in the loft at night, something Freddie always insists is the wind.

But I know what that sounded like.

"Fuck it," I say. "Here goes nothing."

I climb the stairs. Slowly. And every step I take feels more and more protracted than the last.

I reach the top step. Sweat pooling down my face.

I stand there on the landing.

Silence.

I raise the clock. Move towards the bathroom. Push the door open.

Nothing in there.

Nobody in there.

Nothing but that opening, still unattended to, still unfixed.

I move across the landing. Just two more rooms. The main bedroom and the spare.

I check our room first.

Empty.

And then I walk down towards the spare room.

Open the door.

Also empty.

I lower the clock a little. Sigh. Maybe it was just the floorboards creaking.

I go to turn around when I hear something above me.

I frown.

Look up.

That's when I see the loft hatch.

My stomach turns.

I don't want to go up there. I don't like the thought of being in the dark, in the pitch black.

But for some reason, at this moment, something possesses me.

I look up at that loft hatch.

I lift my phone and flick on the torch.

"Fuck it," I say.

And then I reach up and click the release button.

The hatch falls down, and with it, an air of dust, making me cough.

I reach up. Pull the ladders down.

And then I point my torch up there and climb the ladders.

When I get to the top, I want to turn around immediately. It is dark up here. Damp. Claustrophobic. And there're spiders everywhere.

But more importantly than that, there is nobody up here.

I go to turn around when I notice something.

It catches my eye. Only for a moment. Just a brief, fleeting moment.

But when I see it, it makes my heart skip a beat.

Over by the wall—the wall connecting our loft to Moira's loft —I see an old poster. A poster of an old cattle breed sticking to the wall.

And as I get closer, I can't figure out why, but I realise it's familiar, somehow.

I've seen it somewhere before.

It's when I reach it and stand right there that it comes to me.

That it hits me.

And that it almost knocks me to my feet.

I've seen the corner of this poster before.

I saw it in the Snap I received.

The one with the note.

I KNOW EVERYTHING.

And then...

I hear movement. Right in front of me.

Shuffling.

Which can't be possible. Because this is the wall.

It's the wall between ours and Moira's.

It's...

And then it hits me.

No.

It can't be.

It can't...

I inch forward. Knowing full well, I need to turn back. Knowing full well I need to get away.

I step right up to the wall between the lofts, and I push on one of the bricks.

It tumbles away.

I jump back.

And then I pull another away.

And another.

And suddenly, as I pull more and more bricks away, I realise why I have heard movement above for so long.

I realise I am not insane.

And I realise why the Snapchat I received was sent from my own attic, after all.

Because there is a passage between our attic and Moira's attic.

I go to back off, to run away when I hear more movement.

I freeze.

Go completely still.

I turn my torchlight on my phone ahead when I see something staring back at me.

Two skeletons.

Two bodies.

The skeleton of a young woman.

Skull caved in.

And a smaller skeleton.

A small skull.

I almost collapse out of the loft. I can't understand. I just need to get out of this house. I need to find Freddie. I need to find Freddie, and I need to go to the police because I am not insane. This is not in my head.

I drop my phone in the panic. Hear a crack.

But I just want to get out.

I just want to get away.

I race down the stairs and take a left when I slam into someone and scream.

"Sarah!"

"Get away! Get away!"

"Whoah, whoah. It's me. It's me, Sarah. What is it? What's wrong?"

I quickly come to my senses and realise it's Freddie. He's holding me.

"Sarah? What's wrong?"

I can barely speak. I can only point. "It's—it's real, Freddie."

"Slow down a second. What's real?"

"It's... I got a message. A message from Cameron. And I recorded it. Recorded him telling me about how—how Moira's son's involved. Or—or her nephew, Kent. I don't know who but —but it's somebody. He told me everything. How he's the one who stalked me. How he paid Cameron to—to do all these things. And then I got back here and—and I heard something just like I've heard so many times. Then I went into the loft, and I saw it. The place the Snap was taken. The one that vanished from the account with my password as the name. And... and the bricks, Freddie. The bricks. There's a passage in there. And then—next door. There's a... There's something up there."

Freddie looks at me. Calm and composed as possible. "It's

okay," he says. "Sarah, you just wait here. And I'll go up there. I'll see."

"No!" I shout.

"Sarah," Freddie says. "I've got this. Everything is okay. I love you. Okay?"

I want to tell him to stop. I don't want him going up there. I don't feel like it's safe up there or anywhere around here anymore.

But then he climbs the stairs.

And I see him disappear around the corner.

I hear him climb the ladders, and I wait.

I step back. Rub my temples. I wait for a shout. I wait for a scream. I wait for him to beg for help.

And then I hear him come back down the steps of the ladder.

I look up. See him at the top of the stairs. He's holding my phone. He looks concerned.

"Well?" I say.

He steps right up to me. Puts a hand on my cheek.

"Sarah," he says. "You're—you're right."

And just hearing those words makes my body freeze. "What?"

"There's—there's something up there. The walls to Moira's. Something's... Something's not right. I saw it, Sarah. I—I fucking saw it."

I see the horror in his eyes, and I know he sees the truth now. I know he believes me now.

"Freddie," I say. "What're—what're we going to do?"

I curse myself for sounding so weak, but he holds my arms, and in that reassuring way he always does, he takes a few deep breaths and looks me right in the eyes. "This video. This Cameron. Have you saved it?"

I nod. "It's—it's right on there. It's—"

"Good," he says. "Because we'll need it."

He walks past me. He still hasn't handed me back my phone yet.

"What are we doing?" I ask.

"What are we doing? Going to the fucking police, of course."

And I go to respond, go to agree, but something feels wrong.

Something just doesn't feel right.

"You—you've been working up there," I say.

Freddie turns around. Frowns. "What?"

"When we first moved in. You... you said it was rickety up there. And that—that you were doing work up there. Why didn't you see it?"

Freddie shakes his head. "Sarah? You really implying I knew something about this? Really?"

"And you told me not to go up there."

"I *advised* you not to go up there because of the fucking hole in the bathroom ceiling."

I want to argue. I want to fight. I want to disagree.

But in the end, I can feel myself slipping, feel myself spiralling.

He walks up to me. Puts a soft hand on my arm.

"We're going to be okay. We'll beat this, just like we beat everything."

He puts his arms around me, holds me, and I sink into them.

"Everything will be okay, my angel," he says. "Everything will be okay..."

My stomach turns.

I am back there.

The maize fields.

The demon mask.

The hands around my wrists.

And the neck mole.

The...

"Everything will be okay, my angel. Everything will be okay..."

I pull away.

I look at the scar on his neck.

I look there, and suddenly it all makes sense.

He stares at me. Calmly. "I'm guessing the video is saved to your phone, right?"

"I—I—"

"Good," he says.

He drops the phone to the floor and cracks it under his foot in one heavy stomp.

And then he pulls back his fist, punches me across the face, and all I see is darkness.

CHAPTER FIFTY-ONE

I open my eyes, and I hope it's all been a nightmare, a horrible dream.

But then I taste the blood on my lips, and I feel a deep, unwavering sense of dread.

I'm in a room somewhere. It's dark, and it's cold. Dusty. I'm aching everywhere. I have a vague memory of being lifted. Of being carried upstairs and taken somewhere. I have a vague memory of a lot of things.

But one thing I remember clearly?

Freddie.

Dropping my phone.

Crushing it underneath his foot.

And then punching me in the face.

The dread hits me again. Freddie. My sweet Freddie. All this time and he has been involved. All this time and I should've seen it.

Because how else was somebody supposed to sneak into our house after I passed out and take the parcel away from me?

But how far does this go?

How deep does this go?

I look around, and I see I am in the attic. And that fills me with fear. With dread. Because it's dark. So dark.

I think about the sounds above.

I think about the voices and the footsteps I swore to Freddie I heard in the night. The creaking he swore was the wind.

And I think about the number of times he told me not to go up there. Because he was working on something. Because it was a mess. Because the bathroom ceiling wasn't safe.

And how little he needed to convince me, all along.

I hear a floorboard creak behind me, and I know I am not alone.

Footsteps. Footsteps moving closer to me. I sit there. Heart racing. I'm on some kind of chair. Some kind of wooden stool.

I don't know what is going to happen to me. But I know how afraid I am.

I know how decisive this feels.

How trapped I feel.

Because the man I love punched me in the face and knocked me unconscious, then dragged me up here and bound me here.

I hear the footsteps get closer and closer.

And then, they stop.

There is someone behind me. Right behind me. Standing over me. I hear their breathing, heavy. I sense their gaze. And I smell the slight sweetness from their aftershave.

I know right away it is Freddie.

"Hello, love," he says, casual as ever. "Do you need water or anything?"

He speaks with such a casual tone that it actually knocks me for six. This has to be a nightmare. It can't be real. I've hallucinated scenes that seemed more vivid.

But then I wonder. Have I? Do I even *need* the medication I'm on? Did I even need my stint in the psychiatric hospital after all?

I shake my head. This can't be for real. Freddie can't be involved.

He can't know the things I've been hiding from him.

Hiding from myself.

But then he walks around the chair and stands right in front of me.

It's dark, but I can see his face. And there's a look to it. A look I've never seen before.

A look on his face like he despises me.

But a familiarity there, too.

A familiarity I've noticed before, in brief moments, but never truly acknowledged. Never truly registered.

A familiarity I've looked past.

But a familiarity that is starting to dawn on me more and more.

A past I have tried to bury. Tried to suppress.

Rearing its violent head, all over again.

"I'm serious," Freddie says. "You look like you could use a drink."

I try to say something when I realise I am gagged. The taste of sickly saliva clings to the back of my throat. I'm woozy. Shaky. Weak.

"I'm sorry about the nose," Freddie says. And it's only then I realise how painful it is. How bunged up with blood it is. "I realise that was a rather... dramatic way of proving a point. But everything has fallen into place, Sarah. Everything has built up to this moment. I'm just sorry it's come about so soon. I was hoping we could stretch this out a little longer. We both were."

I frown. I still don't understand. My heart races. My chest is tight. I can barely breathe.

Freddie steps forward. Right before me, then. He crouches in front of me. Puts his hands on mine. And then he smiles.

"You really don't recognise me. Do you?"

I want to say I do. Because a part of me does. A part of me senses I know him.

But it's that part deep, deep within the darkest recesses of my brain.

The part I least want to go.

"I thought that would be the hardest part. Convincing you I'm a stranger. I mean... sure. We hardly knew each other too well. But we knew each other enough. I knew you better than you knew me, anyway. A lot about you."

He looks at me, right into my eyes, and I can sense him pulling at the doors of a part of my mind I don't want him to go.

"First of all," he says, sighing. "Before I go any further. I just want you to know you're right. All the events of the last few months. They were real."

Hearing Freddie saying those words punches me right in the gut.

"I would say I'm not proud of what I did. But honestly, I'm pretty proud. Even the small details. Printing all those mock newspapers with Charlie's death on there. Convincing you you'd imagined it. Really think it was so hard for me to just rip up some other newspaper, Sarah? Didn't think to check?"

I feel sick. I want to vomit.

This can't be real.

It can't be true.

"And the photos, too. The screenshots you took of the Snaps. Didn't think that maybe, just maybe, I might know a thing or two about logging into your iCloud? Deleting them before you got to me? Especially having your bloody iCloud password as that Snapchat account name of mine. Really, I almost sympathised with you. I would've done, anyway. If I were on the outside. But I'm not. Am I, Sarah?"

It's the way he says those last words that convince me.

It's the way he says them that makes me understand.

Makes me realise.

"I've searched for you for a long, long time. When you left the Family, it became difficult to track you down. Especially when names are so easy to change. But when I found you... well. I knew it would take time to break you down. I knew it would take many, many years. But I knew it would be worth it, too."

I look into Freddie's eyes as tears stream down my cheeks, and as much as I don't want to accept it, as much as I want to run from it, I know I can't deny it anymore.

Who he is.

How he knows.

What he knows.

"But it isn't just me involved, is it, Sarah?"

He looks around, over to the darkness behind. And I realise then that this is the attic. It's my attic.

And up ahead of me, there's that gap in the bricks.

The gap to the room.

The room where I saw the skeletons...

No.

I don't want to think about that.

I don't want to think who it might be.

"Mum?" he says. "You can come through now."

A woman appears in the darkness.

I hear footsteps up ahead.

"You know, that's the part I thought might be difficult. But when this house came up for sale... Let's just say I had the perfect plan. To link the two houses. And then to start."

A woman appears in the darkness.

And I see right away that it is Moira.

She is dressed all in white.

Just like I used to dress when I was a little girl.

And she certainly isn't struggling anymore.

Not struggling with her mobility at all.

I think of her upstairs when I went around to find the contents of the parcel.

I think of her at the top of the stairs, and how weird it seemed.

I think about it all, and I see it right before my eyes.

Freddie wanted us to buy this house.

He wanted us to buy it.

And he did it for a reason.

"Well?" Freddie says. "Aren't you going to say hello?"

Moira steps forward, and a smile widens across her face. And suddenly, I know why I recognise her. I know why I found her familiar when I first saw her. It's because I've seen her before. A long, long time ago. But it's her.

"Hello, dear," she says. "Long time no see. I've waited a long time to make you pay. We both have. For what you did..."

CHAPTER FIFTY-TWO

The door in my mind is open now.

I think of my life in two distinct segments.

The days before Charlie went missing.

And the days after he went missing.

Those two distinct segments are real. Very real.

It's how I told myself the story that isn't quite as it happened.

* * *

"HELLO, SARAH," Moira says as she stands there opposite me in the darkness of the attic. "Is it starting to make a little more sense now?"

I look up at Moira. I look at Freddie. I look at them both in this attic as I sit there, bound to the chair. Taste of blood in my mouth. My nose throbbing, swollen, undoubtedly broken.

And it's the burn on Freddie's neck that keeps on catching my eye.

That, and Moira's white dress.

The same dress all the women in the Family used to wear.

I see it all, and I know what they know.

I know *how* they know.

I know *who* they are.

I remember her standing there that day when I stared down at the dying rat. Smile on her face. Cheering me on. Encouraging me. She looked so much different then. So much younger.

But I see it now. Clearly.

It's quite clearly her.

She is one of them.

"Did you think you could run from your past forever?" Moira asks. "After everything you did?"

I want to speak. I want to fight my corner. I want to say so much.

But the gag around my mouth suffocates me from saying anything.

And even if I *could* say anything, I'm not sure any words would come out.

I am broken.

I am totally and utterly destroyed.

My worst nightmares are playing out right before my eyes.

"My nephew, Kent. Not my nephew at all. Nothing more than a handyman. My son here couldn't go compromising his identity. So we got someone to help us out. To visit and threaten onion-breath Cameron to do the dirty work. Just a pity Cameron spotted him leaving my place that night. But anyway, that is irrelevant now. Maybe you should've paid more attention to just how often your beloved fiancé here headed up into the attic. But no. So self-absorbed. As you always were."

Freddie walks over to me, then. He pulls the gag away. Pushes a water bottle into my mouth and pours it down my throat. There's no sensitivity there. Not anymore. It's as if he doesn't recognise me anymore. Doesn't love me anymore.

"When I heard about your breakdown about a son you 'never

had'," Freddie says, "I didn't know whether to sympathise or be insulted."

I shake my head. I want this to stop. I want this to end. I want it to all go away.

"Because on the one hand... at least you were being haunted by your actions. By your past. Especially when I heard the name. *Charlie*."

My skin shivers.

"But on the other hand... it almost felt like you were taunting me. Like you were taunting all of us."

I shake my head because it's not true. None of this is true.

I wasn't taunting them.

It wasn't a game.

It was just... what happened.

And it's such a huge part of who I am.

The hidden iceberg under the surface of the water influencing my every move.

"But we had to stay patient. Both of us had to stay patient. We had to create the perfect conditions for the grand reveal, so to speak. We had to put you through hell to get you to this point. Just like you put *us* through hell. Both of us. And hell. Who knows how much further we might've got if Cameron didn't open his big old onion-stinking mouth? Jeez. So many things I can't believe you fell for. Cameron coming round to service the boiler? You actually believed that shit? Honestly, it was too easy. Didn't quite realise how crackers you actually were. Close, but not quite."

I shake my head, and I want to cry, and I want to beg because I didn't mean it I didn't mean any of it I just did what I did to help save myself I—

"But the truth is," Freddie says, "I've learned that as haunted by the past as you are, you're still just the same jealous, deceitful, lying bitch you've always been. The same malicious cunt you were back then. The same selfish witch who did all the things you did."

"Please," I say.

"What?"

"Don't. Just... just don't. Please."

Freddie looks at Moira. Moira looks back at him. And then both of them look back at me, bemused smiles on their faces.

"'Don't'?" Freddie says. "'Don't'? That all you have to say?"

He walks right up to me again.

Crouches right before me.

"Love," Moira says. "Don't get too rough with her."

But he grabs me by my cheeks and squeezes them tight.

Stares at me with hateful eyes.

"'Don't'?" he says. "Really? That's all you've got to say?"

I try to speak, but he's holding my face so tight that I can't say a word.

He shakes his head. Smiles.

"No," he says. "I'm going to make you remember."

"Freddie, please—"

"I'm going to make you remember, and I'm going to make you confess it all," he shouts. "Because that's all I've wanted. All along, I've pushed you further and further because it's all I've wanted. For you to admit it. To look me in the eye and admit it. Once and for all."

"Please, Freddie. If you've... if you care at all about me, please. Don't do this."

"Care about you?" He snorts. "I only care about one thing from you. One fucking thing."

I close my eyes and shake my head because I know it's coming.

It's coming, and I don't want to hear it.

"I want to hear you say the words," he says.

"Freddie—"

"I want to hear you admit it."

"Please!"

"I want you to admit to me and admit to your fucking self

what you did to Charlie! And what you did to Elana! Your own fucking sister! And her child! My child!"

* * *

I HEAR THOSE WORDS, and I am back there again.

CHAPTER FIFTY-THREE

I am back there again, and this time I know the memories are real.

They are *memories*. Not visions. Not hallucinations.

They are memories spilling out of a box I wanted to keep closed all this time.

I am in the field first. It's a warm day. For a moment, I wonder if it's Charlie's hand in mine. His sweaty palm, as I stand there in the middle of this field.

But it isn't.

I look around and see my sister, Elana, standing beside me.

She's crying. Tears cover her beautiful, perfect skin as she stands there in the white dress we all wear. I always was jealous of her, a little. Jealous of how beautiful she was. And jealous of just how much more attention she got than me.

As much as I didn't want to admit it. Because jealously is wrong. It's a sin.

"It won't happen," she says. She's only eighteen, but she looks older. Like a young woman. Ready for the world outside? The dangerous world outside we've heard all about?

Somehow, I'm not sure whether we're ever going to see that world.

"It will happen," I say, squeezing Elana's hand. Maybe a little tighter than is comfortable.

"But it won't," she spits. "I think it's my eggs. I think—I think maybe I just can't have a baby."

I don't know a lot about boys or eggs or sperm or how they work. The boys and the girls are kept separate here in the Family until they're old enough to meet each other and marry and have a baby. I've never met Andy, the guy my sister has fallen in love with. But I know he's older, and I know there's a chance this might not all be Elana's fault.

"Who's to say it isn't him?"

"It's not him, Sarah."

"But—"

"It isn't him, Sarah. Okay?"

She looks at me then with those toxic eyes. With such venom. Because even though Elana is my sister, we've never been close. I've tried to be close to her. But even though she gets all the fuss and attention, ever since I was born three years after her, she's always been jealous of me.

"Maybe... maybe it's not such a bad thing that you can't have a baby."

Elana narrows her eyes. Frowns. "What?"

"I'm—I'm just saying. You're still... young. And the boy."

"You can call him by his name."

"Okay. Andy," I say, a hint of frustration to my voice. "I haven't even met him."

"What does that matter?"

"I mean, I'm your sister."

Elana opens her mouth as if she's going to say something nasty. Then she closes her lips. Sighs. "Are you still bleeding?"

I feel my face go warm. I've been bleeding for a couple of years now. I still find it icky. A bit disgusting. But I'm getting more used to it. "Yeah. What does that have to do with anything?"

She looks at me, and just for a moment, I see a glint in her eyes.

The glint of somebody planning something.

"Nothing," she says. "When did you last... you know..."

"I don't see what that has to do with anything."

"Nothing," she says. "I'm just checking... checking my little sister is okay. That's all."

I sigh. "A week ago. Something like that."

"A week ago," Elana says.

And once again, she isn't there.

Once again, she is distant.

Once again, she is lost in thought.

Lost in a plan.

A plan that I can see now.

A plan I should've seen at the time, but my fifteen-year-old self couldn't quite comprehend.

Not so naive and innocent and living in a community like this.

I see Elana smile.

Then I see her lean over and kiss me on the cheek.

"Everything will be okay."

She steps away.

"What will?" I ask.

She never answered me as she stood there in the middle of the maize fields. The place we'd always run to. The place we'd always get lost.

But I know now exactly what she was talking about.

* * *

I'm BACK in the darkness of the attic, and Freddie and Moira are standing opposite me.

Freddie looks down at me. Smiles.

I see the burn mark on his neck, and I know.

"You're remembering," he says. "Aren't you?"

I shake my head.

I want to fight the memories.

I want to resist.

"You're remembering how it played out. What happened. And what you did..."

* * *

IT's a week after the conversation with Elana, and I am in the maize fields.

I'm supposed to be meeting her. It's a warm, stuffy day. She told me she has something to tell me. Something important. And as I sit there, twiddling daisies, I wonder if it's good news.

News about the baby.

But she isn't here yet, even though it's getting later, and it's a bit chilly.

I think about turning back and walking when I see him standing there in the maize fields.

I don't see his face because he is wearing a red demon mask.

All I see is that he is naked.

And he has this mole.

Right on his neck.

I try to turn, and I try to run, but I don't get very far.

I don't like to think about what happened next.

Him holding me down.

The tight pain around my wrists.

And the words he whispers into my ears.

"Everything will be okay, my angel. Everything will be okay..."

* * *

IT'S NINE MONTHS LATER, and I am heavily pregnant.

Mum and Dad give me more attention. Everyone gives me more attention. Even Elana has been particularly nice to me, which I find weird because she usually loves being the centre of attention. They're all so happy I'm having a baby. That I'm adding a new member to the Family.

But I can't tell them all how scared I am.

And how much I want to get away.

It's because I've met a boy. Gregg, he's called. He's nice. Sweet. We got matching rings with elephants on. I wear it sometimes, and I don't think anyone has noticed.

But he's on the outside.

I sneak off into the maize fields some days and actually end up sneaking into the outside world. The world outside the sect I've grown up in. It's only when I see Gregg that I realise the life I've been living in the Family is so different from every-body else's. It's like I have been sheltered from a normal life. And yet, weirdly, it's the world outside that seems like the weird one, and the life I've been living seems like the normal one.

But everyone is nice with me now.

So much nicer.

Yet beneath the smell of flowers and the happy smiles, some-thing still just feels so... rotten.

* * *

AND THEN BEFORE I know it, I'm holding a screaming baby in my arms, and I don't know what to do because I'm only sixteen now. Just turned sixteen and no idea what to do for this little boy, for the best.

I am exhausted. People have stopped being kind to me, and keep on telling me how much harder everything is going to get. I have been left to my own devices. People keep telling me I need to step up my act. That I'm going to have to go out into the wider world and find a job because I'm a mother and I need to provide for my baby.

But then there's Gregg, too.

Gregg, who keeps telling me to escape with him and my baby.

That the pair of us can start our own family.

But he doesn't get it. He doesn't understand.

He doesn't see that I am trapped and that I can't run.

It's when the baby is just three weeks old that Elana finally comes to me in the woods, right by the stream.

"Don't you think this is too much for you?" she asks.

I sit by the babbling brook, Elana by my side. She has been sweet these last few months as I sit there, baby in my arms. Really, it feels like she's the only person I can trust anymore.

Like the baby has brought us closer than we've ever been.

So I speak to her.

I confide in her.

"Yes," I say. "I... I really do."

Elana puts a hand on my back. "Don't you think maybe... maybe it would be better if I had him?"

I look at her, and I frown. "What?"

"The baby," she says. "Charlie. That's the name I wanted for him. Charlie. You haven't even named him yet."

I take in a deep breath and look down at this little life I don't know what to do with, and I wonder if my sister could take better care of him after all.

"Just think about it, Sarah. You can live your life. The life you want to live. With Gregg."

I look at her. Narrow my eyes. "You know about him?"

"Of course I know about him."

"Don't tell Mum. Dad. Anyone."

"Sarah, I won't tell a soul. You know how much trouble it would get you in, seeing someone secretly. Someone without the Family approval. And that's not the kind of trouble you want to face when you're on your own with a baby, no world skills, is it?"

I don't know the word "blackmail" at the time, but I get the sense that my sister is doing it to me.

"But then you'll be on your own."

Elana leans closer to me. "That's where you're wrong. Andy. Me and him are still together. We're going to get married. And we can be a family. Me. Him. And baby Charlie. And you can go off with Gregg and live your perfect life. And I won't tell a soul."

I look at my sister, and I want to believe she's helping me.

I want to believe she's got my best interests at heart.

I look down at my screaming, wailing baby, and I almost see the logic in what she's saying.

Almost.

That's when I hear her say the words that change everything.

"Everything will be okay, my angel. That's what Andy always says to me when I'm sad. Everything will be okay, my angel. Everything will be okay..."

They hit me like a punch to the gut. "That's what he said."

Elana narrows her eyes. "What?"

"The—the boy. The man. The one who did this to me."

"Sarah, calm down—"

"I think it was him, Elana. I think it was Andy. We need to tell Mum. We need to tell Dad—"

"Sarah."

"I don't think you're safe. Because he did this to me and..."

And then it clicks.

I don't know if it's the way she's looking at me.

I don't know if it's the memory of her sitting there, a glaze to her eyes when she asked when I'd last bled nine months ago.

When I told her a week ago.

And when a week after that—at my most fertile—it happened.

I don't know what it is, but I just have an instinctive sense at that moment that I know.

"You knew about this. Didn't you?"

I can see her prepare to tell a lie she's planned on telling me for so, so long.

But then something slips. Something slips, and suddenly, it all becomes clear.

"You—you arranged this. The pair of you. You arranged this."

"Sarah—"

"You made him rape me. Made him—made him get me pregnant. So you could—so you could have the baby for yourself."

"It wasn't rape."

"It *was* rape," I spit. I'm angry. I have never felt anger like this before. "You did this. God knows how many of you did this. How many of you knew about this."

"I did it because I was desperate, Sarah. I—I didn't think. I just wanted a child more than anything in the world. But I... I can't have them myself. I know because me and Andy were trying for a long time."

She's saying all these words, but I can't take them in. Because as much as I've always known she hates me... this. This is something different. This is something else entirely.

"But you have a chance now, Sarah," she says. "A chance to start again. A chance to be free."

I stand there holding my crying baby, and I want to run away. I want to vomit. I want to throw everything up.

"Hand him to me, Sarah. Hand him to me, and nobody finds out about you and Gregg. Hand him to me, and we can both be happy. In our own ways."

I want to tell her I hate her.

I want to tell her how much trauma I've experienced.

The compartments I've created in my own mind to lock away the memories of the man in the demon mask pinning me down in the maize fields.

Squeezing my wrists.

And saying those words.

"Everything will be okay, my angel. Everything will be okay..."

The mole on his neck.

I want to tell her all of it, but all I can do is listen.

"Hand him over. And this ends. All of it ends. Or go running to Mum and Dad. Your choice. We can see who they believe. Who everyone believes. And then we'll see how a single mother at sixteen gets on all on her own in the world with a baby she doesn't know how to look after, hmm?"

I can barely believe the words coming out of her mouth. "You don't care about him. Not at all. Do you?"

Elana shakes her head, sighs. "I care. Of course, I care."

"You care about having a baby. But not about him. Not about... about my baby."

She looks at me, and I see her eyes are bloodshot now.

I see her threatening glare.

"Hand him over. Right this second. It ends, one way or another, right now. Do the right thing."

I stand there, and I want to run. I want to run and keep running, forever.

I see this opportunity.

I see this chance.

And as much pain as I am in, as much as I want to stand my ground... I find myself reaching the baby towards my sister.

Her eyes widen as I hand him to her.

Her hands outstretch, grab him from me. Like he's a little toy.

She stands there, baby in her arms, and I see her face light up.

"Thank you," she says, a smile on her face. "Now you can finally leave us alone. Now, you can finally go. And you can leave me, Andy, and Charlie, and everyone else in peace."

She walks past me, my baby in her arms.

I look at the edge of the woods.

At the maize fields.

And I know this is my opportunity.

I know this is my chance.

But then I turn around.

I see Elana walking away from me.

Baby in her arms.

And I stand my ground.

"No," I say.

She stops. Looks around.

"What did you say?"

"I said no. Because that's *my* baby. That's my son. Not yours. Even if he's hard work. Even if I don't know how to look after him. I'll learn."

She looks at me, and then she scans me from head to toe, and she smirks. "Well. Not a lot you can do now, is there?"

She turns around like I am nothing, and I can't control my next actions.

I can't control the anger.

I reach down and grab a rock from the babbling brook.

I walk over towards Elana.

Clenching the rock in my hand.

I walk towards her, and I lift that rock.

And I feel his hands on my body.

His breathing on my back.

His fingers on my throat.

"Everything will be okay, my angel. Everything will be okay…"

"I said *no!*"

It all happens so fast.

The rock against Elana's head.

The sound of cracking. Like an egg.

And then lifting that rock over her head, again and again, and again.

* * *

"Don't you remember now?" Freddie says. "Don't you remember what you did to her? To my beautiful Elana?"

* * *

I see her lying before me.

I see the way her skull is crushed.

The way her dark red blood seeps through her bright blonde hair.

I see her eye dangling out of her eye socket. Staring up at me. Bloodshot.

And then beside her, I see the baby.

My baby.

I see him lying there. Crying. And I know that time is running out.

So I pick him up.

I pick him up, and then I turn to the maize fields, and I run.

* * *

I see all these memories.

I see Freddie standing before me.

Moira by his side.

"Oh," he says. "How rude of me not to introduce myself. The name's Andy. Although I figure you've probably worked that out by now, hmm?"

I see the scar on his neck.

Right where my rapist's mole used to be.

* * *

And I understand.

CHAPTER FIFTY-FOUR

"You remember now, don't you? I can see it in your eyes. You remember. And for real this time. The whole truth. Don't you, Sarah?"

I look at Freddie, and suddenly, I don't even see him as Freddie anymore. I don't see him as the man who has been so supportive to me for so so long. I don't look at him as the man who proposed to me just yesterday.

I look at him, and I see Andy.

The man who raped me when I was fifteen.

The man who was dating my older sister, Elana. Who was destined to marry and have kids with her, but she couldn't get pregnant.

The man who Elana wanted to steal my baby to be hers and his.

And the man who loved the girl I killed.

"I knew it was you," he says. "The second I found her body lying there. I knew it was you. There was just... something about it. The way the pair of you always met up out there. I could tell you were a fighter. Right from the first time we met."

He smiles. And I can almost see him with that mask over his face, hiding him from me.

"The mole on my neck," he says, smiling a little, rubbing it. "You keep looking at that. Well, I figured I had to do something. Nothing a little surgical removal can't do to cover up a really fucking visible mole, hmm?"

I sit there on this chair. Stare at Freddie. Stare at Moira. Both of them looking back at me, here in the darkness.

"You look a little speechless, Sarah," Moira says. "It's almost like you weren't expecting this. After all these years and still, you weren't expecting it."

I close my eyes. I want to disappear. I want to run away.

Just like I ran away that day into the maize fields.

The skeletons.

The skeleton with the crushed skull.

And the smaller skeleton.

That *baby* skeleton.

I see myself in the maize fields.

Charlie in my arms...

No.

I don't want to think about that.

That's the last memory.

The last door.

The one that I will never open.

"There was no absolute proof it was you," Freddie says. "And of course, the Family, some of their activities were... let's say, not so legal. So drawing the eyes on us with a murder investigation wasn't exactly top of the list."

"But we never stopped searching for you," Moira says. "You were notoriously hard to find. But eventually... yes. We found you. Living a nice, comfortable little life with your husband, Gregg. The man you left the Family for, I believe. And where? Right here in Preston. And all we needed then was to break you. A little seductive encouragement from one of the school dads. Who didn't take much convincing. Not really."

I think of Glynn.

I think of the bruises on his neck.

The fear in his eyes.

I think of the whole affair, and I feel betrayed.

"He's not so involved, don't worry. Let's just say we paid him well. But in the end, the whole affair situation was beside the point. Because you gave us a gift. You cracked. You proved your mental health wasn't where it should be, back then, three years ago. And you proved there was a chance. A chance for us to use that. To exploit it. A chance to have some... well. Fun, along the way."

I feel sick. I feel betrayed. By everyone.

"In the end... you broke yourself. Gregg took off. It all fell so neatly into place for us. It was perfect. At that point, well. We just had to be practical."

I don't know how she knows this. How *can* she know this? That was between Elana and me all those years ago.

"We spent some time working on you. Breaking you down. Building you up. But when we found you, you were at a low ebb."

"And that's when I stepped in," Andy says. "Your knight in shining armour. I thought it was going to be difficult. And trust me. Living with you and keeping up the guise *was* difficult sometimes. But we got here, in the end, didn't we? Fourteen long years later, and here we are. And yet somehow, it still feels like I haven't punished you enough for what happened to Elana. For what you did to her."

I think of meeting him in the bar that day. Of how different he seemed to the other blokes.

I think about how he just seemed to know my sense of humour.

How much we clicked.

How patient he was.

I think of making love with him, and I feel sick…

"I'm sorry," I say. "For what I did. To her. And I… I live with it every day—"

"That's a lie," Andy snaps. "Because I know you, Sarah. You push things away. Push things into the deepest corners of your mind. So far down, you convince yourself it isn't even real. So you haven't been living with it every single day. And that's the unfair thing. But you're living with it now. Boy, are you going to live with it now."

I look around at Moira. Look at her in her white dress. And I realise why she looked familiar, now. The woman who waved at me and smiled the day Elana killed the rat. Who reassured me.

"The child was ours," Moira says. "Andy here may be hell-bent on revenge for different reasons. But that child was never yours. It was always Elana's."

"Your—your son raped me. Raped a teenage girl."

"He did what the dear Lord above asked of him."

I open my mouth to respond, but I can barely speak through the anger, through the frustration. "I… I… You're insane. You're actually insane."

"No," Andy says, stepping in. "You're the one who is insane. And you're going to face up to what you did. To *everything* you did."

I hear those words, and it isn't a road I want to go down.

It's a road I want to run away from.

Far, far away from.

"You're going to look me in the eyes, right this second, and you're going to tell me what happened to Charlie."

"No."

A slap, right across the face.

Moira tuts. "Andy, dear."

But Andy isn't listening, and Moira's protestations are half-hearted at best. "You're going to tell me how it happened. Exactly how it happened. Right now."

I look up at them both, and as desperate as I know I sound, as pathetic as I know I sound, I shake my head. "No."

Andy swings another punch against my face.

I am dizzy. Disoriented. In pain.

But I wonder if maybe that's the better way.

If perhaps that's the easier way.

"The truth, Sarah. The truth about Charlie. Now."

I look up into his eyes, and as much as I want to run from it, as much as I want to turn away from the locked door I've kept unopened inside my mind for so, so long, I can only stare at its contents.

"Confess," he says. "Now. To me. And to yourself."

I shake my head and try to run and hide and disappear.

But the door is open.

The lock is on the floor.

"No. Please, no. Please, please, no..."

But it's already too late.

Because I am in the maize fields.

I am running.

And my baby is screaming in my arms.

I know now that I cannot hide anymore.

I cannot hide from what I did.

To Charlie.

To my son.

CHAPTER FIFTY-FIVE

I am running through the maize fields with my son in my arms.

It's hot. Blisteringly hot. I am sweating. I can barely breathe. The sun hides behind the clouds, and everything just feels so humid.

I am covered in blood.

My sister's blood.

I look down at my son. His face is all scrunched up, like always, as he screams in my arms. And I need him to be quiet. I need him to stop crying. Because if he doesn't stop crying, the Family is going to find me. They're going to find me after they find Elana and they're going to see I'm covered in blood and they're going to *know*.

I need to get away.

I need to get to Gregg.

And I need to leave this life behind me.

I run through the tall maize fields near the Family home. I've run this way so many times in the past already. So much so that I know it like the back of my hand. I know it better than anyone.

The maize is so tall, and it never gets cut. Only trimmed. Abandoned.

I know all the places to go.

All the places to hide.

But right now, I feel lost.

I run. I keep running for what feels like forever, but what I know is nowhere near as long. I know my life is going to change from this day on. For good. I've dreamed of living a life with Gregg for a while now. I'm sixteen. I'm old enough to start making my own choices.

Maybe this is the kick I need.

And maybe Gregg and I can start our own lives. A life away from this. From all of it.

I hear my son screaming in my arms.

I look down at my baby, and as much as I love him, instinctively, I wonder.

I wonder if maybe he's better off without me.

Because how can I care for him?

How can I provide for him?

I barely even know how to live in the real world outside the confines of the Family.

How am I going to look after a baby?

Raise a child?

And if anything happens with Gregg and me... I'll be all on my own.

I look over my shoulder. I swear I can hear footsteps. I swear I can hear the maize rustling as I race through them. I swear someone is following me. Chasing me.

And I think about Mum, then. Mum and Dad. I want to believe they'll stand up for me. I want to believe they'll support me. I want to believe they'll understand why I did what I did, especially when I tell them about Andy, about Elana's boyfriend, and what he did to me.

But deep down, I know I was an accident.

I heard them speaking about that once. How they never really wanted me. How Elana was their favourite, and I was just a disappointment. How I was too... curious.

I know they'll never forgive me for what I've done.

I know I'm an outcast, whatever happens here.

So the best thing I can do is run.

The best thing I can do is...

The baby.

Crying in my arms.

Screaming.

The air is thick with heat now.

The clouds are thick, too.

And this screaming, in my head, ringing in my ears.

I look down at the baby, and as much as I love him, as much as he is mine, as much as I will always try to do what's right for him... I know I will never be able to think of him as anyone other than Charlie.

Elana's child.

Andy's child.

I look down at the baby in my arms, my hands covered in blood. And I am in a haze now. I am in a haze because... my memory shifts. There's a gap.

In the middle of the maize field.

Standing over him.

Then by a stream.

Then lowering him down as he cries and tears fall from my face towards the stream, closer to silence, closer to—

But no.

I didn't do that.

I lifted him down and wrapped him up and left him in the middle of the maize fields, and then I ran.

And all the time, I couldn't stop myself saying the words.

"I'm sorry, Charlie. I'm sorry. I'm so, so sorry. But you'll be better with them. You'll be better with them."

I remember running away.

I remember running and running as the clouds thicken, and the sky hurls rain down.

I remember reaching Gregg.

And I remember him holding me and telling me everything was going to be okay.

* * *

AND THEN I REMEMBER NOTHING.

* * *

I OPEN MY EYES.

Andy stares at me.

Moira stares at me.

Both of them stand there above me, tied to this stool in a place I called home, and they look at me like they know *I* know now.

"So now you remember," Andy says. "How you killed him. How you killed my Charlie. How you killed my son."

CHAPTER FIFTY-SIX

"You killed my son, Sarah. You killed my girlfriend—your sister—and then you killed my son."

I shake my head because that's not how it happened. Because I wouldn't have hurt Charlie. I wouldn't have laid a finger on him. Harmed him in any way.

But my memory is blurry.

Fuzzy.

It's like there's another hidden door in my mind.

One I don't want to open.

One I don't have the keys to unlock.

"Say it!" Andy shouts. And suddenly, he's inches from me again. His saliva is on my face. "Admit what you did. Every single bit of it. Admit it. To me. To my mother. And to yourself."

I lower my head. I can barely speak. I just want to get out of this. I just want to get away.

Andy grabs my face. "Say it. Admit it. Now!"

"I killed her," I mumble.

"What was that?"

"I said—I said I killed her. I killed Elana. My sister. I killed her because she wanted to take my baby from me. She wanted to outcast me. I killed her because I was mad. Mad at what—at what she did to me. At what *both* of you did to me."

I look around at Moira. And as much as I know she's complicit in my capture, I hope she understands, on a human level, if anything.

"Your son raped me," I shout. "He raped me, and he impregnated me at fifteen. And that's something he and my sister planned. Planned so they could use me for the baby. Use me because she couldn't get pregnant. Then take it away from me and outcast me so I wouldn't be a problem. Can you imagine how that made me feel? Finding out my own sister did that to me?"

Moira stands there. Silent. I look into her eyes, and I see nothing. Just a void. An empty void.

"Don't you see?" I shout.

"What I see," Moira says, "is that you killed your sister, and then you went to the brook and you killed that poor child. You drowned him there. I found him, face down in there. That ring your boyfriend gave you, the one you always wore secretly. The one with the elephant on it. The one you thought none of us ever noticed. Right there beside him."

The brook.

The cold water around my fingers.

But my ring?

No. I never lost my ring.

This isn't right. It doesn't make sense.

"I don't... I don't remember—"

A slap across the face. Andy again.

"What my mother is trying to say is she doesn't give a fuck. Because that's what everyone wanted. That was the plan, Sarah. Are you starting to get it now? Are you starting to see?"

I open my mouth to speak, but I can barely comprehend it.

"Every... Everyone knew?"

"Everyone knew. Mother knew. Your own mum and dad knew. It was a plan, Sarah. Elana was meant to inherit everything. Every last bit of it. And I was supposed to be by her side. But she couldn't get pregnant. We needed to keep the bloodline pure and consistent. So we needed to find another way."

My head spins. I am still here, in my attic, but I could be in any dark void right now.

They all knew.

The whole Family knew about what happened to me.

They pretended to care. Pretended to search for the man who did it to me.

But all along, they knew.

All along, they wanted Elana to have my son.

"We wanted you gone," Moira says. "Because you were nothing but trouble. You mingled with the outside too much. And it seemed like the best, neatest way. You got the life you wanted. We got the life we wanted. But you just couldn't accept it, could you?"

I shake my head. I feel sad. Broken. Defeated.

But more than anything, I feel angry.

"You're evil. Both of you. All of you. You're evil."

Moira rolls her eyes. "You broke your poor parents, you know? Dad died of a broken heart two years later. Mum couldn't hack it, so she took her own life. The Family fell apart not long after. The others, they might've been able to let this go. They might've been able to move on to their normal lives. But not us. Not me and my Andy. Because you broke everything, Sarah. We had the perfect life, and you broke it. The Family, we might not have been ordinary people, but we were good people. We acted within the realms of the law, mostly anyway. We never harmed anyone. Everyone was there by choice. And our leader. Our dear leader, Father. He knew there was no choice, not in the end. Because of the poison that you allowed to enter. Elana. She was supposed to be the princess. And my Andy was the prince. They were the future. You poisoned us. You cursed us all and destroyed everyone's faith. And now you're going to pay for it."

I sit there. Breathing heavily.

I think about how I got the train that day I was supposed to be at the doctor's. How I'd gone to head back there on the train, back to where I lived with The Family, all those years ago.

How I'd had a panic attack and got off the train and gone straight back home not long after.

I think about everything, and something haunts me.

Because something still doesn't seem right.

I remember leaving my son.

I remember running away from him, through the fields.

Landing in Gregg's arms.

But the stream.

The drowning.

I don't remember that.

Or am I just hiding from the truth?

Am I just...

Andy and Moira grab me. They lift me to my feet, Moira with a strength I didn't realise she had.

They pull me up, so I am standing on the stool.

Then Andy reaches up and wraps what I realise is a noose around my neck.

"So now is where it ends," he says.

And I understand.

I see him staring at me with those cold, loveless eyes, and I understand.

"You broke down. You stopped taking your meds. And after so much concern, you go into the attic, and you take your life. It's simple. You pay for what you took from me. You pay for what you took from all of us. It ends. All of it ends. Right now."

CHAPTER FIFTY-SEVEN

I think about my life in two segments.

The days before I left my son in the maize fields, the days before he went missing.

And the days after I left my son in the maize fields, the days after I ran away from the Family.

The beginning of my new life.

* * *

I STAND on the stool with the noose around my neck in my own attic and stare through tear-drenched eyes at Andy and Moira. I see the way they stare up at me. I see the blankness behind my eyes, and I can almost feel the warmth of the summer air I always associate with the Family. I can almost hear them chanting as I stand around that dying rat.

Go on, go on, go on...

And I can hear the crack of my sister's skull underneath the rock.

Feel the blood crusting on my hands.

The tension in my chest as I run away with a screaming baby

in my arms, just wanting to get away, just wanting to escape, just wanting to...

Do I see myself by a stream?

Do I see myself holding my son's head under the water?

I can envision it. I can picture it. I can feel the cold water against my knuckles. I can smell the freshness of the trees. And I can hear the little glugging sounds as I hold him down.

And I can hear Gregg, too.

I can hear him telling me it's okay. That everything is going to be okay now. That we're together now, and he has me, and he...

But the stream.

Holding the baby in the water.

Holding my son in the water.

That doesn't feel real.

That feels like something my wayward mind has just produced.

That does not feel like a memory.

It feels like something that has been planted there.

And I'm not sure what that means. Not sure what to make of this sudden clarity.

But if I know one thing for sure from the last few months, it's that I am *not* insane.

I have been able to differentiate reality from fakery.

I have been able to tell the difference. It's been the people around me terrorising me. Lying to me.

I have been right.

So why am I so certain I did not kill my baby?

Why am I so certain the last time I saw him was when I left him, painfully, in the maize fields and ran away to be with Gregg?

And if that's the case, why are Andy and Moira claiming they found the baby drowned by my hand?

Andy walks over to me. He stands right opposite the stool. "You're going to do it yourself. Aren't you?"

He looks up at me as I stand there crying, and I want to scream. I want to call for help.

But I know it's no use. I am the madwoman. The crazy lady. Nobody will hear my screams.

Andy smiles. And it's as if he senses my thoughts and fears. I hardly recognise this monster before me. This spectre that has haunted me from the shadows my entire life. And like shadows, they are always closer than you think.

"You're going to step off the stool. You're going to drop. And you're going to die, Sarah. Because that's how it should be. That's the right way it should be. The natural order of things."

I stand there, and I shake my head. I want to fight. But I'm not sure what fight is left in me. I'm not sure how I can possibly fight anymore.

I am out of fight.

I don't have anything left.

Only the anger.

The anger I felt for this man all those years ago.

The anger I felt for *all* of them, all those years ago.

"Any last words?" Andy says. "Before the end of the line?"

I close my eyes, swallow a lump in my throat, and I see my son. I feel my hand against his. Only that's different now, too. The school field. I *can* feel a hand there, but it's my own sweaty palm. The rest is something I added later. Something I invented.

Because Charlie wasn't there that day, and I know it.

I snook off with Glynn and fucked him in the maize fields.

And it brought it back.

It brought it all back, and that's what fucked me up, all three years ago.

My longing for my son.

A missing son.

But the thought of holding Charlie down in the water.

That isn't real.

I left him behind because I thought somehow he might get a better life inside the Family.

I left him behind, and I ran because I wanted to give him a chance.

I left him because...

And then I remember something else.

"I have to go back, Gregg, I have to go back."

It's just a snippet. Just a fragment of a memory.

But it's there. And it's clear.

And I don't understand where it fits into things.

Because as much as all this is happening and as much as it is all true, so too is my dissociative amnesia. So too, is my false memory syndrome. So too is my trauma.

I am a mess.

"You're going to do it," Moira says. "And it might be the most gutsy thing you've ever done."

I open my eyes, and I look at these two people.

I look at them, and I want to cry.

I look at them, and I want to beg.

And then, in that instant, a snotty, snivelling mess, I remember something.

The GoPro.

The one I attached to my chest when I went to meet Cameron.

The one uploading to that remote space with a different password because I was worried about the last time I was hacked.

The camera, still recording all this with its six-hour runtime.

I look at them, and suddenly my broken phone doesn't feel like it matters.

If I can just reach into my pocket, hit Share, it'll all be on Facebook.

It'll be on YouTube.

The whole damned thing will be online, and there isn't a thing they can do about any of it.

I feel my sadness changing, as Andy and Moira stand there, those cocky, confident looks still on their faces.

I feel it changing to something else.

To strength.

To power.

"What're you smiling about?" Andy asks.

I didn't realise I was smiling. But I am. I've got a big smile across my face. And I'm laughing, now. Actually laughing.

Andy and Moira look at one another. And I see their concern. Their confusion.

"Shut her up," Moira says.

Andy walks over to the stool.

I can see he is getting ready to kick it from under me.

"You might want to wait," I say, reaching for the GoPro.

Andy stops. Suddenly, he's calm again. "What is that?"

"This is a GoPro. I've used it to record everything. The meeting with Cameron. I forgot to turn record off. So it's been on. It's been on this whole time. What a shame, hmm?"

They stare at me, both of them. I can see Andy's face turn, and it is delightful.

"Bollocks. You'd never—"

"Never what, Freddie? Or should I call you Andy, now? Never be clever enough to set a GoPro up? Never be so wise as to do something like this behind your back? Well, that's where you're wrong."

"Give me that."

He reaches for it, and I hover my finger over the Share button. "Don't come a step closer. One step closer, and I hit share. It goes online. It goes to YouTube. It goes everywhere. This whole conversation. This entire exchange. It goes online. And you know too well, Mr Technology Man. Once something's online, it stays online, whether you delete it or not. Whether you destroy this device or not. Right?"

Andy is actually speechless.

"What on Earth's she talking about, Andy?"

"Mum, not now," he says, raising a hand. And then he takes a step towards me. "Sarah. Hitting that button would be a big mistake."

"No," I say. And as in pain as I am, as betrayed as I feel, as much as this feels like the end of the road, I feel strong.

For the first time in my life, I feel like I have some control over the demons of my past.

And it's even fucking sweeter knowing that this is the man who broke my life in two.

That these are the people who broke my life in two.

"I haven't had the best life," I say. "But I can tell you one thing. One fucking thing. There'll be a lot of stories about me. A lot of tales, when all this goes live—"

"Sarah—"

"But I am adamant about one thing. I did not kill my son. I was raped. I was betrayed. And I was lied to. And I have told lies myself, sure. I have done some bad things. I turned my back on my baby in a moment of panic. I cheated. I slept around. And I haven't been the best person. I killed my sister, and I do not fucking regret it. I'd rip her fucking head off again and rip the fucking heads off the lot of you if you were all here lined up before me right now. For what you did."

Andy steps forward, but Moira pulls him back, the anger bubbling in his bloodshot eyes.

"But I did *not* kill my son."

I lift the GoPro in the air.

Tighten my grip around it.

My thumb on the Share button.

"Get down, Sarah," Andy says. "There's... there has to be another way. Right, love? Right?"

I hear the softness and the fake care in his voice, and I find it pathetic. I find it hilarious. Desperate. Weak.

I see the desperation in his eyes, and I hate him.

"If there's one thing I regret more than anything, it's falling for your bullshit. But for the first time in my life... no. I'm not going to do what you want me to."

"Sarah—"

"Enjoy prison, Andy. Really. Enjoy it. Because you are not in control here. For once in your life, you are not in control over me."

"Sarah!"

I hit the Share button.

"No!" he shouts.

And then I look down at him and smile.

"This is the moment your life splits in two," I say.

Then I take a deep breath.

I close my eyes.

And I think of Charlie's hand in mine as I step off the stool.

As the noose tightens around my throat.

And as the darkness fades to light.

CHAPTER FIFTY-EIGHT

I am running through the maize fields, my baby crying in my arms, and I know I need to get away.

Because if I don't get away, and they find out what I've done to my sister, they will punish me for what I've done.

I want to get away from here. I'm supposed to be meeting Gregg. I've told him I'm meeting him at four, so I can take the baby, and the pair of us can leave. I twiddle the ring around on my finger. The one Gregg bought me. The identical rings we both have, each of us, to remind ourselves of each other. The one I can't always wear. The one I have to hide to avoid any questions. Elephants on there, my favourite animals.

We can leave, and we can be away from this. From all of it. Forever.

But something is stopping me running. Something stopping me from going.

And that something is the *fear*.

The fear I feel about being a mother at sixteen.

The fear I feel about taking a baby who was put inside me, against my will, by Elana's boyfriend, Andy.

The fear I feel about looking into this child's eyes and

knowing how he came about, and knowing what life was intended for him by the people who were supposed to care about me.

I look at the edge of the maize fields, and I know the future is ahead. I know I can walk out there. I know I can walk out there, and I can end this. Once and for all.

But then I look back, and I know, deep down, that if I walk away with the baby, I will never be free of the Family.

I will never be free of this life.

And they can do a far better job of raising a child than I can, that's for sure.

I look down at the baby. Look at him in my arms. *Charlie.* That's what Elana called him.

And as he lies there, contrasting the blood on my hands and my wrists with his pale skin, I feel love. A deep, deep sense of love.

And also a sadness.

Because I know exactly what I have to do.

I lower him down. Right down, right to the ground.

I lower him there, and I rest him in a thicker part of the maize.

So he's protected from the wind. From the rain which is starting to fall, cutting through the summer heat. From all the elements.

"I'm sorry," I say as I cry. "I... I really wanted things to work out. I really wanted to be a good mummy to you. But I'm—I'm not ready. And these people. Even though I never fit in... They'll look after you. They'll care for you. Way better than I can."

He stares up at me. Clutches for me.

And as I pull myself away from him, I want to reach right back down for him. I want to fight all the logic in my mind and pick him back up. Because he's my son. He's my son, and I love him.

But then I stand up, and in the heavy wind, in the clouds, I squeeze my sweaty palms together.

Smell the warmth of the summer air.
And I run.

* * *

I DON'T STOP RUNNING until I reach Gregg.

I'm in his car. He's telling me everything is going to be okay, but I don't believe him. I am hysterical. My memories of what happened here are blurry. Muddy.

"It's okay, Sarah. I've got you. I've got you."

And I remember sitting there in his passenger seat and his hand on my thigh and feeling like I've killed my son.

And hearing his words.

"We're together now. It's just us. We don't have to worry about them anymore. We're together. We're—"

* * *

HIS HAND IS DAMP.

Sodden.

And his ring is missing.

His ring.

His...

* * *

THAT'S when I open my eyes, and light fills my vision.

CHAPTER FIFTY-NINE

I open my eyes, and I see bright light shining down from above.

I don't know where I am, but my neck hurts. I've got a sore throat. Really sore. Feels like I haven't drunk a thing for a week.

Fuck. It feels like I haven't done *anything* for a week. My body is so stiff. I'm in agony. Total agony, everywhere.

I lie there with this light shining down at me, and somehow, I feel comforted. I feel the warmth of the light, and it reminds me of being in hospital. Or being in the psychiatric hospital. I felt comfortable there. Safe. Like nobody could get to me. Like I was totally resistant to whatever threats there might be outside.

Or inside my own mind, even.

I open my eyes wider, and I see two people standing above me. They're doctors; I'm convinced of it. Doctors or nurses. I can hear them mumbling things, but I can't make out their words for the ringing in my ears.

I close my heavy eyelids again. I'm in pain everywhere. I don't know where I am or why I'm here, but I get the sense that it's something big. That something big has happened to put me here.

.

That pain around my neck. It feels familiar, somehow. It feels...

I remember.

Standing on the stool in my attic.

Stepping off the stool.

And the rope tightening around my neck—

"What should we do with her?"

I hear those words, and my skin turns cold.

The light in my eyes fades.

The buzzing in my ears fades out.

The warmth turns to ice.

I open my eyes.

I am in my attic still. In the darkness, still.

Only I am on the floor now. On the wooden floor. The taste of blood and dust filling my mouth.

Andy and Moira are standing at the other side of the room, chatting amongst themselves. They seem bothered about something as Andy stares at his phone screen, rubbing his fingers through his hair. They seem bothered. Fixated on something.

They're so fixated on the phone screen that they don't even seem to see me.

And then it clicks. It clicks because I hear my own voice coming from that video.

"Well, can't you log in and delete it?" Moira asks.

"I could. But she's changed her password. Changed her frigging password."

"How many friends are on there?"

"It doesn't matter. She's gone live."

"How are we going to counter this, Andy? What are we going to do?"

They both look at one another. So fixated on one another. And I sense an opportunity. A chance.

I turn around, but my neck is so stiff. Either the rope snapped, or they cut me down after I sent the video of their confession of everything online.

They are trapped. They are cornered.

They need me alive.

But I can see the hatch of the attic.

I can see my opportunity to get away.

To escape.

I stretch out my fingers. My arms. Try to drag myself along this wooden flooring. Try to avoid catching their attention. To avoid drawing any attention my way.

I keep on going. Keep on dragging myself along. Keep on pulling myself, faster now, even though my body aches, even though it's wracked with pain.

I pull myself further and further when I feel a hand around my ankle.

"I don't think so."

And then I am thrown around onto my back again. And Andy is above me, practically drooling.

He has hold of his phone. Shaking in his hand. Points it right at me. The GoPro in the other hand.

"Delete it," he says.

I look up at him, and I can't help smiling. Because he needs me now. He needs me more than he's ever needed me.

He hits me across the face. "Delete it. Now. A couple of people started watching it on Facebook. But not a lot. Delete it, and we can find another way through this. You need my support, and you know it. Delete it, and we can get you back to the hospital. We can treat this like some kind of episode. And then one way or another, we can start again."

I laugh louder this time. And then I find myself spitting right in his face. "I love how much you need me. I love how much you are begging. Because it makes me realise just how weak you really are.

He looks down at me. His nostrils twitch. He is not the man I fell in love with. Not the man I thought cared about me. Adored me.

"Andy," Moira says. Almost sensing danger. "You need to keep calm here, love."

But I can see from the look in Andy's eyes that it's already too late.

He lifts me up with immense strength.

Tightens those big hands around me—the ones that used to stroke my back so tenderly.

And then he throws me.

Throws me like I am nothing.

Right to the other side of the attic.

I crash against the outside wall. Dust and debris tumble down, cover me.

He walks over towards me.

"You're a bitch," he says. "A murdering bitch. You murdered my Elana. You murdered my son."

"I didn't murder *my* son."

"And you killed everything good in our lives. All of our lives."

I see him stepping forward, I see the rage in his eyes, and I know he is beyond the point of rationality and reason anymore.

I know he is going to kill me.

He steps further forward. I am cornered. I am trapped.

But at least I have this one thing over him.

At least he's going down with me.

At least he's...

Going down.

I remember something.

The hole in the attic.

The one in the bathroom ceiling.

Just how fragile is it, really?

He walks towards me.

His footsteps are heavy.

His eyes look possessed.

His fists are clenched. Tight.

"You took it away from us. But you won't have the last laugh. I swear to God you will not have the last laugh."

He comes at me. And I see the section of floor above the bathroom. I see how loose it looks. How weak it looks. Right where that gap is.

And I see that possessed look in his eyes.

He walks towards me, and I know I have a chance.

I run.

Run as quickly as my agonised body will allow.

"I don't think so," he shouts.

He grabs me.

I slam down, face first, against the floor.

I hear it creaking.

Hear it move.

Stare down the gap towards the bathroom, a single wooden beam crossing between the two rooms.

Andy laughs. "Thought you could trick me, did you? Actually thought you could get the better of me here? Well, you're wrong, Sarah. You're very wrong."

I feel his hands against my ankles, and I know my plan has failed.

I know my time is up.

I know...

And then I see it.

The Stanley knife.

The one he said he'd lost ages ago, right when we first moved in.

The one he'd been looking for for months.

His favourite Stanley knife.

It's right there.

Right on that wooden beam beneath me, between the attic and the bathroom.

"Come on," he says, tightening his grip on my ankles. And I

know he's going to drag me away. I know my time is running out. "It's about time we finished what we started here."

I clench my jaw.

I reach down, as far as I can, for the Stanley knife.

For a horrid moment, I feel it wobble, like it's going to fall down to the bathroom below.

And then it's in my grip.

It's between my fingertips.

It's—

It falls.

I see it drop down below.

I hear it hit the bathroom floor below.

And then I feel Freddie's hands tighten around my ankles again and feel him drag me away from that gap in the ceiling.

He yanks me away. Grabs my hair. Holds himself up to me. Right up to me. Looks at me with those manic eyes.

"How about we do it like you did it to him? To your son?"

I narrow my eyes. I don't know what he's talking about.

But before I know it, he has me on his shoulder.

"Andy," Moira says.

He pushes past her.

Pushes past her and drags me out of the darkness of the attic.

"We'll see how you like it. See how it makes you feel."

"Andy, I don't know what you're—"

"We'll see how you like being drowned. And we'll drown you right where you deserve to be drowned."

It's only then that I realise where he's taking me.

The bathroom.

He opens the door. Drags me across the tiled floor. He opens the toilet lid and the seat. And then he takes a piss and drags me right over to the toilet. Flushes it a few times, so the water is really high.

But all I am looking at, beside the toilet, is that Stanley knife.

The one that fell from above.

"Any last words?" he asks. "Anything to say? Before I make you go through *exactly* what Charlie went through?"

I look down at the water.

I look down at the Stanley knife.

And then I grab it.

"You could learn to be a bit more careful with your tools," I say.

"What—"

It all happens so fast.

I pop the blade out.

I spin around.

And then I bury the knife deep into his neck, right by his jugular.

He looks at me with wide eyes. With surprise. He tries to hold his throat, but blood spurts out, trickles right down his white T-shirt, some of it splashing onto me.

And as pathetic as it sounds, as much as I hate this man, as much as I despise him for terrorising me, for breaking my life so many times... I see a glimpse of Freddie in his eyes—the man I fell in love with. The man who betrayed me.

And then it's gone in a flash as he falls to his knees.

I stand over him. Stanley knife in hand. Watch as he splutters. Watch as he crumbles.

And I stand defiant over him.

I feel a total sense of calm now.

A total sense of peace.

A total sense of ease.

I take a deep breath, knife in hand, and I smile.

For I am free now.

PART FOUR

CHAPTER SIXTY

SIX MONTHS LATER

I sit on the Preston Docks and smile as I take a deep breath of the warm, spring air.

It's the start of June, and it is scorching. Everyone is out today. Parents and children wandering along the edge of the docklands. The ice cream stall with the drunk-looking guy standing behind the counter, that creepy smile about him as always. The smell of fast food powering from the nearby McDonalds, the drive-thru absolutely ram-packed with cars.

It's been a beautiful summer so far. Stunning. The best since that one in lockdown, where the sunny weather made the whole miserable endeavour a lot more palatable.

But somehow, this summer feels even nicer. The entire last few months have felt nice. Weird, but nice.

I raise a hand to my neck. Feel the slight roughness from the scar there. It hurts. Hurts bad. To this day.

But I am still here.

I am still alive.

And I have to be grateful for that.

I hear him before I see him. The footsteps, approaching the little wooden picnic bench I'm sitting on, tucked away from the main promenade of the docks. Away from the seagulls bothering people walking with their fries.

I look around and see him standing there.

He nods at me. It's the first time I've seen him for months. Ever since I went to his house in the midst of what I am now calling my breakdown.

And four months before it happened.

The fire.

The tragic death of my beloved fiancé and innocent neighbour Moira next door, not to mention her poor, poor cat.

He stands there in that awkward way he always used to, and his eyes don't quite meet mine, and he nods at me.

"Sarah," he says.

"Gregg," I say, smiling at him.

He sits down. We don't hug. We don't shake hands.

"How've you been getting on?" he asks.

It makes me laugh a little. How have I been getting on? That's an interesting question, isn't it? Six months after my boyfriend tried to kill me. Six months after I killed him to save my own skin.

No, wait. That's not how it played out, is it?

It's six months after the fire that broke out afterwards, burning the entire block of semi-detached houses down and seeing me almost lose my life to burns and smoke damage.

All because of that dodgy hob in the kitchen. Freddie always worried about it, didn't he? And he never got around to fixing it.

And there was Moira, too. Always smoking. Always falling asleep with her cigarette in her mouth. So, so dangerous. So, so careless...

Or was it the Christmas lights that did it?

So careless, Freddie. And all to cheer me up, too.

"Honestly, I'm doing good," I say. "Really good."

"And the little one?" Gregg asks.

I look at my belly, and I shiver for a second. I can still hardly believe it, seeing that baby bump. I know it is Freddie's. And that does fill me with terror. Andy put Charlie inside me. I abandoned Charlie. Left him to die.

And then Freddie, the same man but under a different name, got me pregnant again, so many years later.

Only this time, I see it as an opportunity. I see it as a chance. A chance to do better. A chance to right the wrongs of the past.

A chance to try again.

"He's good," I say. "A real kicker. But I guess that's a good sign. Maybe he'll be really athletic. A top footballer. And he can look after his mum all his life."

Gregg smiles. He still can't quite make eye contact with me. "Maybe."

I feel sad because I always wanted a child with Gregg. But he wasn't on the same page about having kids. I can admit that now. As much as I fooled myself that we had a son called Charlie, I know that isn't true now. And I've believed it for a long time.

Really, I'm doing well on that front. There are no gaps in my knowledge anymore. No parts of reality I am fooled by.

I was raped as a fifteen-year-old girl.

I found out it was a ploy to get my sister a child.

I killed her and fled.

Then I turned around and left my baby behind.

I struggled. I was traumatised by what happened. Suffered from dissociative amnesia. PTSD. False memory syndrome.

And Gregg was there to help me through all of it.

And things were good. Until I had a fling with Glynn in those maize fields—a fling I now know was orchestrated by the Family —and the memory of being raped brought it all back and sent me into a spiral of disbelief that I had a son, and he was missing...

Something that happened again when I moved house with Freddie.

Only this time, it turned out Freddie and Moira next door were contributing to my false memories and my dissociative amnesia, all for their own gain.

Because Freddie was Elana's lover.

Freddie was Andy.

And he'd wanted revenge. All this time.

And he went to crazy lengths to secure it. Both of them did.

I think of Freddie lying there in a pool of blood, and then I push that image away.

Stick it back in a compartment in my mind.

It was a fire that killed them both.

A tragic accident.

Nothing else.

Honest.

"The place you're living. It okay?"

I smile. "Little studio flat. Not exactly luxury. But it'll do. It has all I need."

Gregg nods. "Work okay?"

"It's good," I lie. I don't want to tell him I haven't worked for months. That I've been living off state support and savings. But I do have plans. Plans to set up a new business. A few online interviews with new tutoring prospects, things like that.

Truth be told, I've just needed some time.

Time to process everything.

Time to heal.

Time to recover.

But I'm not here to chat work and life with Gregg.

I am here because there are questions I still have.

Questions that need answering.

"You knew," I say. "When I had... when I had my breakdown four years ago. You didn't tell me the truth about what happened. All those years before. Did you?"

He opens his mouth and sighs. "I wanted to protect you. I didn't want you to go through the hell you'd been through as a teenager. Not again. I thought it would be better to keep that hidden. For... for you to believe it was all in your head. I know it was wrong. I know it probably just added to the trauma. And I know that's probably what... probably what made this fester, all these years. I felt bad about it. So, so guilty. That's the main reason I left. I was ashamed. I'm sorry, Sarah. I'm so, so sorry."

I look at him, and a part of me hates him. I've suffered for four years because of him hiding the truth about the cult, about Charlie, about my sister, about everything from me.

But a part of me can't help thinking his intentions were pure, too.

A part of me.

"That day," I say, staring out at the docks, at the beautiful blue water, at the people cycling past. "The one where I... where I ran from the maize fields. When I met you."

"Do you really want to talk about this?" Gregg asks.

I'm comfortable talking about it now. More at ease. "I remember... I remember leaving Charlie behind. And then... things are a little blurry. But I remember something. Your hand on my leg. Telling me everything was going to be okay. The water on your hand. Why was your hand wet, Gregg?"

He looks at me, and I swear I see his face turn a shade pale. "You—you didn't want to ever talk about this."

"Talk about what?"

He opens his mouth. Then he closes it. Looks away. "The video. The one you put on Facebook. I don't... I still don't see why you didn't take that to the police. Why you took it down."

It's a fair point. A change of subject, sure, but a fair point. I have all I need to pin everything on Freddie and Moira. All the confessions I need.

"Although the more time passes," Gregg says. "Maybe I *do* understand."

I deleted the video after escaping the house fire. Took it down immediately.

Because the video complicates things.

As certain as I am of my innocence where Charlie is concerned, the video complicates things.

"What are you trying to say?" I ask.

Gregg closes his eyes. He takes a deep breath. "I made you a promise. A long, long time ago. I made you a promise never to talk about what happened."

"What happened?"

"Sarah, all I know is you came out of those maize fields covered in blood. Drenched. Traumatised. You kept—you kept saying you'd done something. Something terrible. That Elana, your sister. That you'd done something to her. But there were other things, too. Things—things making me worry even more about what you'd done. I—I wanted to go back there. Because you were saying things about Charlie. So I did."

It hits me like a ton of bricks.

A memory door I didn't know I had.

"What..."

"I went back there, and I found him. He—he was drowned. Face down in the water. Dead."

"No," I say. Because this can't be right. I didn't do this. I didn't kill my son. I didn't...

"And I can remember something. You getting into my car. The water on *your* hands. Too much water to be rain. But I promised not to mention this. I promised not to bring it up. Because last time... last time, it sent you spiralling. Last time you remembered, it sent you spiralling. So I tried everything. Tried to—to create a new memory. One where we went away and where I never went back to check on him. And then other memories. Nicer memories. Memories of being on a school field with Charlie. Of watching music with him."

I feel his sweaty hand in mine, and I realise it isn't sweat anymore.

It's water.

Water from the stream.

And I can barely say a word.

"I don't... I don't judge you for what you did, Sarah. And I can't accuse you of anything. But I... I think we both know what happened. And I think that's why we both know you deleted the video. And the fire. The accidental fire. We both know about that. Don't we?"

I think back to stabbing Freddie in the throat.

Then going into the attic.

Stabbing Moira repeatedly, again, and again, and again.

I think about pouring gas everywhere.

Burning the two houses to the ground.

I think about waiting until it was just burned enough and just smoked out enough before clambering my way out.

Being sure to delete the videos first, of course.

"I don't know what you're talking about," I say. "It was an accident. A tragic accident. One I was lucky to survive."

Gregg nods. But I see he isn't convinced. "I didn't want to tell you this. And... and trust me. It caused me a lot of soul searching over the years. It's the reason we drifted. That knowledge. The elephant in the room. That knowledge of what you did. And what... and what it made you."

I try to think of myself holding Charlie's face down in the water, but I can't.

There is nothing real about the memory.

I remember running through the fields.

I remember running away and leaving Charlie behind.

And then I remember landing in Gregg's arms and his damp hand and—

"You're lying," I say.

Gregg narrows his eyes. Frowns. "What?"

"I know I left my son. And that's... that's almost as bad as consigning him to his death. But I know I did not go back into those fields. I know I wanted to... but you wouldn't let me."

Gregg shakes his head. Almost nonchalant about it. "We went through this last time. The accusations. It's not true, Sarah. None of it is—"

"Then why did I receive *this* in the post with a strand of blonde hair and note saying *I KNOW EVERYTHING* last year?"

Gregg looks down. He opens his mouth. Then closes it. "What... I don't... I don't know what that is."

"But you do, Gregg. You do. Because it's exactly like the one you gave me. Remember?"

He looks down at it, and I look at it too. Okay. Maybe I wasn't totally frank about *everything* I received in that parcel. But it's all been for a good reason. Because I need to be careful what information I share. I need to be careful what I tell anyone these days. Nobody can be trusted. Not really.

"Sarah?" Gregg says. "What is this?"

"Do you remember these that we wore? These rings? The ones with the elephants on?"

"I... I remember something about them, yes."

"Do you remember losing your ring that day? Not being able to find it?"

He narrows his eyes. Looks right at me. "No. No, I do not remember that."

"I think... I think *you* went back. I think you killed my son because you didn't want him finding his way back to us somehow. You never wanted children. You only ever wanted it to be the two of us. Only you left something behind. Something Freddie linked to me. Something that was yours."

He's quiet. Speechless. He doesn't say a word.

"I think you made me believe neither of us went back that day.

I think you used my mental breakdown to your advantage to make me forget. Or worst-case scenario, to make *me* believe I went back there. But I know what you did. We both know what you did."

He looks across the table at me. He looks calm. Cool. Collected.

And then, unexpectedly, he shakes his head and smiles.

"I wish you the best with your new life, Sarah. Truly, I do. You. The baby. With everything. I am sorry for the things you've been through. I am sorry for the life we have led. But I don't want to hear from you again. I don't ever want to hear from you again. Enjoy your fresh start. And I will enjoy mine."

He stands.

"You tell yourself whatever story you want to to make yourself feel better, Sarah. As long as you stay the fuck away from me."

And then, without looking at me again, he turns around. Walks away.

And when he disappears, I feel free again.

I feel the warmth of the summer sun again.

I look around and face the docks, and I smile as the kids bike past. I think about my child and me. How I'm going to get it right this time. I'm older now. I'm more wisened now. I'm a better person now. Far, far better.

And the links to my past are gone.

I think about Moira. Freddie. And I don't see myself stabbing them anymore. Killing them.

I see the terrible accident that led to the house fire, which cost Freddie, Moira, and even Moira's poor cat's life.

I see these tragic truths and nothing else.

Because the truth is only the truth if you believe it.

And if you tell yourself enough lies over the top of it and really, really believe them, you can convince yourself anything is true.

Just like painting over old wallpaper.

And if any chips in the paint reveal the past... well, you just paint over it again.

And harder this time.

I put the ring in my pocket.

And just for a second, just for one momentary flash, I see myself in an antiques store just two weeks ago, buying it.

Just for a second, I see myself holding my son down in the water.

Bubbles spluttering from his mouth.

And I see the horror in Gregg's eyes when he comes home that night.

I see all of this.

I see the old wallpaper peeking through the inches and inches of paint.

I feel horror.

I feel terror.

I feel shame.

And then I paint over it again. I put it away, all in a compartment in my mind.

It's not real.

My version of events is real.

I didn't buy the ring. I received it in the parcel.

And the reason I never mentioned it is simply because I thought it was irrelevant.

Or might be useful to keep to myself.

That's the truth.

The God's honest truth.

Do you believe me?

I really hope you...

Actually, no.

Fuck it.

Believe whatever the fuck you want to believe, because I don't have to prove myself to anybody anymore.

Believe what is the paint, and what is the wallpaper underneath.

Believe my version of events or Gregg's version of events.

I know the truth.

I know *my* truth.

I put my hand on my tummy, and I smile.

I have made mistakes.

I have done horrible things.

But I am going to get things right this time.

I get up from the picnic table, and I see a flyer for a summer fete at Ashworth's school in Broughton.

I have a flashback.

A flash of his hand in mine.

A flash of the summer heat.

Of him letting go of my hand and—

I take a deep breath, and I smile.

It's not real.

None of it is real.

There are problems, sure. There is Glynn and his involvement, however passive. But I hear his marriage is collapsing anyway, and I could always give him a hand on that front if need be.

And Cameron, too. He is far away. He is long gone. I don't have to worry about him.

As long as things stay that way, I don't see why he would ever come back to haunt me. Because the tragic fire benefited him just as much as it benefited me.

No. I can't think of it that way.

I am Sarah Evatt.

I lost my beloved fiancé in a tragic fire, where I almost lost my own life.

And I escaped with his son inside me.

A chance for a fresh beginning.

For a fresh start.

This is my truth now.

This is my life.

I am going to be okay this time.

I really, really am.

I look down at my tummy, put a hand on it, and I smile.

* * *

I THINK of my life in three distinct segments.

If you want to be notified when a new R.A. Casey psychological thriller is released, sign up here for new release notifications: ryancaseybooks.com/racasey

Ryan Casey also writes post-apocalyptic thrillers. If you want to be notified when Ryan Casey's next novel is released—and receive an exclusive post apocalyptic novel totally free—sign up for the author newsletter: ryancaseybooks.com/fanclub

If you enjoyed this book, check out Dying Eyes, a gripping detective mystery from Ryan Casey.

Printed in Great Britain
by Amazon